The Chocolate Box Girls

Gracie Hart was born in Leeds and raised on the family farm in the Yorkshire Dales. She writes sagas with a focus on the wars and her native Yorkshire.

She began her career as a glass-engraver before raising her family, Gracie has now written several family sagas.

Gracie Hart also writes as Diane Allen and averages a 4.5 star review rating across her titles.

The Chocolate Box Girls

GRACIE HART

PENGUIN BOOKS

PENGUIN BOOKS

UK | USA | Canada | Ireland | Australia
India | New Zealand | South Africa

Penguin Books is part of the Penguin Random House group of companies
whose addresses can be found at global.penguinrandomhouse.com.

Penguin
Random House
UK

First published 2024

001

Copyright © Diane Allen, 2024
The moral right of the author has been asserted

Set in 11.5/15.6pt Calluna
Typeset by Jouve (UK), Milton Keynes
Printed and bound in Great Britain by Clays Ltd, Elcograf S.p.A.

The authorized representative in the EEA is Penguin Random House
Ireland, Morrison Chambers, 32 Nassau Street, Dublin D02 YH68

A CIP catalogue record for this book is available from the British Library

ISBN: 978-1-405-96330-5

www.greenpenguin.co.uk

MIX
Paper | Supporting
responsible forestry
FSC® C018179

Penguin Random House is committed to a
sustainable future for our business, our readers
and our planet. This book is made from Forest
Stewardship Council® certified paper.

For Zoe Allen with love

I

York, 1935

'Molly Freeman, this may be your last day in school but I am still your teacher.' Mrs Stanley yelled loud enough for all the pupils at Haxby Road School to hear, let alone the day-dreaming Molly.

Molly quickly brought herself back to the world of the schoolroom as she heard Mrs Stanley shout at her to concentrate on the job at hand, just as a blackboard rubber whizzed past her ear and landed on the varnished wooden floorboards of her classroom, leaving a cloud of white chalk dust floating in the summer's air like a host of tiny fairies.

'Sorry, Mrs Stanley, I was just looking out of the window, it is such a nice day and I've only another hour before I leave school for good anyway,' Molly said quietly, hoping that her teacher of the last year would understand.

'There is another hour for you to learn and put some common sense into your head, Molly Freeman. You will need every ounce of knowledge when you join the real world because, believe me, you will look back and realise just how happy your days here at school were.' Mrs Stanley looked over the top of her glasses and glared at the girl she had tried to prepare for the rest of her life, just like she had prepared countless pupils before her. However, in Molly Freeman's case, she pitied her future bosses; she was by no means the brightest button in the box and if her siblings had not already been working for York's main employer, Rowntree's, she would have struggled to get herself an interview even.

'I'm sorry, I'll try to concentrate.' Molly put her head down and looked at her arithmetic book, but could not see the need for any of the elaborate fractions and equations that she was supposed to be able to work out. What would she need these for? She was going to make chocolate like the rest of the family and would have no need for such knowledge. Her mam had always said, 'Do your best and that's all you can do,' and that's what she had always done, regardless of what Mrs Stanley said to her. She glanced over at William Allen as she put her head down and tried to concentrate on her sums, but he stuck his tongue out at Mrs Stanley and then grinned cheekily at Molly as she sniggered.

'You might think that I cannot see you, Molly Freeman and William Allen, but believe me I do have eyes in the back of my head. Any more disrespect from either of you and it will be a caning that you will be receiving on your last day in school.' Mrs Stanley turned and stared at both of them as she finished writing on the blackboard.

'Sorry, Mrs Stanley,' William and Molly said together, not daring to look at one another.

'Just get on with it, and then you can leave with your heads held high,' Mrs Stanley said and sat down in her chair. This was one of many classes that she had seen through the last year of schooling. Most of them were following in their parents' footsteps in family businesses, some were leaving to work in the local shops and some of them, like Molly, were hopefully going to work at the sprawling chocolate and pastille firm that had spread over the outskirts of York. The unshowy, philanthropic Rowntree family were to be praised for bringing much-needed work to the ancient city; not only had they helped people afford their own homes and take pride in themselves, but with their strong Quaker values they had put York onto the map. They had also made her own life easier, especially when it came to the likes of Molly, who she knew would be nurtured by them once at work. Elizabeth Stanley put her head down and started to check the papers that she would have to take home with her that evening, but for now, at least, the classroom was quiet and that was just how she liked it.

Molly concentrated on her arithmetic, but her mind was focused on going home and leaving the school that she had attended since the age of five. It wouldn't matter what she put in her book, she thought, nobody would be bothered once she had walked out of the doors. So, instead of figuring out the set sums, she sketched pictures of her classmates in the margin, cartoon-like and funny, just like she thought of them. Finally, just before the bell rang for the end of the lesson and the end of the summer term, she sketched Mrs Stanley as a long, tall skinny woman with extended arms and huge glasses and whiskers – every pupil laughed about the whiskers on the end of her chin, which she obviously didn't know were there. She sat back and grinned and added a caption, 'Mary Hairy Stanley, the worst teacher ever!' Then she closed the book and watched as the minute hand finally reached half past three and a child in a lower year rang the home time bell.

That was that, then: school was done for good and at long last she could hope to make some money to help the family. She stood up and pushed her school chair under the oak desk which so many past pupils had scratched their names into when bored with their lessons, and placed her book under the desk lid. School was over and now it was out into the wide world, whether she was ready or not.

'Well, that's it and it's about bloody time – my father has been wanting me to help him in the shop for weeks now. I can learn far more working with him than I can in this place,' William Allen said as he walked out of the school with Molly, not giving it a backward glance.

Unlike Molly, who lingered at the doorway and wondered if Mrs Stanley's words were right about school days being the best. She had struggled at school some-times, but she had always known that it was for her benefit that she attended. Unlike William who was often absent, only to be found working in his father's butcher's shop on Haxby Road – for he had a future working in the family business. She, however, did not have secure employment yet and even though her siblings already worked for Rowntree's, and she was to attend an interview on Monday, she was dreading entering the sprawling works of the chocolate factory. She had heard her two sisters gossiping and talking about their work life and coming home each evening smelling of the chocolates that they made and packaged, and it sounded a completely different world to the safety of the school. They both came home exhausted and full of moans most days, having to think for themselves but at the same time sharing the comradeship of working together and gossiping around the kitchen table.

'I'll see you then, Molly, I'll probably be serving you or your mam in the shop next time you see me,' William said, pushing his hands into the pockets of his tight-fitting trousers. He was a big lad, well fed at home, unlike most of the rest of her class, whose families struggled to feed them.

'Yes, I'll see you, William. You take care,' Molly said, watching as he walked down the road towards home as a pang of panic overcame her: she was about to enter into the world of work and she was scared.

'Is that you, our Mol? Well, that will be that then.' Winnie Freeman had just finished making a pie crust and was wiping flour from her hands onto her cross-over apron. She looked up towards the kitchen doorway as she heard the front door slam on the small terraced house that she and her three daughters lived in.

'Yes, Mam, I'm home. Is there anything to eat, I'm

starving,' Molly said as she entered the kitchen and slumped into one of the rickety wooden chairs set around the kitchen table.

'You can make yourself a sugar sandwich, but only one, mind. I only got that loaf of bread this morning and already it's half gone because your two sisters insisted on taking their own dinners to work with them. You would all eat me out of house and home if I let you.' Winnie sighed as she ran a knife around the edge of the enamel pie tin, tidying up the crust before placing it into the oven of the Yorkshire Range. 'I don't know why either of them can't have their dinners in the dining block with the rest of the workers instead of taking what they can get from under my nose.' Winnie watched as Molly sliced a doorstep from the loaf and buttered it liberally before sprinkling a good spoonful of sugar on it and biting into it. 'Don't make another, you have meat and potato pie for your supper. Although there's not much meat in it . . . I'm sure that Thomas Allen's scales are wrong; I don't seem to have got much for my money.'

'William is starting work for him full-time now, he says,' Molly said, licking the sugar crystals away from the side of her mouth.

'He might as well have been this last month or two; he never seems to be at school, from what I hear. The truancy officer is always knocking on the door, according to Lizzie Mason, but they'll not get any sense from that family, no matter how many times he knocks on their door.'

'Well, he's no need of school, he's known all along that he is going to work for his father,' Molly said, looking at the loaf and hoping that her mother would allow her another slice.

'No, you don't, miss, you'll thank me in another year or two when the boys are showing interest in you. Nobody wants to be walking out with the plump one; a slim waist and a petite figure are what's wanted. Especially if you are to attract somebody with a bit of money in the bank,' Winnie said, smacking Molly's hand as she reached for the carving knife. 'And as for William working in his father's shop, he still needs to be able to weigh things correctly and to charge properly. Although perhaps that's what is wrong with his father, perhaps he makes it up as he goes along,' she continued, as she started to peel four potatoes to boil in a pan to accompany the pie.

Molly retracted her hand sharply and watched her mother as she filled a pan with cold water for the potatoes.

'Mam, I don't want to go to work for Rowntree's, I've been thinking I'd rather go and work in a shop or happen to learn to type and be in an office,' Molly burst out, looking worried as she saw her mother's face cloud over. Nobody ever questioned her mother's decisions, she was the matriarch of the family, and she had held her family together since the death of her husband from a particularly bad bout of influenza nearly ten years ago. Her word was set in stone.

'Don't be daft, our Molly! You, work in an office? You can barely spell; you even say to yourself that the words don't make any sense to you, no matter how much you look at them. You should be thankful that Rose got you the interview on Monday; she's put her neck on the line for you. It was either Rowntree's or Terry's on the other side of town and you wouldn't want to trail there every morning. Besides, you haven't even been taken on yet, but you should be all right, as long as you don't say you struggle with reading.' Winnie looked at her youngest – she knew she had problems, but at the same time she was not daft, she just couldn't make sense of letters like she should.

'I won't, Mam, but they may ask me to take a test, our Annie says they will, so they'll soon find out. That's what I'm worried about.' Molly sighed. Annie had tried to get into an office job, and she was a lot brighter than Molly, but she had frightened Molly with her talk of the test that she had been put through. Even though Molly knew that she would not be given a second look at an office job, she was worried about any tests that she would have to do for even the most menial of jobs.

'They are a good, understanding firm, they'll find you a place. They know your sisters are good workers and you've come from the same stable, so they'll take you on,' Winnie said as she added salt to the handful of potatoes and hoped that she would be proved right.

But Molly hoped that her mother was wrong for once; the smell of chocolate filled the house and the surrounding streets all the time and she had wanted to break the trend in the Freeman household.

'Hey up, the other eggs have chipped,' Winnie said, meaning her other two daughters had arrived home from their shift, as she heard them entering the house chattering excitedly. 'They'll just have to wait for their teas for a minute, I must be running late.'

Rose, the tallest and oldest of the sisters, entered the kitchen first, pulling off the white turban that protected her blonde hair that was immaculately held in place by hairgrips. Her make-up was like that of a movie star too. Rose loved to look just right and she had taken the eye of many a fella as she walked the two streets to and from the factory. She had also impressed the management and been told that she was going to be put in charge as a Grade A overlooker once the new product that they were developing was in place. This was good news for Rose as she was walking out with Larry Battersby and everyone knew that wedding bells would soon be ringing – every penny would be needed for them both to set up home together.

'Now then, our Mol, how was the last day at school then? Are you ready to join us Chocolate Girls come Monday?' Rose said cheerfully, leaning against the pot sink as her other sister Annie lit a longed-for cigarette and sat down across from Molly with her legs crossed and her turban still covering her head of tight dark curls.

'I don't know. Annie, do you think I'll be all right? I'm beginning to worry about working there,' Molly said,

9

looking at her other sister who, unlike Rose, didn't care about how she looked, or what folk thought of her; she was the tomboy out of the trio.

'Of course you'll be all right; we'll be there to look after you. Just try not to be put into the Card Box Mill, the stink of glue really gets on your chest,' Annie said, taking a long drag on a Craven A cigarette, which made her cough.

'Not as much as those things do, our Annie, I wish you would stop smoking, it is most un-ladylike,' Rose complained and then turned to look at Molly kindly. 'You'll be fine, love, wherever they decide to put you. The Rowntree family might be strict but they are fair and care about their staff, they have to, or else they wouldn't be honouring their religion. Quakers are known for their caring ways.' Rose put her arms around her youngest sister briefly to reassure her.

'Listen to her! No wonder she is getting a promotion, creeping and sticking up for the management. They are like any other business; if you don't make them money then they will get rid of you. Just like they sacked Brenda Crosby the other week,' Annie said, shaking her head as she remembered that one of her friends had been given instant dismissal without listening to a word in her defence.

'That's because she had been helping herself to the chocolate bars and selling them on to her friends. What else were they supposed to do?' Rose said, glaring at Annie.

'She swore to me that she didn't, that that old bag Agnes Moore, her overlooker, just held a grudge against her. I believe her as well,' Annie said, flicking her butt end into the fireplace and hoping that her sister would not argue back.

'You need better friends, our Annie, everyone knew what she was doing and it was just a matter of time before she was caught. She's lucky that she didn't get the police knocking on her door.'

'Girls, please, no arguing, just for once let us have our supper in peace,' Winnie said and smiled at Molly. 'You will be just grand, love. Just do your best, keep yourself tidy and mind your own business, that is all that they will want. Now, Annie, put the kettle on and change that look on your face, it's as black as the chimney back and it will stay that way if the wind changes.'

'Well . . .' Annie moaned.

'Well, nothing, kettle filled, please, and stop your whinging. We will have a game of rummy after supper, that will pass the night,' Winnie said as she prodded the potatoes with a fork to check if they were ready.

'Count me out, Mam, I'm meeting Larry, we are going to the pictures. There's *Shall We Dance* on at the Odeon and I love Fred Astaire and Larry loves Ginger Rogers.'

'Fred Astaire, Ginger Rogers, listen to you, what's wrong with Laurel and Hardy, now they give you a good laugh,' Annie said as she filled the kettle and placed it on the range.

'Annie, you would argue with your own shadow if you

could. Now all of you, let's have some peace and enjoy our supper together in a civilised manner.' Winnie sighed, her girls had all had the same upbringing but none of them were alike in their ways and it often led to many an argument. However, all her girls had spirit and knew right from wrong so she couldn't have done too badly, even though sometimes it had been hard bringing up three girls on her own for the best part of ten years. With Molly finally going out to work and Rose heading for marriage, life should finally become a little less hard.

2

Monday morning had come around all too soon for Molly's liking. She lay in bed listening to her two sisters who shared a bedroom getting ready for work and could hear her mother in the back yard filling the boiler in the outhouse for the Monday wash. She pulled her bedcovers over her head, blocking out the sunshine that was coming through the skylight window of her attic bedroom. She felt sick as she thought about what she had to do that day: it would be the start of her new life as a Rowntree's employee if things went well, and if they didn't she had no idea what to do. There wasn't much employment in York except the chocolate and confectionery factories of Rowntree's, Terry's and Craven's, and out of the three, Rowntree's was the nearest, being only a couple of streets away from where she lived. So it went without saying that she should hope to get taken on there.

'Molly, move your shanks, its seven fifteen and your interview is at nine,' her mother shouted from the bottom of the stairs, and then her bedroom window shook as her sisters slammed the front door in their hurry to get to work and to clock in on time, running down the street arguing with one another as ever.

'I'm coming,' Molly replied and felt a wave of nausea overcome her yet again as she climbed out of bed and looked at herself in the wardrobe mirror. She analysed every inch of herself as she pulled her nightdress over her head, did up her skirt and buttoned the ditsy patterned blouse that her mother had ironed especially for her interview. She studied her reflection as she pulled her knickers and socks on and realised that she was still a schoolgirl in looks, unlike her sisters, who were grown women and beautiful. She had bobbed, short, mousy-coloured hair that she held back with a hair clip, and freckles over her nose. She was gangly and not yet fully grown where it mattered, unlike Rose, who had the best figure anyone could ask for. Nevertheless, it was what God had blessed her with. There was no way she could change it now, she thought, as she washed her face in the bowl that stood on the washing stand and hoped that she looked the part.

She ran down the stairs and outside to the back yard to spend a penny on the wooden-seated lavvy next to the outhouse. Steam was coming out of the outhouse where her mother was preparing the weekly wash and she could hear her putting the tin lid on the huge pot that she washed the whites in and smell the carbolic soap and Dolly Blue that her mother used religiously every washday. She sat on the lavvy seat and wished she could disappear and not have to face the day, but her mother was not going to let her, and sure enough here she was knocking on the lavvy door.

'Tea's on the table and there's some porridge in the

pot. We can't have you fainting at your interview. I'm about to scrub the front doorstep, so move yourself,' Winnie called as Molly reached for a sheet of last week's cut-up newspaper to wipe herself clean.

Monday was her mother's busiest day; it was washday, step-scrubbing day and it was the day the rag 'n' bone man came. Shouting his usual call of 'Rag 'n' bone!' and exchanging a new supply of Dolly Blue bags, or donkey stones that her mother scrubbed the front doorstep with until it was almost white, for leftover bones. The bones went to be sold to the glue factory, and any outgrown clothes or rags traded were to be sold on as shoddy to the nearby mills. The rows of terraced houses might not be the wealthiest ones in York but there was pride within the women who lived there, and if a standard was not kept then it would be worse for the woman who let the row down. Windows were cleaned, steps scrubbed and the nets kept pristine just to prove that you were a good housewife.

Molly looked at the porridge that had been left for her in the pot. It had skinned over and congealed and she didn't fancy it, even though she was hungry and her stomach was churning, so she poured a cup of tea and looked at the clock. Another half hour and she would have to be out of the house and walking the few streets to the Rowntree's works. She looked at the washing-up that had been left behind and decided to do that to distract herself and help her mother. Pouring hot water from the kettle into the sink she washed everybody's breakfast pots and left the porridge pan to soak. Another ten minutes and she would go, she thought, it was always better to be early than late, so her mother had told her.

'Oh, Molly, look at your skirt, it's soaked from you washing up, and you can't go to an interview with that big wet patch on you,' Winnie exclaimed, looking across at her daughter as she made her way back through the kitchen. 'Go and get changed, you'll have to go in your other skirt, the one you had on yesterday, although it's not as good or as pretty, but at least it's not covered with washing-up water. But hurry up, it is nearly eight thirty and your interview is at nine.' Winnie sighed, noticing the panic on her daughter's face as she ran up the uncarpeted wooden stairs as fast as she could. Poor Molly, she was the kindest out of her three daughters, but nothing ever went right for her, no matter how she tried.

'That's better, not as posh as the one you were supposed to go in but at least it is clean,' Winnie said as Molly pelted back down the stairs and stood in front of her. 'Hands, nails, are they clean? They always look at your hands,' Winnie told her and held her hands out for Molly to place them in hers for inspection. 'Yes, you'll do, now remember your manners and no matter what they ask of you, you do it. You need this job and it's good of our Rose to get you this interview. Now, get gone and don't dally.' Winnie wondered whether to give her youngest a hug for good luck, but hugs were few and far between on her busiest day of the week and Molly would only cling to her and cry by the look on her face.

'Mam, I don't know if I want to go,' Molly said, looking pitiful as her mother walked her up the oil-clothed hallway to the front door.

'You go, and you come back and tell me that you start working at Rowntree's tomorrow. We need the money; you need the money now that you've left school. You are not a little girl any more, Molly, now go.' Winnie virtually pushed her out of the front door and over her newly cleaned step and watched as she walked down the street, giving a final backward glance at her as she turned the corner. 'Please let them take her on, I know that she will be looked after at Rowntree's,' Winnie whispered under her breath, before going to find the bones that she had kept for the rag 'n' bone man who she could hear yelling at the end of Rose Street.

With each step, Molly felt more butterflies in her stomach and more fear as she neared the sprawling complex of the Rowntree's factory. It was a huge complex, covering most of the north side of York, with its own railway sidings and a small station called Rowntree's Halt and its own wharf on the Foss Lock. Along with the huge factories that filled the air with the smell of chocolate, there were tennis courts, a library, a swimming pool, dining rooms, a cinema and even garden allotments to keep their employees happy and fit. There was everything an employee wanted and needed as long as they were willing to work hard and be proud of the job they did.

Rose and Annie had told her everything about the

place and she had often met them outside the blue fence and gates that surrounded the factory after work, but as she reached one of the main gates, she could easily have fled, the terror inside was so bad. She looked up at a large clock positioned just inside the fence, reminding the employees to hurry if they did not want their pay for the day docked. Ten minutes to go, she was in good time, she thought as she passed the red-stoned arts and crafts building that was the library, and the flower beds which contained a memorial to the founder Joseph Rowntree, as she made her way to the sprawling dining block where Rose had told her the interviews were taking place. She tried to compose herself and smiled as one of the workers passed by her with a smile and a reassuring word.

'They don't bite, you'll be fine, love,' said the woman with the same white turban on her head that her sisters wore.

Molly smiled back and breathed in. 'I will be all right; I will get this job and make my mam proud of me,' she whispered to herself as she pushed the heavy oak doors open.

'Here for the job, are you?' an efficient-looking young woman asked her, showing little interest beyond that.

Molly nodded.

'Wait over there then, somebody will be with you shortly,' the woman said, pointing to a wooden desk where another young girl was sitting.

Molly tried to say thank you but only a squeak came out and the secretary looked at her as if she was an inconvenience to her day.

'She's a flarchy one, as my mam would say, couldn't work all day in those heels,' the lass sat next to her said and grinned. 'You here for the job and all? I didn't want to come but my mam said I had to and besides there is a train that brings me straight here, which is not something you can knock when you live out at the end of the world in Selby.' The lass grinned again. 'Besides, I need some money, I don't want to live at home for ever, it's hell there at the moment. My mam lives with this fella and my baby brother Billy is always bawling. I need to get out before it drives me crackers.' She pulled a face behind the secretary's back as she turned and gave her a black look.

'I only live two roads down, it'll be easy for me to come back and forward to work,' Molly replied, trying not to look at the lass whom her mother would have called a bit common.

'Well, that's all right for you then, I don't suppose you've got a spare room at yours, I could leave home then and have no travelling.' She looked at Molly with a twinkle in her eye.

'No, I live with my mam and my sisters; I sleep in the attic bedroom as it is,' Molly said quietly.

'Bedroom to yourself, eh! Luxury, I share with two of my sisters when they are at home, I dread when they come home from tattie picking. Mucky back-breaking job, you wouldn't get me doing that,' the lass said. 'Anyway, what's your name, I never heard you give it when you came in?'

'It's Molly, Molly Freeman. Should I have given my name when I came in, she never asked for it?' Molly looked worried and thought of walking over to the secretary who was now sitting behind her formidable oak desk.

'Nah, there's only me and you waiting, they'll know who we are. I'm Connie, Connie Whitehead. Whitehead by name and whitehead by nature. My mam says she doesn't know why I'm so blonde when all the rest of us are quite dark. I think I must have been the milkman's.' Connie laughed and then went silent as the secretary put her finger to her lips.

'I'm just a little nervous, I babble too much when I'm nervous,' Connie whispered and then went silent as she could hear footsteps coming down the winding stairs towards them both. Looking up they saw a young girl not much older than themselves but dressed for office work, and with an air of superiority about her.

'Interview? Are you two here for the interview? If you are then follow me,' she said, turning back up the stairs expecting both girls to follow, walking with confidence and not even bothering to wait for their answers.

Connie shrugged her shoulders and stood up, followed by Molly, and they both followed the untalkative girl to the top of the stairs where she motioned for them to take a seat on a long leather bench next to glass cabinets filled with commemorative chocolate boxes for special occasions like Easter and Christmas. Both girls gazed at them and knew to be quiet.

Molly felt her stomach churn as a door along the corridor opened and a woman dressed in a smart plain suit stepped out and looked at them over the top of her spectacles. Her hair was tied back in a neat bun and her facial expression did not change as she looked at both the girls.

'I'm Mrs Spencer, now come this way with me, we need you to fill in a form or two and take some tests to see which part of Rowntree's you will fit into the best.'

Mrs Spencer led both girls to individual desks not too dissimilar from school ones and gave them a form to fill in giving details of themselves.

Molly looked at hers and felt a panic come over her; could she fill it in correctly and without making a mess and blotting the ink? She picked up the ink pen and started to complete her personal details. She was aware of how quickly Connie had completed hers and looked up at Mrs Spencer as she finally finished her form, a look of worry on her face.

'Now we want both of you girls to take some tests to see what part of Rowntree's you would excel in,' Mrs Spencer said, and noticed both girls look at one another with worry on their faces.

'It's nothing to be anxious about and won't take long, and then we will need you to visit the doctor and dentist.'

Molly felt sick; she had never been to a dentist, and what if she couldn't manage the tests? Her sisters were always making fun of her for sometimes not being as sharp as them. She said nothing as Connie was sent through one door and she through another across the way where two women were waiting to assess her skills.

'Hello, Molly, don't worry, it's not like an exam,' said

the younger of the women, and it was then that Molly noticed a man in the corner taking notes, which made her even more worried.

'Here you will find different shapes to go into these holes in the board, but not all the shapes will have a matching hole. It is up to you to decide what goes where and how fast you can do it. Do you understand?'

Molly nodded and felt her stomach churn as she waited until she was told to start. All she could think was, why hadn't her sisters told her there were so many tests, and then at least she'd have known what she was in for. Next it was about putting coloured cards into matching boxes, and then came a set of puzzles to solve. After this, somebody took her temperature and felt how cold her hands were. This, she was told, was to see if she would be able to use a chocolate piping bag, as if her hands were too warm the chocolate would go white once cooled. Molly's head was spinning when at last she was asked to pack shapes into a box. The shapes were made of plaster of Paris and the tester smiled as Molly's face fell when she realised that they weren't edible.

'Pack them in exactly the same way as you see in the completed box just there and make sure each one is contained in a frilly paper cup. When I say go, the gentleman over there will time you,' the instructor said, and watched as Molly stood at the table and waited, a determined expression on her face.

'GO.'

Molly felt her hands sweating and her brain tried to

calculate where each chocolate should go. Could she do it quickly and correctly enough to get into the chocolate packing department along with her sister Annie? She had told her how fast they all worked in there, so she knew her hands had to be nimble and her mind sharp. Suddenly she dropped one of the pieces and it landed on the floor, causing her to lose precious seconds. She did not dare to look at the inspector's face as she hurried to finish the task and at last heard the man click on the stopwatch as the last shape was given its allotted place. She sighed and stepped back; surely that was all the tests over.

'Thank you, Miss Freeman, if you could go and take a seat out in the corridor we will come to a decision and let you know.'

Molly's legs felt like jelly as she walked back into the corridor and sat down with relief on one of the leather seats. There was no sign of Connie, she was either still taking part in the tests or she had already left, Molly thought as she clenched the palms of her hands together and just hoped that she would not be going home with disappointing news. Had she put the coloured cards in the right boxes, and would dropping a pretend chocolate count against her? It was too late now, the instructors would have made their decision and there was nothing she could do. Her heart beat wildly as the door opened and the instructor stepped out and smiled.

'Providing that you pass your medical, I'm pleased to say that we would like to welcome you to employment with Rowntree's, to work in the Card Box Mill, making and printing the various chocolate boxes that we have for our products. Well done, Miss Freeman.'

Molly sighed. She had passed the test, and that was the bit that she had been most worried about, but she had really wanted to be a part of the chocolate icing team. 'Thank you,' she said, trying to smile. Perhaps she would eventually get there if she proved herself. She would try and ignore what her sister Annie had said about the Card Box Mill, she always did exaggerate slightly.

'Don't thank me yet, let's get you through the medical and then you can. Follow me,' the instructor said, and walked a little further down the hallway, stopping to open a door with an 'Occupational Health Department' sign on it.

Molly walked into the room. It was large and airy and smelt of carbolic soap, and she was greeted by a man in a white coat.

'Ah, you must be Miss Freeman, please take a seat and I will then examine your eyes and ask you to read from the board over there as far as you can, then my colleague Nurse Jenkins will ask you a few questions and will ask you to undress for a full-body examination.'

Molly sat down in the chair and looked up towards the light that the doctor shone into her eyes, and then once he had made notes she was asked to read a series of letters that got smaller line by line.

'Excellent! Now you just have the nurse to see and then on to the dentist.'

Dentist – she had seen a doctor before but never a dentist, and she didn't want to undress in front of somebody she didn't know. She was acutely aware that her knickers were patched and worn and was embarrassed by the state of them as she stood in front of the nurse and answered question after question about her health before being asked to strip off to her underwear.

'Hold out your hands. Now turn them over so that I can see both sides.' Molly held her hands out and noticed them shaking as the nurse ran her hands down her spine and legs and then parted the hair on her head. 'Just looking for nits,' she said, 'and then we will measure your height and weight.'

Standing under the wooden measuring stick and then being weighed, Molly felt thankful that her ordeal was nearly over.

'You are a bit thin for your height but it's something and nothing. Tell your mam to give you a slightly bigger portion at dinnertime,' the nurse said, and smiled as she wrote her notes down.

'I don't think she'll do that, there's not that much to go around anyway,' Molly said, and wondered why her weight was so important.

'There will happen to be a bit more, once you have started working for us, every penny counts,' the nurse said, and then walked her to the door once Molly had pulled her clothes back on. 'Next door down, just knock and enter, the dentist is waiting for you.'

'Thank you,' Molly said, and felt a tingle of excitement

and fear as she left the nurse and walked into the dentist's surgery.

'Ah, Miss Freeman, welcome, come and sit in my chair and let me examine your teeth.' The dentist, dressed in white, ushered her into his chair and pressed a pedal to make it recline as he hovered over her with a dental mirror in one hand and a steel thing that Molly had never seen before in the other. 'Now this should not hurt, but if it does, then let me know.'

The smell of the surgery and the all-new experience frightened her and if she could have got up and run away she would have done, but Molly knew that she needed the job too much to show how scared she was and to leave. So she closed her eyes tight, blocking out the dentist's face as he prodded and poked about in her mouth.

'Ow!' Molly yelped as the steel probe hit a nerve in a decaying back tooth and then wished that she had said nothing as the dentist pushed the pedal to bring the chair upright again.

'I'm afraid, Miss Freeman, that back tooth is very badly decayed and will have to come out immediately. We will do that right here and now and have you home in no time.'

Molly felt the blood drain from her face. 'I've never had a tooth out before, will it hurt?'

'No, you'll not feel a thing, I'll give you some anaesthetic and some gas, and it will put you to sleep for a short while, just until I extract the tooth. Now when did you last eat?'

'I didn't have any breakfast this morning, I was too nervous,' Molly said and felt like crying, but if a tooth was stopping her from making money for the family then she would have to put her faith in the dentist.

'Excellent. I'll get my nurse just to place you in a white gown, we don't want you walking home with blood on your clothes now, do we?'

Molly felt like crying as the nurse prepared her for the tooth extraction. She watched as clinical devices were put into an enamel tray next to her chair and finally, a stand with two bottles of gas and gauges was wheeled up, to which a mesh mask was attached. The nurse checked that the white gown was tight around her neck and then the dentist loomed over her.

'You won't feel a thing, my dear, you will only be asleep for a short while and when you wake up we will take you next door into the nurse's room where you can recover.'

Molly looked at the dentist and noticed every vein and blemish on his face as he placed the mask over her nose. It smelt of rubber and something stranger that she had never smelt before and she wanted to run as she heard a hissing sound and her mouth went dry and her head went dizzy and she felt slightly sick as the gas did its work and she slipped off into sleep.

Molly had no idea how long she had been asleep when she heard the nurse speaking. 'Molly, Miss Freeman, are you back with us?' She felt a gentle hand on her shoulder and then tasted the horrible irony taste of her blood in her mouth as she tried to sit up and leave the chair. 'Not so fast, you will be dizzy and disorientated for a while. Take your time,' the nurse said as the dentist came back over and asked her to open her mouth for a final check.

'Everything looks fine, now don't wiggle your tongue in the cavity, else it will start to bleed, don't eat anything until teatime, and remember to brush your teeth twice a day and then you won't have to return to me in a hurry, hopefully.' The dentist indicated that the nurse should help Molly back into her room.

'Oh, and no toffees or chocolate,' the dentist added as Molly found her legs with the aid of the nurse and made her way to a chair to wait in until her full senses returned.

Molly felt groggy as she took the nurse's arm. Toffees or chocolate, she never had either except at Christmas, and was he supposed to say that to someone when after all he worked for a chocolate factory? She'd never go back and sit in his chair ever again if she could help it, she thought, as she spat a mouthful of blood into the clean white hanky that her mother had made her bring.

After a short while the nurse looked across at her and smiled. 'Feeling better now? Do you think you can stand and walk all right?'

Molly nodded, she had to get away from the smell that she now knew to be the anaesthetic. She never wanted to smell it again.

'Right then, I'll walk you back to the main office where you took your aptitude test. There are a few things that you will need before you start work in the morning.' The nurse opened the door for Molly and waited for her to slowly gain her ability to walk and for her head to clear from the fumes of the gas.

Work in the morning, she was to start work in the morning, she thought as she sat across from Mrs Spencer, who nodded to the nurse, taking Molly's new dental records for her files.

'Right, Miss Freeman, you start with us tomorrow morning at seven thirty sharp in the Card Box Mill. You will work a forty-four-hour week and will be paid eleven shillings a week. This is a copy of the Works Rules and Regulations: make sure you read them before you start in the morning.' Mrs Spencer hesitated and looked at Molly for acknowledgement.

'Yes, Mrs Spencer, that sounds fine,' Molly said and then realised that school hours had been a doddle compared to the hours she was about to work.

'You need two white turbans and two white aprons that you can buy from various stores in town. I advise that you wear stockings and flat shoes, no high heels, no sandals and no jewellery, other than a wedding ring. You need money for whatever you eat, dinner can be bought and eaten here in the dining block, the food is good and is cheap.' Mrs Spencer must have said the same thing over and over again and had got the patter off to a fine art as she looked across at Molly's pale face. 'Are you all right with all that, Molly, have you heard all that I've said?'

'Yes, thank you. I already know most of that; I have two sisters that already work here, one in the boxing room and one I don't know where at the moment, she isn't allowed to say.' Molly looked across at Mrs Spencer who looked quizzingly at her.

'Oh, you should have told the dentist that you had sisters that already work here; they would have been allowed to stay with you when you had your tooth removed. Would you like me to fetch one from their work to make sure that you are all right?' Mrs Spencer asked, leaning over and looking at Molly closely.

'No, I'm all right now; it was just when I woke up that I felt a little light-headed and queasy,' Molly replied, saying nothing more.

'Now, let me see. When you say you don't know where your sister is presently working in the factory, that must make you Rose Freeman's sister, she is helping us with an exciting new product that is about to be released. She is sworn to secrecy so it is good to hear that she has not discussed her present work. So, that also makes you Annie in the packing department's sister. We like to give employment to full families, so I'm glad to welcome you into our family, Molly,' Mrs Spencer smiled.

'Thank you, yes, I'm the youngest and my sisters have told me how good it is to work here.' Molly wasn't entirely telling the truth: Rose spoke nothing but well of the Quaker chocolate factory, but to Annie, it was just a job to be endured. She would soon be finding out which she agreed with.

'You'll know then to report to the timekeeper each morning and not to be late else you will lose your morning's pay and will be locked out?'

Molly nodded. Annie had been late a morning or two and had come back home to get a good dressing-down by her mother, and she wasn't going to let that happen.

'Right then, seven thirty sharp, report to the timekeeper's office and someone will meet you and take you over to the Card Box Mill, where you will be taught your job.'

Molly made her way home past the larger houses of Hambleton Terrace and the terraced houses of Rose Street, turning onto her home street of Belgrave. She could see her mother standing outside talking to their next-door neighbour, her brush in hand from sweeping the small front path.

'Been sweeping the muck up from the rag 'n' bone man's horse. I've just put it around the rose that's flowering at the back door; waste not want not,' Winnie said.

'Well, how have you done Molly? Do you start work in the morning?' Jenny Campbell asked, showing more interest in her neighbour's daughter than her own mother did.

'I start in the Card Box Mill in the morning,' Molly said. 'But Mam, they had to take one of my back teeth out, they said it was rotten.'

'Only one? You won't remember, but our Rose had three out when she started. We never warned you because we thought you wouldn't go.' Winnie ignored the fact that she had just got a job until she saw the upset on her youngest daughter's face.

'Well done, lass, it will be work in the morning with

the other two. You'd better do what you want this afternoon as it will be the last time you will have some time to
yourself for a while. I've already bought you new turbans
and aprons, I knew you'd get a job there.'

'Thanks, Mam, I might have a walk into town while
I've got the chance,' Molly said and thought that she
would make the most of having some time away from
school and home.

'There's threepence on the kitchen table, you get what
you want, my lass, but perhaps not toffees, not until that
gum heals over. My treat.'

'Thanks, Mam, that's a real treat.'

3

It was rare for Molly to walk into town by herself and she felt as if things had really changed in her life in just that one day. She had got herself a job, been to the dentist for the first time and now she was walking into the busy city of York on her own with threepence burning a hole in her pocket. It was a lot for her mam to give her and she would have to spend it wisely on things that she really needed and not fritter it on sweets and chocolate. After all, if she was going to start work at Rowntree's, chocolate would be the last thing that she would want to eat if she was anything like her sisters. They complained about the smell of chocolate all the time and hardly ever ate it because they worked with it all day.

She waved at William as she passed his father's butcher's shop and saw him serving behind the counter. It was as if he had always been there and not just left school. It was time for both of them to grow up and join the real world of grown-ups whether they wanted to or not. However, today she would dawdle in York and enjoy herself until teatime, and then she would go home and see what her sisters thought of her working in the Card

Box Mill, although Annie had already made her thoughts known as usual.

The York Molly loved was a sprawling city still surrounded by ancient stone walls built by the invading Romans centuries ago, and its busy streets were filled with shops and alleyways. They led to many a historic place of interest and Molly smiled with pleasure as she passed under the remains of a Roman gatehouse at one of the main entrances into York called Gillygate. When she was younger she used to imagine Roman centurions and Roman ladies going about their business as they sped from perhaps the bakers or the fish sellers. Even now the streets were huddled and packed together and hardly touched since Romans had walked them, so it didn't take much for her to romance about them. Not far from the Gillygate entrance, she walked into the Minster Yard, where she sat for a while on one of the wooden seats and looked at the towering medieval minster that York had been built around. It always took her breath away and she gazed at the majestic spires reaching up into the sky. She had never been inside it but she wondered if she dared do so now as she sat on her own. She had heard about the beautiful stained-glass rose of the main window and the towering arches inside but had never dared to enter. Molly moved up to make room for an elderly lady on the bench next to her and smiled as the woman took her hand and clenched it tightly.

'It's wonderful, isn't it? The minster is just wonderful. We are truly blessed and do you know I have actually seen the Lord within it?' She held Molly's hand so tightly and shook it so violently that Molly was scared. 'He's come to save us, everyone of us!' She stood up suddenly, raising both hands in the air and giving Molly an opportunity to retrieve her hand. 'He can save you, my child, if you let him.' The old woman stared down at Molly, who took the second chance to get up and hurry away from the religious zealot.

'Repent and he will save you.' Molly heard the words being yelled at her as she walked briskly across the square and then broke into a run as she made her way down the overhanging medieval row of houses called The Shambles and then quickly turned into the marketplace, her heart pounding as she mingled with the shoppers and people browsing the market stalls. She felt scared. Had the old woman really seen the Lord and was she a sinner? If that's what happened to you in the minster then she would rather not go in. She stopped for breath next to the fruit and vegetable seller and looked at the apples that were lovely and fresh but knew if she bit into one it would hurt where she had just had her tooth removed. She listened to a conversation between a housewife and the stallholder.

'That silly old bag Mad Martha is in the Minster Yard, she's claiming the Lord is amongst us again and she is trying to save souls,' said the housewife as she passed him a cauliflower.

'I hope she doesn't come this way, I have had to tell her many a time to move on; she needs locking up, that's what she needs. One day it's the Lord and the next day it's the devil she talks to. A century or two ago she would have been burnt for being a witch.' The stallholder laughed as she handed him his money.

Molly sighed; so everyone knew her, she hadn't just been singled out as a bad person. That was a relief, she thought, as she made for the stall where she had decided to spend her money. Perhaps one day she would look in the minster, but not today: not if that was the effect it had on people. Instead, she would buy the hair slides that she had wanted for so long and now, with the threepence that her mother had given her, she could just afford them. She could wear them on her day off from work as no jewellery was to be worn at Rowntree's, and besides, they would be hidden under the white turban that she would now have to wear like everyone else to keep any stray hair from getting into the chocolate. She stood looking down upon the rows of ribbons, clips and slides. She was too old now for ribbons, those days were gone, but the two black hair slides with a small paste diamond at one end were just right for her. Not that her hair was long, but it would hopefully make it look more glamorous, giving her a look of Judy Garland, who was starring in all the pictures of late. She picked them up and looked at them.

'Tuppence each them, love,' the stallholder said and smiled as she looked at them in her hand. 'They'll look right bonny in that hair of yours, catch the eye of many a young man, those will.'

Molly smiled and felt in her pocket for the threepence. She had just enough money for one of them and a penny lick from the ice-cream seller on Monkgate before she went home. That would be her money spent wisely and hopefully, the taste of ice cream would get rid of the irony taste of blood from her mouth, she thought. She paid for her slide and made her way out of the walled area of the city, back up to where the air smelled once again of chocolate, to the place she called home.

'Now then, our Mol, I hear that you are joining us in the morning. Another year or two and we will be able to run Rowntree's. One of us in the new developments part, one in the Packing Department and now one in the Box Mill, we just about cover it all,' Annie said and laughed as she sat back in the chair, took her shoes off and rubbed her aching feet. 'If you had any sense at all you'd keep a million miles away from the bloody Rowntree's factory and do anything but make boxes.'

'Annie, hold your tongue and watch your language! Molly's done right well to get herself a job and well you know it,' Winnie said sharply as she laid the table and listened to her girls talking.

'You'll be fine, Molly. Mrs Spencer said that you impressed them all at your interview. Besides, you can always start at the Card Box Mill and then work your way into another part of the factory once you have proved yourself,' Rose said as she passed her mother the knives and forks and scowled at Annie. Her sister had no work ethic: Annie hated anybody in authority and trusted nobody, and she was friends with lasses that also thought the same way. But Rose knew that Rowntree's was good to you if you were good to Rowntree's. It was as simple as that.

'Well, I don't know, but I'll just do what Mam has always told me to do, and that's to do my best,' Molly said as she looked at the mince and onion pie that her mother was dishing out for the main meal of the day and suddenly realised how hungry she was.

'That's it, lass, just do your best and that's all that can be expected from you. Now all of you sit down and have your suppers. I managed to afford some good mince today, your mate William, Molly, undercharged me, his father will not put up with that for long. But I wasn't going to say anything, they charge enough anyway.' Winnie pulled her chair up to the table and looked around at her girls as they all helped themselves to boiled potatoes and carrots. Molly was the last one she had to see into employment, and once Molly was happy in her work, she would be able to look after herself and survive in the world if the worst came to the worst. It had been a hard life since her husband, Alf, had died, but she had brought her girls up now and her work was nearly done. She was proud of each one of them.

'He never was very good with his sums, I suppose he will have to learn just like me,' Molly said as she tucked into her supper, trying to forget about the coming morning and starting work, and listening to her sisters talking.

'So when are you stuck-up lot going to tell us what the new chocolates are going to look like? Are they in a fancy box or fancy wrappers?' Annie quizzed Rose. She had been asking her the same question for weeks now but Rose ignored her as always.

'Molly, you'll be able to tell me if there's anything fresh happening in the cardboard box department. You'll tell me now, won't you? I want to know if there's a different job to be done shortly or if I'll not be needed any more.' Annie looked at Molly.

'You leave our Molly alone; it will not have anything to do with either of you. So stop asking questions, everybody will know by next week, it's to be launched and announced on Monday. However, I will tell you it's the best thing that we have ever done because everyone will like it. And it came about after an idea was found in the suggestion box.' Rose rushed down her supper and pushed back her chair. 'Now, I'm off round to Mary's, she looks terrible and she whispered she had something to tell me when I was leaving work.'

'I hope that she's all right. Give her dad my best,' Winnie said as she took Rose's empty plate and placed it on top of her own.

'She's something to tell you all right, but half of Rowntree's already know her news. We all feel sick sometimes with the smell of chocolate but not on a regular basis like Mary has been of late. I've seen her dash out and the supervisor making a note of her rush to the toilet for the last six weeks and we all know what that means.' Annie looked across at her mother, who looked back at her sternly.

'I didn't think you could eat the chocolate when you

worked there, so why does she keeping being sick?' Molly asked innocently, seeking an answer from Annie.

'She's . . .' Annie tried to say but was stopped quickly by Rose.

'She's probably got a stomach ache because, no, you can't touch the chocolates we make. Now you stop listening to idle gossip, our Annie.'

'It's a big stomach ache, if you ask me, it grows bigger every day,' Annie said and finished her supper as she looked at the puzzled expression on Molly's face.

'Now, stop your gossiping, give my love to poor Mary, it sounds like she will be needing it, and you, Annie, you can wash up tonight. It's Molly's last day of freedom so she can get away without doing anything tonight like you all did when you first started work,' ordered Winnie.

Annie grunted and started clearing the table. 'I'm going to meet Joan down by the wharf after, just to pass an hour or two before bed.'

'Right, you do that, but no flirting and dallying with the lads on the barges that bring the cocoa. We don't want another Mary, now do we?' Winnie said sharply, looking at Molly who was obviously confused and wondering what the conversation was about. Perhaps, Winnie thought, it was time to tell her one or two basic facts, just like she had with her two sisters before they started work. She would take the opportunity when her two girls were out. Winnie watched as Annie washed the plates and cutlery as fast as she could.

*

Molly lay in her bed. It was hot and stuffy and she pushed back her sheets and eiderdown; she either froze to death in winter or sweated like a stuck pig in summer in her attic bedroom. However, she wasn't bothered, it was better than sharing with Rose or Annie; they rowed nearly every morning, especially about who had to get out of bed and acknowledge the knocker-upper who acted as their alarm clock every morning as he tapped on their bedroom window. Although the girls had an alarm clock, their mother still employed old Tom Spencer to knock on their window with his long pole. It gave him some pocket money and some dignity, her mother always said, when she was questioned about still needing him. In the morning he would be knocking for her too, she thought, as she hugged her pillow and ran her tongue over the sensitive gum where her tooth had been. She was still trying to understand what her mother had said to her, *Don't let a man or boy lift your skirts and don't drop your knickers for anyone!* Why would she do that? She knew not to show her knickers to anyone, and besides, they had more patches on them than a cabbage leaf as they were hand-me-downs from Annie.

Then she started to think about her new job. Would she be able to do it? What if she hated it and what if she felt sick every five minutes like poor Mary? They wouldn't want her then. She looked up through the skylight; darkness was creeping in just for a few brief hours through the warm summer night. She heard Rose talking to Annie in the bedroom below her and she listened for her mother pulling on the chains of the grandfather clock at the bottom of the stairs before she came to bed. She was only young when he died but she could just remember her father doing the same thing and then looking into each bedroom to check his girls were asleep. She missed her father, she used to squeeze her eyes tight shut and pretend to be asleep as he bent down and kissed her on her brow. She squeezed her pillow and remembered the smell of tobacco on him and his soft gentle fingers caressing her hair as he left her to go to sleep. If only he was there to comfort her tonight, she thought, as she tried to forget the coming day and fall asleep looking at the white apron and turban that she was going to have to wear every day, folded neatly on the chair next to her bed.

4

'Molly, come on, stir your shanks, didn't you hear Annie?'
Rose burst into Molly's bedroom and pulled back her
covers. 'First day and you are going to be late, that's not
good.' Rose left Molly to get ready for her first day at work
and she stumbled out of bed, went through her morning
routine and then put on the white apron, and then the
turban over her hastily brushed hair. She quickly glanced
at herself in the mirror, heart pounding, and ran downstairs into the kitchen. Her mother was already up and
the fire was lit, a loaf of bread, ready sliced, in the centre
of the table.

'Bread and jam for your breakfasts this morning, but
don't spill it down your apron, our Molly, you don't want
a mark against you on your first day.'

All three girls stood up as they ate the bread and jam
and took quick slurps of tea as they looked at the kitchen
clock above the fireplace. They couldn't be late, not even
a minute late, or they would lose a morning's pay.

'Hands, lady?' Winnie said to Molly. 'They'll do, now
tuck your hair under the turban, there's a lock hanging
down at the back, and smile, for heaven's sake. They are
not going to kill you.'

43

'I feel sick, Mam, I don't want to go,' Molly said as a wave of nausea and nerves came over her.

'Don't be daft, now all three of you get yourselves gone, finish your bread and jam on the way to work, another ten minutes and the gates will be closed. Now get gone!' Winnie opened the front door for her trio to leave.

'Thanks, Mam,' Rose said and gave her mother a peck on the cheek as she walked out of the house with her bread already eaten, while Annie followed, still eating hers as she made her way out into the early sunshine.

'See you tonight, Mam,' Molly said, although she could have turned back there and then as she felt a sense of panic come over her.

'You'll be all right, pet, they'll look after you,' Winnie said and could nearly have shed a tear herself as Rose and Annie linked their arms through Molly's and marched her off down the street to make sure she got there on time and to the correct place. She would be fine, but she was the baby of the family and had always been protected; now she was out in the big world and would have to fend for herself.

The roads into Rowntree's were thronged with white-aproned and -turbaned women, all rushing to get to the gates and clock in on time. Amongst them all were some men on bicycles. There was a blockage at the main gate as workers queued up to use the card machine to be timed into work.

People jostled Molly as she stood in line, not knowing quite what to do.

44

'You need to go to Grumpy Davis over there, he will have your name on his clipboard and he will give you a clocking-in card, or a Blick card as we all call them, and then he'll point you in the right direction. We aren't allowed to come with you once we're past these gates.' Annie smiled, remembering her first day at work and how lost she had felt, and looked angrily at a woman who pushed poor Molly to one side. 'You'll be all right, we will both see you in the dining block at lunchtime, or I will even if Rose can't make it. She works over her dinner hour sometimes, that's how she got where she is.' Annie grinned up at her oldest sister.

'Yes, see you at lunchtime. Now Mr Davis is free, go and get your card. You'll be fine.' Rose watched as Molly made her way to Dennis Davis, who checked in everybody new and held a handful of new Blick cards.

'Ah, another fresh face, so come on, what's your name, I'm not a mind reader.' Grumpy Davis lived up to his nickname as Molly told him her name and he looked through his handful of cards.

'Eh? What was it, Molly Foreman? Speak up, I can't hear with all this lot going past me.'

'Freeman, Molly. It's Molly Freeman,' she said loudly and watched as her two sisters walked across the yard and out of her sight.

'Here it is, you'll need this every morning to clock in at the Blick Time Recorder, you just put it into the machine and wait for the ping and then retrieve it. It has your name and department on it. Make sure you don't lose it or give it to somebody else to clock you in. There's a guide waiting over there with a new bunch of employees, she will show you the way through to the Card Box Mill.' Dennis Davis then moved on to the next fresh-faced new employee.

Molly walked over to the yard where another girl was waiting with the guide. She smiled as she recognised Connie and gently touched her arm as she stood beside her before walking quite a distance to the Card Box Mill at the north-eastern corner of the factory. The air was thick with the smell of chocolate and steam, and noise was coming from every part of the factory as they made their way to the long low building where the chocolate boxes were made.

'So you got chosen too. I'm glad,' Connie whispered as they walked down a windowless corridor with offices on one side and a storage area filled with cards ready cut to shape for the boxes.

'Yes, I'm glad to see you,' Molly said as they followed the guide up a flight of stairs to where the main production area was. The two girls stopped with the guide and were mesmerised by the wall of sound that met them, with busy machines clattering and the women workers shouting above it all.

'Lord, it's noisy, and look at all these women, there must be five hundred – and the smell!' Connie said and held her nose.

'You'll get used to it,' said the guide sharply. 'And you'll learn to cope with being red hot in summer and freezing cold in winter; I'm afraid it is one of the oldest buildings that Rowntree's have and should really be replaced. Now, time to clock into your department, girls. I know that you have already clocked in at the gate, but we also need to know that you are in your department. Present your cards as you must do each morning if you want to get paid.' The guide watched as the new recruits punched their cards through the clocking-in machine and then followed her onto the factory floor.

'I hate this smell, it makes me feel sick,' Molly whispered to Connie. 'I bet it gives you a bad head by the time you get home, even if the noise doesn't.'

'We've got the worst job of all, I'm not going to like it here,' Connie said, ducking her head as a low-flying pigeon flew over the working women and roosted on a beam next to the hanging electric lights and a broken window pane which it must have come through.

They said nothing more as both were given a workbench next to one another and realised that the smell came from the pots of glue on each bench and a pot that was bubbling over a lit Bunsen burner at the side of the factory floor on another workbench.

'This is your work station. Mrs Beaumont will show you the job we wish you to undertake and perfect in the weeks to come. However, being juniors on the production line you will for now be expected to keep other workers topped up with the card, glue, ribbons and decorations for the boxes. That is until you have perfected the job in hand.' She then turned to an elderly woman,

47

Mrs Beaumont, who had been working in the Card Box Mill most of her adult life, as she took control of the situation and thanked the guide.

Connie nudged Molly and grinned as the stout well-spoken woman took a piece of card and folded it here and there, quickly making it into the perfect box and then lining it with paper, pulling the printed paper taut and then finishing it off with a ribbon and tassels.

Molly watched and felt a sinking feeling she would never ever be able to do that, as the woman picked up the box and passed it to them to inspect. She looked at the beautiful box that Mrs Beaumont had made and feared that she would not have a job by the end of the week.

'I've been making boxes for forty years, we do not expect you to pick the skill up overnight so don't worry, we are here to train you,' Mrs Beaumont said, passing Molly and Connie what they needed to copy what she had made.

Molly was aware that she was concentrating so hard that her tongue was poking out of her mouth as she pulled the printed paper over the cardboard base of the box, and she looked at Mrs Beaumont as she sought her advice on where to fold and glue it to complete the box shape. Finally, she got to the bit that she knew she could do as she affixed the red ribbon just below the wording 'Rowntree's of York Chocolates' on the lid and looked at her work.

It was far from perfect: the lining was bubbling and not glued in places and there was a big crease running through the picture of the Roman walls of York that adorned the box of chocolates. Molly felt hopeless and ready to get her marching orders as Mrs Beaumont inspected it and showed her where she had gone wrong, before inspecting Connie's.

'Not bad from either of you, given it is your first attempt. Now, there's a pile of seconds here that you can practise on until dinnertime and then you can both make yourselves useful and go around filling the glue pots on everybody's work stations and making sure they all have enough boxes to get on with their orders. That way you get to know who you are working with and watch at the same time how people manage the job. You will soon get used to it; we all had to learn when we first started.' Mrs Beaumont looked at them both. 'I'm over there right in the centre, you can't miss me. I'll inspect what you have done while you go for your dinners and then will tell you what problems I find and how you can resolve them.'

Molly felt nervous as she picked up the first piece of card and the decorated cover, this time making sure that it was totally covered with the foul-smelling glue, and that she folded every corner of the box in tight. She stretched the paper cover as she had seen Mrs Beaumont do, but as she did so the cover tore: she had pulled too hard. She sighed, and felt like she would never get such a simple-looking job right; however, she did see a glimmer of hope as she watched Connie who was having exactly the same problems. Dinner could not come fast enough as she tried her best to complete a perfect-looking box and hoped that she could get some advice from Rose who she knew had worked in the card box part of the factory for a short time when she had started here.

'Lord, am I ready for my dinner, my mam has given me enough money to buy it this week but I don't know if she will next week,' Connie said. 'Bertha next door to me says we won't get paid till next week for what we do this week, that they are always a week behind with your pay.'

The sound of the horn telling everyone it was lunch-time sounded and the workers started filing out of the Card Box Mill across to the large dining hall above which both Molly and Connie had been interviewed in the works offices.

'I don't think I want any dinner, the smell of the glue is giving me a headache and making my stomach feel as if it could gip at any time,' Molly sighed, and looked at her meagre attempts at box-making, hoping that she had improved with each one that she had made.

'Yes, it does stink and it is so noisy, you can't hear yourself think with the card-cutting machine and stamper working all the time. Not to mention Old Bag Beaumont watching us like a hawk. Come on, let's make the most of the time we have for lunch – at least this afternoon will be easier if we are to just supply every-body with what they need.' Connie put her arm through Molly's and followed the queue of women making their way to the large building that looked more like an aircraft hangar than a dining hall.

'My sisters said they would meet me for dinner, just to see how I've got on this morning. Annie works in the piping department and our Rose is really important, she's working on a new product that she's not allowed to talk about until next week when it is going to be announced.'

'Oh, you never told me that she was one of them up there, the posh lot. No wonder Old Bag Beaumont looked upon your boxes more favourably than mine.' Connie grinned and laughed. 'Why can't she say anything to anyone, it's only chocolate?'

'They never want another firm knowing what they are doing, just in case they copy it and get it made before them. At least I think that's what she told me. My boxes were no better than yours anyway,' Molly replied, and then smelt the rich aroma of dinner: her sisters had always talked about the meat and two veg that you could get for seven pence halfpenny; or a full three courses for less than a shilling that included a steamed jam pudding. Her mother had only given her sixpence and Annie had told her that she would be able to have fish and chips and a cup of tea for that. However, with the smell of glue still in her nose she didn't even feel like eating that.

'Just look at that dinner, beef and mashed potatoes with cabbage, that's what I'm having,' Connie said as a young woman walked past carrying a heaped plate of food.

'I think I'll just have a dish of soup, I hope they have soup, otherwise I might be sick. I've got to look out for my sisters, they sit at the far end of the hall next to a greenhouse where the gardener grows some fancy vegetables, so they said.' Molly queued up with a wooden tray for their order to be taken by an army of cooks that were serving an array of heated dishes.

'Looks like it's women in one end and fellas in another, that doesn't give you much chance to flirt. I thought I could flutter my eyelashes at a good-looking fella while I had my dinner but there's going to be no chance of that, is there?' Connie sighed and asked for the roast beef, pulling out a shilling from the small bag that she had tied around her neck.

'What do you want to do that for? My mam said to keep away from fellas last night,' Molly said, and shook her head at the main meals as she moved her tray on towards where the soup and puddings were served. Usually, she would have relished a pudding as it was a luxury at home and her mouth watered as she watched custard being poured on a portion of steamed ginger pudding, but her stomach told her not to risk it and she settled for a plain vegetable soup as she looked around the dining hall for her sisters.

'There they are, sitting with a few others, and they have room for us two,' Molly said, feeling happier that she had her sisters to sit next to. 'Come on, come and meet them.'

'They'll not want me, you go to them, and I'll find somebody else to pester.'

'No, come on, of course they will want to meet you.' Molly smiled and made her way through the crowds of women carrying trays of lunch or heading back to work, and made for the long table where her sisters sat.

'Hey up, you have survived then? Have you been sick yet, because I know you have a weak stomach and always retch when our mother is cleaning a hen or boiling fish?' Annie grinned as she took in the dish of soup with just one slice of bread and butter next to it.

'Not yet, but I might be this afternoon when we have to fill the glue pots up.' Molly put her leg over the wooden bench and sat next to her sister. 'This is Connie; she started to work in the box factory with me this morning. She's from Selby and comes in on the train every morning.'

'Hello, Connie, we both told her not to worry and that there would be somebody in the same situation as her – another new starter – and that she wouldn't be on her own. How are you finding it?' Annie asked, as Rose looked at the young girl who appeared to be a little more worldly-wise than their sister; even dressed in her white uniform and turban she looked older than her age.

'It's all right, it's a job and money at least and it might give me a chance to leave home.' Connie sighed. 'I need to have somewhere of my own, there are too many in our house and my mam has a man in her life.'

'Oh, that sounds interesting, and how old are you, Connie? Are you the same age as our Molly, fifteen? I take it you are.' Rose glanced at Annie who she could tell was thinking exactly the same thing as her, that Connie came from a bad home.

'Yes, I'm fifteen and there are sometimes six of us in

our house, not a minute's peace. Oh, this meat is good, but I can't afford one of these every day, else I'll not be taking any money home with me when I get paid and then my mam will be throwing me out whether I want to leave or not.'

'Yes, the meals are always good here, saves you making something substantial when you get home. Although our mother always makes us sit down to a dinner together and then she can hear our news every evening and make sure we are all all right, even though we are old enough to run our own houses. She doesn't seem to realise just how grown up we are.' Rose smiled as she watched Connie eat her way through her dinner as if she had never eaten before.

'You are lucky, mine is never at home, I'd often come home from school to find my baby brother on his own, my mam is never there. Bread and drippin', or if there is some, jam, that's our tea. I can only afford this today because I helped myself to some money that my mother's fella had dropped out of his pocket this morning.'

Molly felt herself blushing. Connie came from the sort of family her mother would call common, though her looks and clothes belied that. Until that moment Molly had not really worried about Connie's background, but now it was becoming clear that Connie had bigger family issues.

Rose got up from the table and smiled at Molly. 'I'll see you after work. I've got to get back, we have a supervisors' meeting in ten minutes.'

'Yes, I'll see you, Rose.' Molly knew full well that Rose

would have something to say about her new friend, but she didn't care, she had been the only one that had made her welcome that morning and she was grateful for her company.

'Yes, and I'm going out into the rose garden for ten minutes now I've finished my dinner. I'll make the most of the sunshine; before we know it, it will be winter and then we will all be freezing,' Annie said as she followed her older sister and left the two new workers together. 'I'm not keen on that Connie,' Annie whispered to Rose. She too hoped that Molly would soon find a new friend other than Connie. She didn't know the lass but she could tell, even after the briefest of meetings, that she seemed to have a lot more experience of the world and would perhaps not be a good influence on her little sister.

'You never know, it might be just the sort of friend our Molly needs. At least she's more mature,' Rose replied, and hurried to her meeting.

'You can tell that your sister is hobnobbing with the bosses. No wonder you got a job, I'm just surprised that you are even anywhere near the Card Box Mill. Couldn't she get you in higher up?' Connie leaned back and patted her now full stomach.

'It doesn't work like that here, you start where they think you will fit in at what they think you will be good at and then they promote you. Our Rose started in the packing department but she kept getting ideas about how to improve products and put them in the sugges-tion box. Now she's in the department that tries out new recipes and she can't talk much about her job, she has to keep it to herself.' Molly stood her ground, she knew a little of how Rowntree's worked and there certainly was no favouritism, you had to prove yourself first and then perhaps be given a job with responsibility.

'That'll mean I'll always be in the Card Box Mill, that is if I decide to stay, but I must if I want a life of my own away from my mam and her fella.' A cloud came over Connie's face and Molly felt bad that her home life was not a good one.

'Well, our pay will go up once we have learnt the skills, then you might be able to rent a room or something. In fact, I think Rowntree's have housing of their own. It's called New Earswick, you want to put your name down for a house there. Our Rose and her fella keep talking about getting one once they are wed. She was only on about it the other night when she came back from the pictures.' Molly looked up as her fellow workers started returning to work ahead of the end-of-dinner bell being rung.

'They'll not want a single woman, they'll be for families, but talking about the pictures, can we go? I can pay for us, I'll manage to get the money somehow. It would make a real change and I could perhaps stop at yours that night,' Connie said hopefully.

'Err . . . go on then, I'll ask Mam for some money and if you can stay, but now we had better get back to work.' She knew what her mother would say straight away, it would definitely be no, once she found out what kind of family Connie came from. Connie might sound and act like sweetness and light but upbringing was everything to her mother and although the Freemans were nowhere near rich, they had morals and cared for one another.

Molly looked at her barely touched soup and braced herself to tackle the smell of bubbling glue pots and cardboard-cutting machines. She and Connie walked back to their posts and awaited their orders.

'Right, girls, this afternoon you can go and help your fellow workers, get to know them and keep them supplied with cards, glue and decorations. Every new starter does this. It helps you to get to know who you are working with, and where everything is kept, and you will also see how other workers handle the box-making. Your legs will be tired by the end of the day but it teaches you well.' Mrs Beaumont looked at Molly and spotted what she had seen so many times in new employees. 'Is the glue making you feel ill?' she asked sympathetically. 'You'll soon get used to it, just like you will making the boxes, you'll not notice or think about it twice in the coming weeks. I've looked at both of your efforts and they are not so bad, I've seen a lot worse. Another week or two and you will be doing it with your eyes closed, you should fit in well. Now, jump to it, go to each worker's bench and see what they are short of, and fill them up where needed.'

Molly went from workbench to workbench seeing how she could help. Between her and Connie there were five hundred women to support and Molly soon realised that she would rather be sat at her desk making chocolate boxes, no matter how intricate the job was. Some of the workers talked to her and gave her the time of day, some just grunted and nodded at what they wanted. All those who did talk to her said the same, that they had been in her shoes and knew how she felt. Molly was exhausted and even though some had shown pity to her, she doubted that they had ever felt like her, else why would they still all be working there? When at last the factory whistle sounded, signalling the end of her shift, Molly had never felt so glad in her life. Her head ached from the smell of the glue, her feet ached from the miles she must have walked around the factory and she was just exhausted from having to concentrate so hard.

'Thank the Lord for that. I'm so ready for home, although that will take another hour and there's not a lot there even when I do get back,' Connie said, in front of Molly as they queued up with the rest of the workers to clock out through the Blick machine.

'I'm so tired! Is this how everybody feels every day? I thought school was bad but the noise and the smell and the long hours have made my head spin and now I just want to flop.' Molly put her card in the machine and wondered if she could face another day, let alone a lifetime of working for Rowntree's.

'We'll get used to it, once we have been here for a few weeks, that is if they keep us on that long! I don't like that old bag Beaumont watching my every move, sitting on her high stool in the middle of everyone, perched like a crow. She shouted at me once or twice for talking. I was only passing the time of day and trying to find out any dodges to our job.' Connie sighed and then smiled as they both left the box factory behind and walked out into the fresh air, even though it was still laced with the smell of chocolate. 'I'll have to get going, I've my train to catch and I want a seat, it'll be a crush with everyone coming out at the same time. See you in the morning.'

'Yes, I'll see you. I suppose it will get easier,' Molly said, almost on the edge of tears as she watched Connie run to the end of Haxby Road to Hambleton Terrace where the Rowntree's workers' own station stood. Connie seemed to be enjoying it more than she was but she wasn't going to let on to her sisters as she saw Annie coming her way and noticed Rose already waiting for her at the main gate.

'You've survived then? And you are none the worse for a hard day's work?' Annie put her arm through Molly's and grinned. 'I bet Bessie Beaumont has been a stickler, she's always got a face on her.'

'I don't mind her; I know she's got to teach us our job. However, Connie doesn't like her, she was pulled up a couple of times today,' Molly confessed.

'Aye, well, I can believe that, she's a bit flighty is that one, our Molly. I wouldn't take all that she says as gospel and don't let her lead you astray, I know her sort. You've just to look at her, common as they come and she could do with a wash,' Annie said quietly as they met Rose, linked arms, and started to walk towards their home on Belgrave Street. Annie had taken a strong dislike to Connie and had decided that no matter how lovely she came across, there was something about her she just didn't like.

'Well, your first day over, our Molly, you'll be just like us now. Ready to get this blessed white apron and turban off and not to smell chocolate or glue.' Rose smiled. 'Bad head and tired, I bet?'

'Yes, that I am, and ready for my bed, I don't know how I'll manage all week.'

'You will, we all have, it helps when you get paid, and that keeps you going. Now, what will Mam have made for supper, because I bet you are hungry now? Soup never fills, but I know you were feeling sick, you looked nearly green. Unlike your new-found friend, who seems to know everything already,' Rose said, and sighed.

'She's all right; I don't think she has got a good home,' Molly said, going quiet.

'Well, don't let her lead you astray, put your head down and concentrate on your work, you'll be fine if you do that,' Rose said, opening the front door to the home she was always glad to return to.

'You will be knackered like the rest of us, but you will be all right.' Annie giggled as they all shouted, 'We are home,' and smelt their mother's cooking welcoming them.

5

'I'm off out, Mam, don't make me any dinner, I'm going to see Mary and then meet Larry,' Rose shouted through to the kitchen, before running directly upstairs to change out of her work overall and turban. Before she did so she flopped on the bed for a quick second. Annie and Molly weren't the only two that were knackered, as Annie had so crudely put it. Rose was finding it hard to keep to herself what was taking place in her part of the factory. It had been a busy year already with the introduction of the new chocolate Aero bar and now they were working on the new wafer bar that they wanted to perfect before launching it onto the market. Sometimes she wished she was still in Molly's shoes, making boxes, not in charge of anybody but herself. She was the new team supervisor, no longer one of the front-line workers, but not one of the bosses either, so was mistrusted by both sides and found it hard to make friends. As it was, most of her friends were settling down and getting married and it looked like Mary was going to have to do the same if her fella would stand by her in her hour of need.

She felt guilty as her mother stood at the bottom of the stairs and called, 'Next time tell me if you don't want dinner, you can have yours warmed up tomorrow, I'm not wasting it.'

Rose called down her thanks as she swung her legs to the side of the bed and started to change into the blouse and skirt that were on a coat hanger over the curtain rail, getting aired by the summer sun's rays. She dabbed a splash of lily of the valley cologne onto her wrists before grabbing her handbag from the wardrobe that she shared with Annie. Everything was shared with Annie, including the double bed that used to be her mum and dad's until her father had died. If tonight's visit to the house of both her and Larry's dreams went to plan, things would be changing, a wedding would have to be planned. Living over the brush would not be tolerated by the Rowntree Foundation, but she had heard the house was about to become vacant and she longed for her own home.

She checked herself in the wardrobe mirror, patted her blonde pinned hair into place and then ran down the stairs shouting, 'Bye,' as she slammed the terraced house's door behind her and headed out across the streets to her best friend Mary's home next to the Deanery Gardens, a little backstreet right next to York Minster.

Mary was in a right pickle, Rose thought as she rushed down and through Bootham Bar, one of the large stone entrances to the original city that had kept the Scots and other raiding forces at bay. She thought she was at least five months pregnant and the father of the baby was somewhere at sea with the Navy. Mary didn't know if he would care or even return to her in the state that she was

in and hadn't dared to tell her ageing father of her predicament. Rose herself had tried to help Mary as much
as she could but it was, as Annie had said, becoming
more and more obvious at work that Mary was with
child, especially when she kept having bouts of morning
sickness. She wouldn't be the first to be in such a state but
it put her in danger of losing her job if she did not tell her
employers soon, whether she wanted to or not.

Rose wandered down the tight snicket towards
the Entwistles' home and stood on the cobbled street,
knocking on the aged oak door and waiting for it to open.

'Ah, Rose, you must have come to see Mary, we
have just had our supper and she is in the back kitchen
washing the pots. I hope that you will forgive me, but I
am just reading the evening newspaper in the comfort of
my armchair. I will let you make your own way to her.'
Edward Entwistle was a well-educated man, some said
too well-educated, for he had no common or financial
sense when it had come to running the family grocery
shop that he had since lost. Now, he tried to make a living
running a small bookshop, while Mary had to earn true
money.

'Not at all, Mr Entwistle, I hope that you are well
and that the book trade is good.' Rose closed the door
behind her.

'So so, I lose faith in our common man, he no longer
seeks to be educated but would rather be entertained
with ridiculous stories of daring deeds. What is wrong
with reading Dickens and Tolstoy? That's what I ask

myself every day. And the world is in such a mess, nobody has a penny to their name and there is a feel of unrest in Europe; bad times are coming, of that I'm sure, Rose, my dear.'

'I'm sorry to hear all that, Mr Entwistle, I hope things improve for you, for us all,' Rose replied, knowing that once he found out that Mary was carrying a baby there would be even more worry for him. 'I'll leave you to your newspaper and go to find Mary.' She was eager to get away from the smell of the pipe Edward Entwistle smoked for comfort, and away from the gaze of the worried old man too, as he walked towards his homely comforts.

'Yes, yes, go through, I am sure you two have plenty to discuss, even though you see one another most of the day. Women always have plenty to talk about I have discovered, it amazes me.' Edward made for his chair, with his pipe and newspaper in hand.

Mary stood next to the pot sink with a tea towel in her hands. 'I thought it was you when I heard father talking. He seems to be a bit upset about some news that he's heard about Germany forbidding marriages between Germans and Jews. If he's upset over that, what is he going to be like once he realises that I am expecting and the baby's father is across the other side of the world and may not even come back to me?' Rose could see the tears welling up in Mary's eyes.

'Shh . . . Mary, as soon as Joe hears the news he will come back to you, I know he will.' Rose looked at pale-faced Mary; if her mother had still been alive it would have been clear to her that her daughter was pregnant, but with Mary's father being left alone and wrapped up in his own worries she had no one to turn to. 'Let us go and sit out in the Minster gardens, there are still a few roses flowering and it is quite warm. We can talk freely there.'

'Yes, that's a good idea, I need some fresh air, we had some left-over mutton for supper and it has left me feeling queasy.' Mary untied her cross-over apron and tried to smile. 'I'll not keep you long, I know you are meeting Larry and having a walk to the village at New Earswick and are planning for a happy future together. I'm so glad for you both, I just want you to know.'

'Oh, Mary, I feel so guilty, there's me positively gloating about my life and there's you surrounded by worry.' Rose closed the door to Mary's home and walked her friend across to the gardens, sitting on a bench as the minster's clergy went back and forth to their worship.

'Well, it's my own fault, isn't it? I shouldn't have been so eager to please Joe, our first time and it leaves me like this,' Mary said, and put her hands on her stomach. 'It's beginning to show, although I don't feel quite as sick as I used to.' Mary wiped a tear away from her eye. 'What do you think them at work will say when I tell them that I'm having a baby and am unmarried? Will they sack me? I can't afford for them to do that. Not until Joe returns – if he returns – and tells me his intentions.'

'I don't think they will sack you, Mary, it's why Rowntree's employs the people they do. They will give you the benefit of the doubt until Joe makes clear his intentions, I'm sure. You'll just be another soul for the Quaker firm to say they have saved by hard work and religion, and you are a good worker, they know that. You will be fine and by the time the baby arrives, Joe will be back and placing a ring on your finger.' Rose was glad that the doubt in her mind didn't transfer to her voice as she squeezed her friend's hand. She knew that Rowntree's would keep her at work for as long as they could but after that, she had no idea how Mary was going to cope.

'I've decided that I am going to tell my supervisor at the end of the week. She must be daft if she hasn't already realised that I'm pregnant. I know that half the chocolate-packing department has cottoned on, just by the looks they give me. The supervisor I'm sure must already know, as she's been logging me going back and forward to the toilet of late,' Mary gasped. 'I've let my father down, I've let myself down and I'm carrying a baby that I don't really want, not yet anyway.'

'It takes two to tango, Mary; this is Joe's problem as well. I hope that you have written to tell him – can he receive letters when he is at sea?'

'Yes, the post gets sent on ahead to where his ship is due to dock or is taken out to them and then distributed on board ship. They're supposed to be good for morale, but I don't think mine will be. He will probably rue the day we walked out together in the spring.' Mary breathed in and wiped her nose. 'Anyway, enough of me. You are going to look at the house in the village? Have you been offered it? Is that not unusual as you are not yet married?' Mary spoke with a hint of envy in her voice.

'We are only going to have a stroll down the avenue and have a look at number ten, where old Mrs Bowen lived. It's got the painters and decorators in and will soon be coming up for rent once the Trust is satisfied the work has been done. Larry thought it would be a good idea to have a nosy through the windows. He's thinking of putting his name down for it although he's not mentioned or even hinted at marriage yet. I think the Rowntree Trust will prioritise a married couple so it is all pie in the sky for now.' Rose blushed, she wanted so much to get married, but at the same time, she didn't want to give up work. She relished her promotion to supervisor in the new products block and could see the firm was getting bigger by the day.

'Well, if he's any sense he will get on with it and put a ring on your finger before the dashingly good-looking new manager Ned Evans gives you the eye. All the girls are talking about him. He is so handsome.'

'Yes, he is, I have noticed, he does have the looks of a film star, doesn't he? However, I'm true to my Larry, and besides, if you married somebody who you worked with every day, just imagine the conversation that you would have of an evening. Work, work, work, that is all it would be.' Rose smiled; Larry might not have had the looks of Ned, and he did smell of engine oil and soot from the steam trains he serviced, but he loved her and that was all that mattered.

'I wish I had someone like your Larry, he's always the same and is here in York, not thousands of miles away doing who knows what. They say a sailor has a woman in every port. Well, am I just the one he keeps happy in his home town?' Another tear ran down Mary's cheek as she sniffed again and blew her nose.

'Now, don't be silly, he will be back before you know it and once he realises the situation it will be you getting married before me. Now, I'm going to have to go, Larry will be waiting for me. I'll see you in the morning and I advise you to tell your supervisor everything, she'll understand, you'll see. Your father will as well, I'm sure, you are not the first to be in this situation and he will be kind to you. After all, you are his only daughter and he loves you.' Rose gave Mary a quick hug. 'Chin up, things will work out fine.'

'I hope so,' Mary sniffed. 'Now, go on, else Larry will wonder where you have got to and it soon comes in dark nowadays.'

'I didn't think you were going to come. I've sat on this bench until my bum has gone numb,' Larry said, standing up to put his arms around Rose as she ran down the river path to their meeting place.

'I'm sorry, I stopped longer than I should with Mary, but she is in such a state, she would feel much better if she told her father and those at work. She's thinking the worst with her Joe as well, picturing him with a different woman in every port. I wish she would write and tell him that he's about to become a father, I'm sure he would stand by her if he only knew.' Rose looked worried.

'It's nice to see you and all, pet,' Larry said in his jovial Geordie accent. 'Now, leave Mary behind for now and worry about us. If it's not Rowntree's, it's somebody else you are worried about. I haven't seen you for a full twenty-four hours, I need a bit of you.' Larry kissed her on her cheek and then linked his arm through hers.

'I'm sorry, she just worries me. How are you, then, are you still game for having a nosy at this empty house? I feel like I've bullied you into looking at it with me but I don't know how much longer I can share my bedroom with Annie, she drives me around the bend most nights.' Rose blushed; she knew he knew damn well why she had suggested that they looked at the empty house together. She couldn't have hinted more about her thinking it was time for them both to be settling down together if she had put a ring on his finger.

'Away with you, it was time we were thinking along those lines, I suppose, we've been courting for eighteen months now and we have both got good jobs. You don't have to make your Annie as your excuse; I sometimes just need my arse punching.' Larry grinned. 'As long as you are not expecting, because I need to save up a bit more before I walk you down the aisle and I can't afford bairns yet.'

'Larry Battersby, what do you think I am, I'm certainly not expecting and well you should know it. I'm not hinting that we should get wed, not just yet; I just want to look at this house and think about perhaps just putting my name down for one with the Trust. It can take years or months to get one, they are so sought after.'

'Aye, well, we'll have a look, put your mind at rest and then we will see. I'm not a man to be rushed, as well you know it.' Larry smiled and looked at Rose's face; he knew what she was hankering after but he wasn't going to let on what he'd got up his sleeve, she'd have to wait just a little while longer.

Rose and Larry stood on their tiptoes and looked in through the bay window at the empty house that was being decorated for a new family to live in.

'It's grand out here, a village on the edge of town, and all the houses have a garden and everything you need, even bathrooms – now wouldn't that be grand?' Larry gazed at Rose's excited face.

'Oh, I could just imagine living here, it's only a stone's throw from my work, and it would be perfect. No Annie snoring in my ear, it would be heaven.' Rose sighed as Larry gave her a mysterious look.

'Aye, well, you could have me snoring in your ear instead.' Suddenly, without warning, in the unkempt garden, Larry dropped to one knee and pulled a small box out of his pocket. 'Rose Freeman, I think it is about time I put this on your finger, that is if you'll have me?' Rose gasped and Larry's face lit up with a broad smile.

'Oh, Larry, you haven't? You have! Oh, Larry! It's beautiful, is it really for me?' Rose picked up the small diamond engagement ring from its box and tried it on her wedding finger. 'It fits, it fits perfectly, I can't believe it and there was you saying that you wanted time and you had this in your pocket all along,' she exclaimed.

'Aye, well, you've been hinting long enough and damn it, I do love you, so let's get both our names down for a house and get married as soon as we can. You are all I want, Rose Freeman, and well you know it,' Larry said, a tear in his eye as he gulped and tried to keep his emotions in check, getting up from his knees and kissing her in front of two young boys who whooped and made fun of them both.

'Oh, Larry, I thought you were never going to ask,' Rose said with a grin. 'Wait until I tell my mam, she kept saying that I'd be getting wed before I knew it. Oh, I'm so happy, just look at this ring; it must have cost you a fortune!' Rose beamed.

'Aye, it cost a bob or two, but you are worth every penny,' he said, smiling. 'I'll feel so proud with you walking down that aisle, and your mam was right, I couldn't let a lass like you slip through my fingers. We'll put our name down for one of these houses, you can stop work and I can provide for a family, two or three of 'em or even four or five, as long as we can make ends meet.' Larry had not noticed the cloud forming over Rose's face.

'I could never stop working, Larry,' she said gravely. 'I love my job, and the pay is too good now that I've got a position of responsibility. Children can come along later, we will just have to be careful, you know, take precautions.' Rose blushed as she broached the subject her mother had always lectured them all about and thought of Mary.

'Well, I'd always thought of myself as a bit of a family man. There's six of us brothers, as you know, and we all look after one another, just how it should be. Just like you three sisters do. Besides, no matter how careful we are, no doubt there will be a slip-up, it goes without saying, but it won't matter when we are wed.' Larry looked awkward as he seemed to realise that children were not yet part of Rose's plan.

'That's just it, we might both come from big families, but we never have any money and I'd quite like to have a comfortable life for a while without worries,' Rose said carefully. She had seen so many women tired and desperate to provide for their children that she had different plans for her life, especially after being given a leg-up into near management status at Rowntree's.

'Well, we'll see. What happens, happens, let's celebrate today and go and tell your mother and then on to mine and see what they have to say. It'll be a surprise for them all, but I know they will wish us well.'

'They will, my mam will be over the moon, although she knew we were pretty serious about one another.' Rose looked at the man she loved and worried yet again that his head was set on becoming a father straight away and, by the sound of it, for her to stay at home. She had more ambition than Larry, he was happy being a stoker on the railway, but she had seen what a good job and education could do for a woman and she wanted more, a lot more!

*

'Oh, my Lord, just look at that ring, it must have cost you a fortune, Larry! Now aren't you a lucky lass, our Rose? I knew that you were serious, but I didn't think perhaps this serious.' Winnie patted the cushions on the sofa as she led the engaged pair into the small front room that was kept for best. 'A drink, we will have to have a drink of sherry to celebrate.' Winnie bent down to open the cupboard door in the dresser that held a bottle of sherry and glasses for special occasions. 'Annie, Molly, get yourselves in here and celebrate with your sister, we are going to be having a wedding in the family,' Winnie yelled excitedly as she passed the open front-room door and put the papier-mâché tray with the sherry and glasses onto a worn wooden table and stood back with folded arms to look at the young couple.

'Aye, my lass, getting married! Do you think you will be able to get the house that you've been nosing around? It would be grand if you could, but you've got to get wed first.' Winnie looked her daughter up and down and then whispered quietly before Annie and Molly came into the room. 'There's no rush is there, our Rose?'

'No, there isn't, Mam; you should know me better than that,' Rose replied indignantly, while Larry looked down at his shoes.

'I didn't think there was, but I thought I'd better ask. Now here, let's raise a glass to you both,' she said with a smile on her face as she measured out what she thought were appropriate amounts for each of her daughters to drink.

Annie and Molly came into the room and hugged Rose

and smiled at the man who was going to be their brother-in-law, but who was also going to split up the close family.

'We are going to have a wedding, that will be special. Are Annie and I going to be your bridesmaids? Can I have a new dress?' Molly asked excitedly. 'Where are you both going to live?'

'Not here, I hope, I'm not sharing with you, Molly, up in that space in the roof you call your room,' Annie said as she looked at the small amount of sherry that her mother had poured her.

'No, we'll not be living here; Rose can come and live at our house until we can get one of our own,' Larry said as he drank his sherry in one gulp and kissed Rose on her cheek.

'We will get a home of our own first before our wedding, Larry. Your mother will not want me living with you all. She's only just nicely got rid of your two older brothers to lodgings of their own,' Rose replied firmly, looking across at her mother for reassurance. The last thing she wanted was to live with the Battersby family in their small railway-built terrace house, which was already filled to the rafters with Battersby men.

'Now, that would be sensible my lass, home first, then a wedding. It'll not be long before one comes up that you can both afford. Rowntree's will see you right, I'm sure, as soon as one comes up for rent. They value you, Rose, you are a good worker and they will know to look after you.'

'I know, Mam, but we will have to see. Rowntree's rent to anybody, not just their employees. We'll keep our eyes open, though.' Rose looked at Larry. 'Are we going to tell your parents before it gets dark? I don't want to be walking across York on my own.'

'I'll see you home; you are not walking on your own. But aye, we'll go and tell my folks the news. Like, it'll not come as a shock to them, they know I've been sweet on you for a while now and my ma spotted the ring when I tucked it into my pocket at teatime.'

'Did she say anything to you?' Rose asked, tucking her arm through Larry's.

'No, not a word, you know my mam, a woman of few words and my father even more so.'

Rose knew all too well what his parents were like, they were true working-class folk from the Durham coalfields who had come to live where the railways had led them, unlike her father's family who had always had desk jobs. She was marrying below herself, but love didn't take account of that.

'We both need to save up before we even think of walking down the aisle, don't we, Larry?'

'Oh, I don't know, we could get married as soon as we can if you came and lived at ours,' Larry grinned, holding her tight.

'No, please, we will wait a decent length of time; we don't have to rush into it, so let's take our time,' Rose said forcefully and grabbed her handbag from the sofa as she and Larry headed to tell the news to his family, who lived on Anderson Terrace, not far from the main railway station.

*

Maude Battersby stood with her arms folded and her pinny tied around her waist and looked at her son and the girl he was to marry.

'Well, I suppose I knew it was coming, you can't carry on like you two have without being caught out. Seeing each other every evening, it had to happen. When is it due then?' Maude asked, glaring at Rose.

'Oh no, Mrs Battersby, we are in no rush to get married, I mean there is no immediate reason for us to,' Rose said sharply to the hard-faced woman who kept her sons in order.

'No, Ma, she's not expecting, we just love one another and want to be together,' Larry said and shook his head. 'I thought you'd be glad for us.'

'What, glad to have another under my roof? Because that's what'll be happening, I bet. You have no brass and you can't afford to keep a family fed, because that's what you'll have as soon as you are wed.' Maude looked Rose up and down.

'I don't think so, Mrs Battersby,' Rose retorted, meeting her gaze directly. 'We aim to save up to rent a house in the Rowntree village and we have walked around there tonight just to have a look. We can wait until one becomes available and I'll add my name to the list tomorrow.'

'Well, he'll not be able to afford one, so I hope that you make good money. He's only a stoker; he's not got many brains,' Maude said, looking at her son as he dropped his head. 'You'll have to be the earner, so I hope that you aren't expecting.'

'That will not be a problem, I love your son and that is all that matters,' Rose said sharply and then turned to her fiancé. 'I'll go home now, Larry, don't bother to walk me, it is still just light, I can make my own way.'

'No, I'll walk you home, no problem, Rose.'

'No, you stay with your mother and I'll see you tomorrow. Really, I need some time to myself. It's been a bit of a day.' Rose walked to the door and kissed Larry on the lips before she left him standing in the doorway watching her walk into the dusk with his mother shouting for him to come in and close the door.

6

All night Rose had tossed and turned thinking about her engagement to Larry. She knew that he thought a great deal of her and had often said he loved her, but she hadn't realised that he had actually been thinking of marriage. Was she really ready for it? That she didn't know. She certainly wasn't enthralled with the thought of being part of the Battersby family; they were tough and hard-working but rough with it, except for her soft-spoken Larry. Perhaps she shouldn't have said yes so quickly, she thought, as she played with the ring that Larry could not afford to give her. However, this was what she'd been wanting, and she had said yes now and she did love him. Or so she thought; her eyes had been opened of late with the promotion at work. However, there was many a worse man out there than Larry Battersby, she thought to herself as she heard Annie mumble at the sound of the knocker-upper clattering at the window.

'I don't know why we still pay him, there's a clock downstairs and I keep my watch on all night. It'll be one less bill for our mam once you have gone off with Larry the lover if we give it up.' Annie yawned and pushed back her covers in the darkness of early morning.

'I haven't gone yet, and when I do go, you'll need him more than ever else you'll never wake up. If somebody gives me another alarm clock as a wedding present I'll give it to you, because you'll need a second one. Larry will be up long before me as he's to stoke all the trains into action,' Rose said lazily and yawned as she watched Annie get out of bed and walk over to the bedroom door to be first in line for the toilet and a morning wash.

'You are not seriously going to marry him, are you, our Rose? You could do so much better. He's not good-looking, he smells of coal and oil all the time and nobody has a good word for his family.' Annie crossed her legs as the urge to wee came over her, but she felt she had to say what had been on her mind all night.

'I've said yes, so I am, Annie. Anyway, I love him, so why shouldn't I? It's what I wanted.'

'Then you want your head seeing to. There's better catches out there than Larry Battersby and you know it,' Annie said, before rushing in a flurry of white nightdress downstairs to the outside lavvy, leaving Rose to ponder over her decision once more.

'Well, it's been a bit of a week in the Freeman house,' Winnie said as she watched her girls quickly eating their breakfast. 'My youngest has started work and my oldest is about to get married. What are you going to spring on us, Annie? I think it's your turn now.'

'Nothing, absolutely nothing, nothing ever happens in my life. I go to work, I help around home and that's my life,' Annie said quickly, one eye on the time as she gulped her mug of tea down.

'You walk out with your mates, you were out the other night, I heard you talking to them outside,' Molly said. 'In fact, you do more than I do, I'm so tired of an evening now when I get home.' Molly stuffed a crust of bread in her mouth and tried to keep it away from her still-tender gum.

'Yes, but we only have a walk down by the canal or head into town to just gaze in the windows,' Annie replied and nudged Molly to stop her from spilling marmalade down her white apron as she quickly spread it on her bread before reaching for her coat.

'Come on, you two, stop moaning and filling your faces, it's time to get to work. It's a big day today; I can tell you now that the first batch of Chocolate Crisp leaves the factory today. I need to be there to see it goes well,' Rose said and stood to wait for them both as they slurped the last dregs of their tea. 'It's got wafer in it, it's like a biscuit and tastes lovely. I bet it sells well once people try it. I bet it is going to be a real success, everyone in my department is excited about it.'

'Yes, I know, you all tried to keep it quiet, but we all found out yesterday what you've been doing. I hope Betty gets some recognition for being the one to put the idea in the suggestion box. I heard her telling everyone it was her who had written "a wafer-filled chocolate bar that a man can take to work in his pack". Then she finds out they've been making just that in your department,' Annie commented, and pushed Molly down the passage and out of the front door into the busy early morning street.

'It will be up to the management to see if she gets any recompense. I should think they will though if it is a success,' Rose replied and waited until Molly caught them both up.

'I could think of some good ideas, like get glue that doesn't smell as much. I still get a bad head when I'm in there,' Molly moaned; it had been a long first week and she was tired and ready for the weekend.

'You'll get used to it eventually. I was talking to Mrs Beaumont and she said you are progressing nicely, better than your friend Connie anyway,' Rose said and walked quickly, she couldn't be late as there was to be a launch meeting before the wafer bars started to roll off the new production line and she had to be there.

'Did she really? She always seems to be picking on me, unless she is genuinely trying to help me. She keeps telling me to pull the paper tighter so that I get better corners on my boxes. And the other day she slapped my hands when I had placed a paper rose in the wrong place. I nearly shake when she watches over me and my boxes. They do look better than when I started though.' Molly grinned with pride as she and her sisters clocked into work and walked across the open yard before having to clock in again at their various work stations.

Rose stood at the back of the management meeting and listened to one of the founders of Rowntree's giving a speech about the new machinery that they had bought for producing the four-fingered wafer bar that was covered in milk chocolate and then wrapped in silver foil with a red wrapper around it. She listened as Seebohm Rowntree spoke loud and clear as he read out the brand marketing:

'Today we launch a golden-baked wafer biscuit, moulded into a block with delicious milk chocolate. The wafer and the chocolate are kept separate – not a mixture. You can see them, quite distinctly, when you snap a piece from your Chocolate Crisp – feel them, quite separately, in your mouth. You can taste them, still quite separately, as you crunch on them. Two splendid foods, each with wonderful flavours, each adding to the enjoyment of the other. Crisp wafer, milk chocolate, giving you the Rowntree's Chocolate Wafer Crisp. This, my dear friends and work colleagues, will be a success for Rowntree's. It is to be marketed at 2d per bar and will at first be retailed at all cafes and shops in London and the south and then if successful we will bring it up north where it belongs. "The biggest little meal in a bar". If the southerners like it then us northerners will follow suit.

'Now, let's get production rolling, and get those chocolate bars wrapped and sold.' At that, Seebohm Rowntree stepped down from the podium that had been erected for his speech, leaving the machinery to be turned on and the workers to start their first shift producing the new snack bar.

Rose walked over to her position and watched as the

girls she had trained dealt with the new processes and hoped that Seebohm's new invention would be a success. He seemed to be always pushing new boundaries and was always looking for new ideas. Aero, the milky bubbly chocolate, had been his responsibility last year and now there were plans afoot to market a new box of chocolates. Molly need not have worried about not getting work in Rowntree's, it was going to need more and more workers, she thought as she walked the new production line and kept her girls in check.

'How's things progressing, Miss Freeman?' asked Ned Evans, one of the managers from the offices above. 'Everything running smoothly? I'm sure it is now that you are overseeing it all.'

'Yes, thank you, Mr Evans, everyone is excited about the new product, it looks just as it should. Inviting and waiting to be eaten and just the right size to be put into a packed lunch, as the initial suggestion said. I'm sure it will do well.' Rose took in the handsome, quiet manager who caught many of the worker's eyes with his film-star looks and quiet manner.

'I'm sure it will. You seem to be fitting in to your new role well, Miss Freeman; I presume you are happy with your new position?'

Rose looked at Ned: he had never shown any interest in her in the past and she was surprised he was doing so now. 'Very much so. I was hoping that now I am in this position I may be able to afford to rent one of the houses in the Rowntree village.'

'That would be a very good move for you, Miss Freeman. I live there and I can totally recommend the lifestyle. Perhaps you would care to come and have a look around. I moved in a year ago and I can honestly say I have not regretted it for a minute. Plus, there is all you need on your own doorstep: shops, a church, a sports hall and with the coming of the new theatre that is about to be opened we will be quite self-sufficient.' Ned smiled and touched Rose's arm slightly.

'Oh, I don't know, your wife wouldn't want a complete stranger looking around your home. But thank you.' Rose blushed, she had never had a member of management ask her to their home before and felt that all the workers were watching her and the dishy Mr Evans talking.

'Well, that's no problem as I'm not married, I live with my mother as my father passed away a few years ago now and she decided to live with me when I moved here. She would welcome your company, as would I. How about you pop around later this evening after work and your tea? Mother will put the kettle on I'm sure and get the biscuits out. But perhaps not a Rowntree's Chocolate Wafer Crisp, I think we will have seen enough of those by the end of the day,' Ned added with a laugh. 'Do you know, I really think the name Chocolate Wafer Crisp needs shortening, I'll suggest that at the next meeting. It's far too long. It needs something that is easier to say and remember. Now, am I to see you later or do you have a beau that will be walking out with you?'

'I do have a boyfriend,' Rose managed, for some reason

suddenly glad that she had not worn her engagement ring to work as she looked at the attractive Ned. 'If your mother doesn't mind, I would like to come and have a look around. I've viewed one that is empty from outside, but would like to see what they are like for room space.' She couldn't believe she was being given the time of day by Ned Evans, let alone being invited to his home.

'Ah, well, we are just next door but one from the empty house. I'll look forward to seeing you at about seven, should we say?'

'Yes, that would be lovely, thank you; I will look forward to it,' Rose replied without giving it a second thought. Larry was not going to visit her that night so what was the harm in visiting Ned Evans and his elderly mother?

'Splendid, however, now I think it is time to get back to our work. We must not set a bad example to the workers now, must we? Especially on such a busy day.' Ned grinned with a twinkle in his eye.

'No, of course not, I will see you later.'

'Indeed you will, Miss Freeman, and it will be my pleasure.' At that, Ned walked off down the production line, commenting to the staff as he went.

'Well, you look like the cat that's had all the cream,' Annie said as Rose came and sat down beside her, Molly and Connie during their dinner hour. 'I take it the new biscuit bar production is going well?'

'It is, as it happens, they look lovely and they will sell.

Here, I've brought you one each for your puddings, these have not made the grade so either the wrapper or the biscuit isn't perfect.' Rose fished three bars of the newly launched confectionery from her pocket and passed them to her sisters and Connie and watched as they unwrapped the silver-foiled bars and bit into them.

'Now, that is good because it's not a sweet, it's more a biscuit you can eat anytime,' Annie said, noticing as Connie just ate a little bit of her bar and put the rest in her pocket. 'Are you not eating all yours? Mind somebody doesn't pull you up for taking it home with you.'

'I was going to take it home for my brother but I don't want to get into bother if I do,' Connie said and wished Annie had not seen her do so.

'You'll get a chance to buy some cut-price rejects tomorrow and take them home then, better to do that than get in bother as soon as you have been taken on. There will be bags of chocolates and all sorts for you to look through, over there at the end of the hall; it's how they get rid of the rejects. Not that any of us want to see another piece of chocolate for at least two days when we leave here for the weekend.'

'Oh, then I'll finish it,' said the hungry Connie, not needing any further encouragement to eat every crumb. She hadn't got the money on her for a large lunch, unable to borrow any more from her mother or anybody and payday was a week away. She had looked in envy as the pay lady had come around with the metal trolley with a safe upon it and paid those who had worked the previous week. Handing over brown envelopes of money made all the work worth it. Next week she too would be paid, but for now, she and Molly had nothing to show for their toil.

'Yes, Annie is right, eat it while you can, everyone will be going for the rejects tomorrow, so you can say you are one of the first to try the new Chocolate Crisp Bar,' Rose said, picking up the bar and looking at the white writing across it and thinking that Ned Evans was right, it did need a more catchy name. Perhaps they could discuss it tonight when she went to see his home. She was starting to feel quite giddy and had a stomach full of butterflies over the thought that Ned Evans, no less, had actually asked her to his home! He hardly ever said anything to anyone, he was a quiet boss who just got on with his work; she felt so special, he was everyone's heart-throb throughout the factory. At the same time, she felt a bit guilty for even accepting his invitation; after all, she was now engaged to be married to her Larry. Still, an hour looking around Ned's home and visiting his mother would not hurt, would it? Pulling herself out of her thoughts she noticed her younger sister looking distracted as she sat back after finishing her bar.

'You are quiet, Molly, what's wrong?'

She looked up at her sister, her expression pained. 'I got told off, spilt some glue over somebody's made-up boxes and she had to throw them away. She was mad with me,' Molly said quietly, now near tears. Molly remembered how the elderly employee called Maggie Appleby had scowled and sworn at her as she dropped glue on the top three or four of her newly made boxes. At one point she thought she was going to slap her, but instead she had spoken her mind and got on with her job. She had apologised, but the look on Agnes's face was still etched on her mind.

'That's probably because she is on piece work and gets paid for every box she makes. It will have cost her money, but you weren't to know, and you didn't do it on purpose,' Rose said and put her arm around her little sister. 'I'm sure she will forgive you, we have all been new starters here, just watch what you are doing and apologise if you do anything wrong.'

'She was really horrible to Molly, I should have stuck up for her,' said Connie. 'She'd piled up her boxes in a stupid place anyway, so it was bound to happen.' She smiled reassuringly at the girl she considered her new best friend.

'You two just keep your noses clean and don't fall out with anybody that's worked here for a long time; those are the ones that you have to learn from. But Connie, thanks for being there for Molly, she needs a friend like you, everybody does.' Rose smiled and looked across at her own friend Mary as she entered the dining hall; her condition was beginning to show, and she was going to have to tell somebody soon of her predicament, but it wouldn't go down well with management or her father, she thought sadly.

*

88

'Where are you going to? Back down to Rowntree's village did I hear you say?' Winnie had asked Rose as she washed the dirty pots after tea.

'Yes, one of my bosses has asked me to come and have a look around his house after I mentioned that I am interested in living down there. He wants me to meet his mother as well, she gets lonely seemingly.' Rose tried not to show her nerves about going to see Ned Evans.

'Oh, hobnobbing with the bosses and their families, are we now? Does Larry know that you are going? I just noticed you said *I* was interested in the houses in the village, not *we*! I take it this boss knows that you are now betrothed?'

'Well, no, there's no need for him to know, he's only showing me around his house and asking me to be polite to his mother. He never usually pays much attention to the team I am on, until today when he was watching the new production line operate.' Rose pulled on her coat and checked her lipstick in the small mirror that hung on the wall in the kitchen.

'Well, do mind what you are doing. Bosses can sometimes take advantage of their workforce. No going upstairs with him, do you hear?' Winnie shook her head; she had seen a spark of excitement in Rose's eye and knew exactly what was going through her head. 'When I was in service them upstairs were devils for taking advantage if they took a fancy to you. Don't you be swayed by his position. Larry might not be the best catch in York but he's a good worker and steady.'

'MOTHER! Stop it! I'm not likely to run away with him or do anything else. He is showing me his home and that's all.' Rose felt her heart beating fast; her mother knew her too well, perhaps she should have waited to put on her lipstick and worn more sensible shoes, she thought, as she walked down the passageway and out the front door.

'Lord, you look swanky, you can't be going to see Mary with high heels and lipstick, and if that's all for Larry then it's wasted,' Annie said as she sat on the small garden wall talking to her friend from two streets down. 'Where are you off then?'

'Never you mind, it's work business, that's all,' Rose said and tottered off down the street trying not to trip in the heels that she had only worn twice before.

'Lord, our Rose is changing; just look at her, all she thinks about is her work. Not like us two; there are better things in life, like the lads that come into the docks with cocoa beans.' Annie grinned and linked arms with her best friend Joan Smith. 'Now I could spend all my time with that new one that came last week. Did you see him, oh so bonny? In fact, let us go and sit on the canal side and see if there's any sign of him now.' At that, Annie set off with Joan in the opposite direction to her big sister.

Rose breathed in and smoothed her skirt down as she opened the white-painted lattice garden gate and walked up the spotless garden path with vibrant dahlias in full bloom on either side of it. She softly pressed the doorbell and for a swift second queried just why she was standing outside one of her employers' doors on a Thursday evening after work. Her stomach was churning and her head spinning. Ned Evans was a different class of person to her. He was suited management, the sort that floor workers did not mix with; what if her mother was right and what if he had only lecherous ideas on his mind? It was too late to turn and run now, she thought, as she heard footsteps and the Yale latch being turned.

'Ah, Miss Freeman, I thought it would be you. I was just telling my mother that we had a visitor this evening.' Ned Evans smiled as he opened the door and Rose thought he looked even more handsome in his hand-knitted cardigan and loose-necked white shirt as he welcomed her into his home.

'Mother is in here, she is just listening to the news on the radio, although I must say it is all very depressing: the economy is under strain; there are murmurings of war and nothing seems to be right in the world. However, please come through into the living room, I'll put the kettle on and make us all a cup of tea. I'm afraid my mother struggles with her arthritis, so I have had to become the maid and cook.' Ned smiled and showed Rose along the hallway which was covered in beautifully painted scenes of York.

'Mother, this is Miss Freeman, she is interested in renting one of the houses in the village when one becomes available,' said Ned as he made Rose welcome in the modern, furnished living room, standing behind her as his elderly mother lifted her head and looked up at her son's visitor.

'Miss Freeman, that's a bit formal, Ned, does she not have a Christian name?' Ivy Evans stared at the young woman who was one of the few female visitors invited within the Evans home.

'It's Rose, Mother, but I should call her Miss Freeman, seeing that we work together,' Ned replied, clearly anxious that Rose wasn't offended.

'Don't be so daft, Ned, she's a guest in our house and you are not at work. Now come and sit down here, Rose, and then I can see you, and Ned, you put the kettle on, where's your manners?' Ivy patted the settee for Rose to sit down beside her.

Ned grinned, then placed his hand out to guide her to the seat her mother wanted her to take. She smiled as she sat down next to the old lady, who had a shawl around her shoulders despite the weather, and started chatting to her as Ned left the room to fill the kettle. He was used to following his mother's instructions.

'Your son was so kind to suggest I come and have a look at your house so I know what they are like from the inside. I'm thinking of renting one. I must say they are very roomy, there is still a lot of space, even with this beautiful dresser and three-piece suite.' Rose looked around the room and smiled as the old woman leaned forward and took her hand.

'He's shy, you know, is my son, I'm amazed that he dared ask you to visit, you must have really caught his eye. You are a bonny bit of a thing, he did right bringing you home.' Ivy sat back in her chair as she heard Ned stirring the tea ready to bring it in to them both.

Rose blushed. 'Oh, I don't think he thinks that way of me, he's just trying to help,' she replied, feeling uncomfortable as Ned returned carrying the tea tray and putting it down on a small table underneath the bay window.

'Milk and sugar, Miss Freeman?' Ned asked, looking across at her.

'Rose!' his mother reminded him sharply, shaking her head.

'Just milk, thank you, no sugar,' Rose said, smiling at his mother.

'Sweet enough, aren't you, Rose, I can tell that straight away. Tell me, what do your parents do? Are they employed at Rowntree's? It seems it is the three Rs that employ people in York: Rowntree's, the Railway or the River. It's not like where we come from in the North-East where it's the pits. I was glad when Ned showed he had the brains to escape having to go down the pit. He's good with figures, you know; don't know where he gets that from because his father was nobbut a miner and I was in service when I was younger. We are not as posh as some that work at Rowntree's, that's why he keeps himself to himself.' At this, Ned passed Rose her tea and frowned at his mother for telling his employee their private business.

Rose took her cup and found her hand shaking as she sipped her tea. 'My mother was in service too, but my father worked on the railway, he was a clerk in the ticket

93

office until a few months before his death. Now my mother stays at home and we three girls bring in enough for her to keep the house on. We all work at Rowntree's now. My youngest sister just started this week.' Rose looked up at Ned as he sat down next to the table and sipped his tea.

'Nowt wrong with being in service. I bet your mother misses your father. I miss my Stan, I'm just thankful I have my Ned, here. He's a good lad and works hard both here and at work. I couldn't wish for a better lad.' Ivy looked at her son and smiled as she sat back and enjoyed her drink.

'That's not what you say sometimes, Mother,' Ned grinned. 'In fact, I couldn't do anything right yesterday.' Ned took her frail hand affectionately.

'That's because you never shut up about that choc-olate biscuit that you have just started to make. It is all I have heard about of late and you still keep moaning about the name they have given it. If you don't like it, tell that boss of yours that you don't, you are usually right about these things.'

'It's not as easy as that, Mother. The board has decided and we have to abide by the decision. Now, no more talk of work, both Rose and I are away from it now.' Ned sipped the last dregs of his tea and looked across at Rose. 'Well, you have seen the living room and the hallway, would you like to see the kitchen and perhaps upstairs?' Ned seemed uncomfortable that his mother had raised his concerns over work to Rose.

'The lass has barely touched her tea, there's no need to rush her, lad,' Ivy said sharply.

'It's all right, Mrs Evans, I need to get home anyway, and I've a few things to do before morning.'

'All right, pet, but you come back, if only to see me, I don't get out and about like I used to.' Rose nodded and smiled as she rose from her seat, placing her tea cup on the tray next to Ned as he stood up too.

'I must apologise for my mother, she's like a leech with any visitors that we have. She gets lonely when I am not there to keep her company through the day. She is also extremely nosy.' Ned smiled as he led Rose into the kitchen of his home and watched as she looked around her.

'That's no problem, she's a lovely woman. I didn't realise that you came from a mining family; I assumed that you must be related to the Rowntrees like a lot of the managers there.' Rose looked around her at the spotless, well-fitted kitchen, with a sink that you could stand up against and admire the garden, and with room for a good-sized kitchen table and chairs with cupboards around the sides.

'No, like my mother says, I was lucky and fell on my feet when I got a job there. I think it helped that our family are Quakers, they value their beliefs, as you can see in all that they do.' Ned went to stand next to Rose. 'It's a good-sized kitchen, isn't it? Then there's a small room back here which we keep for best. It is hardly ever used as we don't have that many visitors as my mother has already pointed out. And when we do, my mother always drags them in to see her and they never get to our best room, just like with you.' Ned opened an adjoining door and led Rose into the room that they kept for visitors, watching as she touched the chenille-covered suite and looked at the photos on the fireplace.

'You have a lovely home. They are a lot bigger than they look from the outside. I think perhaps I am aiming too high for my pocket.' Rose decided not to mention her engagement to Larry as she looked at the handsome, well-groomed man that all the women in Rowntree's swooned over.

'Would you like to look upstairs? There are three bedrooms and a bathroom with a bath, toilet and an airing cupboard that my mother wonders how she ever managed without. Anything is possible, Rose, if you put your mind to it – and you are a very capable young woman,' Ned said admiringly as they both walked into the hallway.

'Oh, no, I could never look around your bedrooms, that is too private; you have already been too kind for showing me around this much.' Rose hesitated. 'Thank you for saying that I'm capable, sometimes when I'm at work I feel anything but.' She blushed and looked into Ned's blue eyes and for a brief moment found herself wishing that she had not accepted Larry's proposal.

'Well, you need not worry on that count. The management knows that you are one of their prize workers and I know they are appreciative. You are a vital part of the new production line,' Ned said warmly as he passed the living-room door, his mother clearly having heard what he said.

'For goodness' sake, my lad, you are useless at talking to women,' she cried, sighing as she heard her son open the door for Rose to leave.

'Thank you, once again, for showing me around.' Rose smiled as Ned shook his head apologetically at his mother's comment. 'Goodbye, Mrs Evans, I'll perhaps see you again shortly,' Rose called down the hallway, hearing a muffled reply that included Ned's name.

'My mother seems to want to run my life at the moment. I do apologise.' Ned smiled and looked at Rose.

'That's what mothers do, mine is just the same. Thank you again. I'd better be on my way, it looks like rain,' Rose said, smiling shyly as she started to walk down the garden pathway.

'Here, let me get the gate.' Ned rushed past her and opened the garden gate for his visitor, looking as if he had something more to say. She waited expectantly and looked at the flustered Ned.

'Erm . . . I know this is perhaps inappropriate of me, but I wondered, would you like to go for a walk with me this Sunday? If the weather is fair and you have nothing else to do? It would be nice to get to know you a little bit better.' He lowered his head briefly, before raising it again and looking seriously into her eyes. 'Perhaps my mother is giving me some good advice for once.'

Rose stood and looked at him. Ned Evans, the most lusted-after man in Rowntree's, was asking her out for a walk and all she was thinking was that she should really say no, she couldn't betray her Larry. But before she knew it the words just came tumbling out of her mouth with a shy smile. 'That would be lovely; I will look forward to it.'

'I thought you would say no. Should we meet at the top of Monkgate at one? I will have seen to my mother's dinner by then.' Ned looked towards his home and noticed the net curtains move as he turned back to Rose.

Rose took a deep breath; she'd not mention Larry. 'Yes, one o'clock at Monkgate will be ideal.' She felt her heart pounding, she had hidden the truth about Larry and was about to two-time him with her boss, but it was worth it just to walk down Monkgate with such a handsome man.

7

Annie's legs ached. It was Friday and nearly home time, the time she looked forward to all week. It was just a blessing to get away from the endless chocolate decorating and packaging and the banter that went with it as each girl talked about what was going on in her life. Unlike Rose, she hated her job, she wanted to break away, leave York and see the world. Rowntree's was not everything to her, it was just a way of getting some money in her purse, although she was never left with much once her mother had taken her board and lodging from it.

'What are you doing this weekend, Annie? Got anything planned? I'm going to get my hair permed. Flo from next door is coming around to do it. My curls keep dropping out and it needs cutting.' Susan, the girl who worked across the other side of the never-ending flowing belt of chocolates, grinned as they both watched the clock count to the last few seconds of the Friday shift.

'I've nothing planned, I've no money so can't do anything. I might sit on the side of the canal and watch the barges come in and out with the cocoa beans and sugar; I like to see what they unload and where it has come from,' Annie replied as she put the last swirl of dark chocolate on the last batch of Black Magic as she heard the end-of-shift whistle blow.

'What you want is a fella, and to take more care with your appearance, you never will get a man if you slop about like you do,' Susan scolded, laughing. 'But happen you are right and I'm in the wrong, fellas are nothing but bother anyway. You keep dreaming and I'll keep trying to make myself as attractive as I can. Thank God that bloody whistle's gone,' Susan said with a grin as she stood back from the conveyor belt and took in the packed and decorated chocolates, thinking that she had done another good week's work.

'Our daft Rose has gone and got engaged to Larry Battersby, she wants her head seeing to. That family is nothing but trouble, even though Larry seems the quiet one out of them. Mam seems all right with it all though,' Annie said as she and Susan walked out of the long low factory in an orderly fashion with the rest of the white-aproned workers who were tired and ready for home.

'Well, that's no surprise, she's been walking out with him for eighteen months, but I'd have thought she could have done better for herself. She's clever is your Rose and good-looking with it. I've got my eye on Brian Mason, but he never looks this way. I think he's so handsome and have you seen him dance? He can dance a real good foxtrot. In fact, I might go to the dance hall once my hair is permed on Saturday night, are you coming with me? We can have a good laugh. We could go to the ballroom in Burton's Buildings, I know it's supposed to be teetotal but I always take a nip of my father's whisky in with me, nobody ever tells and everybody does it anyway.' Susan stood at the clocking-out gates and waited for a reply.

'I don't know, I've got two left feet and I'm not into sitting watching people dance and have a good time, I'll be better off at home,' Annie said and was relieved to see Molly coming across the yard with Rose not far behind her. 'I'll let you know, or if I turn up I turn up. I bet you knock Brian Mason for six with your new perm, he doesn't know what he's missing.' Annie gave her friend a warm smile as she walked quickly to join her two sisters on their walk home. Susan was man-mad; all she wanted to do was find her ideal man and settle down. She had a figure that drew attention, but she didn't seem to be able to catch the eye of Brian Mason, a local lad who seemed to have his pick of all the local women.

'Well, your first week over, Molly. Do you think you will survive?' Rose asked as all three walked back home along with the rest of the workers.

'Yes. I think so. I've made new friends and hope to meet up with Connie tomorrow afternoon, she's coming on the train to go to the pictures with me, despite me trying to tell her I'm not really interested. The trouble is neither of us has any money,' Molly said and put her head down.

'I'll give you your ticket money in and Mam might give you enough for fish and chips,' Rose said, putting her arm affectionately around her youngest sister.

'I'm not keen on your new friend; she's a strange one,

too clever for me, I heard her talking to another worker when she was at our dinner table. She knows every trick in the book when it comes to getting something for nothing,' Annie said, and then decided she should amend what she had just said as Rose seemed to be less hard upon her. 'Perhaps it's because I don't know her well and she is trying to impress everyone. I'm sure Bessie Beaumont will soon put her in her place if she steps out of line.'

'She's all right, she's got it hard at home, and I don't think her mam looks after her family very well. You'd like Connie if you got to know her. What are you going to do this weekend, Annie? I know Rose will be walking out with Larry as she always does, that goes without saying.'

'I am, I think, but he hasn't made plans yet. I some-times think he takes me for granted,' Rose said quietly, silently thinking of her promise to Ned to walk out with him on the Sunday.

'Don't say that, our Rose, you have just got engaged to him, you should be over the moon. Even though I've thought from the start you could do better. At least you have a fella; nobody ever looks at me, although Larry is not really much of a catch,' Annie said, opening the door to their home and the smell of their tea. Connie might not have much of a home life, but their mother looked after them with every bone of her body, and they were each grateful for her love.

'One day, Annie, somebody will catch your eye and that will be that, I just know it,' Rose said, hanging up her coat in the hallway and hoping secretly that Larry would not be calling for her that evening as she would have to lie and tell him that she was doing something other than walking out with him on Sunday. Ned Evans had treated her today like he would on any other day at work but at one point they had shared a knowing look, each of them clearly thinking of their Sunday meeting.

'Well, I'm going to bed early if I'm going out tomorrow afternoon,' Molly said, looking questioningly at Annie.

'I'll just go for a walk down by the canal before it gets dark, get some fresh air and try to get rid of the smell of chocolate,' Annie said, and both her sisters shook their heads.

'You'll not find a fella down there; go for a walk down into town, instead of wandering with Joan like two lost souls. I always think everybody and anybody could be on those barges that come and go, so just be careful,' Rose said as she called out a hello to her mother, her mouth watering at the smell of the ham and pea broth that was going to be their supper.

'We both like watching the things being unloaded, especially the cocoa and sugar, and imagining where they have come from, there's nothing wrong in that,' Annie snapped at her sister. 'Some of us think farther afield than York.'

'Sorry, I didn't mean to sound overprotective, but all sorts of folk come and go on those barges. Just be careful, our Annie. They might pick you up and kidnap you and before you know it you'd be on the other side of the country and wanting to come home.' Rose was half joking but half serious; she had seen some of the canal people and they always looked rough to her.

'I will, but you are totally wrong, they are only making a living like the rest of us,' Annie replied and hung her coat up, thinking about the lad she had seen the other evening. Hoping that he'd be there again if she and Joan sat on their usual seat and talked about what was on their minds until dusk when the bats started to flutter over their heads as they headed out of the city's ruined walls to look for their night feed.

'Now then, girls, another Friday, I don't how where the weeks fly. To think, Molly, you have worked at Rowntree's a full week now, you'll be coming home with a pay packet next week and then you'll realise that it's all worthwhile.'

Molly sat down at the dinner table without replying, she was too tired. She doubted she could keep her eyes open while she sipped her soup.

'She wants to go to the pictures with her new mate tomorrow, Mam, can you sub her enough to get fish and chips?' Rose asked as they all sat down and ate together.

'Depends if her mate is a man or not, she is a bit too young to be making eyes with a fella on the back row,' Winnie grinned as Molly turned bright red.

'You know it isn't, Mam. It's Connie that works with me. She's going to come from Selby if her parents allow her and she can get some money. If it were tonight, I'd be too tired, but a good night's sleep and a bit of a lie-in and I should feel a lot better. Could you lend me some money please, Mam, if she does come? I've told her where I live so she might be knocking on our door.'

'I don't know, I try and save and put a bit away each week from out of your wages for emergencies and every weekend one of you wants some of it back. It's a good job our Rose makes good money and that old Ted Lawson pays me a bit for keeping his house straight for an hour or two a week, else we would be begging on the street.' Winnie looked at her three girls who she would do anything for and they knew it and smiled. 'Aye, if she comes I'll give you enough for fish and chips, but it comes out of your wages next week, mind. So don't be making a habit of it like someone I could mention.' Winnie glanced across at Annie, who despite being the quieter of the three seemed to spend what money she had frivolously on magazines about travel and faraway places that she would never in her dreams ever visit.

Annie said nothing but pushed her chair back and stood behind it. 'I'm off out for a walk with Joan, Mam. Is that all right? I'll be back before dark.'

'I swear if I didn't know better that you had a fella and all, but Joan's mother tells me that all you do is go and watch the barges come and go and moan about work. One day one will appear for both of you, no doubt, just like Larry did for Rose, and then I'll be losing another one of you.' Winnie sighed. 'One day I'll be a lonely old woman living on my own, trying to make ends meet with three daughters who are too busy to visit me because of their own families.'

'Never, Mam. We would never leave you on your own,' Molly said and got up from her chair to put her arms around her mother, whom she could never see being out of her life.

'Happen not for a while then, love. At least I hope not,' Winnie said and hugged her youngest tight. 'Get yourself away, Annie, but take care, don't leave it too late to come home. And I suppose you, lady, will be seeing Larry, seeing it is Friday night?' Winnie looked across at Rose who was suspiciously quiet.

'I don't know, it depends if he calls for me. I'm not walking over to his if he doesn't,' Rose replied.

'Not a lovers' tiff already? Not when you've just announced your engagement, I hope?' Winnie looked at her daughter; something was wrong.

'No, Mam, I just thought I might wash my hair if he doesn't show his face before seven. Have a quiet night because we will be going dancing tomorrow night as usual,' Rose said, hoping that Larry just for once wouldn't call for her.

'All right then, it seems that you are all settled for the evening and I'll sit down and do some knitting. It might not be long before I'm knitting baby clothes, but make sure you wed him before then, our Rose. We'll not have you in the same condition as that friend of yours.' Winnie started to clear the table as her girls made themselves busy.

'I'll see you later, Mam, I won't be late,' Annie said as she took her coat down from the hook in the hallway and put it on, buttoning it up to the top. Autumn would soon put a stop to her walks along the canal and then she would have to retreat into her own world or have a moan to Joan if she could get away from home. She was going to make the most of each evening before the dark nights came and she had to sit around the front-room fire with her sisters and pretend to be content with her lot.

'I didn't think that you were going to come.' Annie turned to her friend as she sat down beside her and wrapped her coat around her legs.

'Well, there's nothing else to do and my father is in a bad mood, so I'm best out of it at the moment,' Joan said as she lit a cigarette and sat back watching the smoke rise from her mouth and wishing Annie would sometimes find a more sociable place to meet.

'I wish my dad was still alive, we used to have some good times together, I miss him so much,' Annie sighed. 'Sometimes I can hardly remember his face; he's been gone so long. He used to sit me on his knee and tell me stories of lost lands and people that he made up just for my amusement. I can't blame him I suppose for always wanting to travel.'

'He was better than my dad; I can't do right for doing wrong. I invariably end up with a clout around the lug, just for being there. Mam says it's his nerves since he was gassed in the war, he can't cope with any sharp bangs or noises; he thinks it's a bomb going off.' Joan nudged Annie sharply. 'Here, look, it's the barge again with that good-looking lad on board; they must be back with another load of beans.' Sure enough, they could hear the chug of a heavily loaded barge pushing its way around the bend and along the murk of the canal waters.

'Oh, he is so good-looking, I don't care what colour his skin is, he's so handsome,' Annie said, lifting her head up to view the red and green barge with the name *Freespirit* painted alongside its bow, to look for the young lad about her age with such exotic looks.

'Your mam would go mad if you took him home, you know she would! It would be bad enough if you took a lad from off the backstreets home with you. But a lad of his colour and off a barge from Liverpool, she would murder you or near as dammit.' Joan couldn't understand Annie's fascination with the lad that came as regular as clockwork to the Rowntree Wharf to deliver cocoa beans. She knew that her family would tan her backside if she came home with anybody but a lad of her own class and race, and there was her best friend losing her heart to a lad who she didn't even know the name of, and knew nothing about.

'He will be just the same as us, Joan, it doesn't matter what colour your skin is. I think he looks so handsome, just look at him walking around the decks.' Annie watched as the barge came nearer and edged up near the canal bank, only a few yards from where they were sitting on the bench. 'Oh, Lord, he's looking at us, Joan, he's looking at us!'

'Well, that's what you want him to do, isn't it? You

have dragged me here often enough and looked at him for long enough. You should be pleased,' Joan said as they watched the fit athletic young man jump off the barge as it bumped up by the side of the wharf and pull on the mooring to tie and secure the barge in place. Both girls pretended to continue their conversation as the captain of the barge came out and made sure all was in order before turning the engine off and patting the lad on his back and walking down the banking side to register his arrival with Rowntree's.

'Oh, my goodness, Annie, he's coming our way. I don't know what to say to him, I've never talked to anyone like him,' Joan said as Annie shook her head at her friend's ignorance.

'Course you do, he's just like us, don't be so stupid,' Annie said sharply and felt her stomach churn. He was actually walking towards them after all these times of sitting and admiring him as he visited York from Hull docks, bringing with him the basic ingredients for Rowntree's business.

Both girls tried not to look as the lad approached them, dressed in a checked jacket and grey shirt with black trousers and a red spotted handkerchief tied around his neck, which gave him a certain swaggering look. The look that had caught Annie's eye from the start.

'Good evening, ladies, admiring the view, are we?' Joshua Ramsey said in the broadest Scouse accent that the girls had ever heard. 'Shove up then, you two, let a tired canal worker rest his weary legs,' he added, smiling at both girls.

Annie moved up closer to Joan, but neither of them knew quite what to say.

'There must not be a lot to do around here, as I see both of you most times when I deliver to the chocolate factory. Do you both work there? Must be grand to be able to eat free chocolate all day.'

'There's plenty to do but we like to sit here and have a natter, it doesn't cost anything and the view isn't that bad,' Annie said with a sly smile. 'We do work for Rowntree's; nearly everybody does in York. But there's not free chocolate every day, and besides, you get fed up with the smell.'

'Well, I'm staying over in York until Sunday, the boss has got us cheap lodgings, he's off to see his other woman and I'm going to be left to my own devices, I could do with two girls like you two showing me around the town,' Joshua grinned. 'That is, if you don't mind being seen with folk like me.'

'No, not at all,' Annie said quickly as Joan kicked her, not wanting to get involved with the lad that they didn't know from Adam. 'Joan's going to be busy tomorrow but I'm free all day. I'm called Annie, Annie Freeman, and this is Joan Smith.' Annie looked over at Joan, who seemed really angry at her.

'Well, Joan and Annie, I am Joshua Ramsey – Josh – and it's a pleasure to make your acquaintance. It's not every day you come across two bonny lasses like yourselves sitting on a bench all alone. As if they were just waiting for you.' Josh gave the broadest smile Annie thought that she had ever seen in her life.

'Good to meet you, Josh, we have seen you coming back and forward for a while, only by chance though.' Joan pulled a face as she heard Annie make him feel welcome. She never thought that her best friend would be so pally with the lad that they had noticed for a month or two, knowing what reaction their parents would give them if they ever found out. Nobody ever went out with a lad of colour, the scandal would be too much.

'Yes, and I've seen you but never had the chance to make myself known. Anyway, I've done it now. So, where are we meeting tomorrow, then, and at what time?' Josh put his head to one side and winked.

'I'll meet you here at eleven. Will that be all right?' Annie asked and felt herself blush.

'If you can make it one, that would be better? I might have to help the boss in the morning, and besides, we could hit the town in the evening,' Josh said, standing up.

'Oh, yes, maybe,' Annie said quietly. It would be fine walking around York with Josh, but to be seen out with him in the pubs and dance halls was another matter.

'It doesn't matter if you can't, I know the problem, and I get it all the time,' Josh said, his face falling as he started to walk away.

Annie was quick to blurt out her reassurance. 'That's no problem with me, people can say what they want!' she cried. 'I'll be here at one, and yes, we will make a day of it.'

Her words were met with a grin and a wink. 'See you then, Annie Freeman. Are you sure that you won't be joining us, Joan?' Josh asked, already looking like he knew the answer.

'No, I'm washing and setting my hair tomorrow, but I hope that you both have a good day,' Joan said, finding the first excuse she could think of to get out of an awkward situation.

'All right, just you then, Annie? We can have a right sweet day together. But now I'm away for some scran, I'm hungry and I've some bacon and eggs waiting for me on the barge.'

Annie and Joan watched as Josh walked back to the moored barge and climbed aboard before linking arms and walking home.

'What have you said yes to that for, Annie? It's one thing to eye him up, but quite another to walk out with him! Your mother will go mad!' Joan said as they set off for home.

'He's just the same as us, why shouldn't I walk out with him? Anyway, you've admired him as much as I have, you are just chicken, Joan Smith.' Annie felt sick to the bottom of her stomach, however; Joan was right, if her mother ever found out she would have plenty to say. She vetted every lad that knocked on the door whether it was the post boy or butcher boy, but a lad that worked on the barges and was coloured would definitely not be welcome anywhere near the Freeman family.

'I may be chicken, but I'm not daft. You don't know

the first thing about him. You just be careful tomorrow. In fact, I wouldn't show my face, I'd keep away.'

'I'll see, it might be raining and then it won't be worth going. Washing your hair! Couldn't you think of something else, Joan? It was so obvious that you had no intention of joining us.' Annie pulled Joan's arm tighter, she was a good friend but useless at thinking of excuses.

8

'You look dressed up. What are you up to, Annie, you never dress up on a weekend?' Molly said, looking at her sister in her best knitted cardigan and tweed skirt as she picked up her handbag and checked her lipstick in the hallway mirror.

'Never you mind, Miss Nosy, it's nothing to do with you. Can you tell Mam that I might not be back for dinner tonight? I might be eating out with a friend,' Annie said, wishing Molly would shut up and let her get on her way before her mother came back from having tea with the next-door neighbour.

'It's a lad, isn't it, you are off out with a lad? You never put that much effort into dressing for going out with Joan,' Molly grinned. 'Who's the poor devil who is daft enough to put up with you, our Annie?'

'Just go back to your bed, you still look half dead, and say nothing to our mam, she'll only interrogate me when I get home and want to know the far end of a fart and where it's gone. Besides, it's nobody you know and none of your business.' Annie tucked her bag under her shoulder. 'If you know nothing, you can't say anything.' Then, with a quick check of herself, she left Molly watching her leave the house as she quietly closed the front door so that her mother would not hear her leaving from next door.

Annie felt her stomach churn as she made her way along the towpath towards where the barge was moored and saw Josh waiting on the bench as promised. He was smoking a cigarette with his spotted handkerchief around his neck, and his dark curly hair was now covered with a checked cap. Should she turn around and return home? It was like Joan said, she had no idea who he really was and she would be talked about and ridiculed for walking out with someone of a different class and colour than herself. She steadied her nerves; it didn't matter to her, so why should it matter to anybody else? The narrow-minded people of York would have to mind their own business. She had heard enough from Joan the previous night, who up to that point had been all too interested in the lad that both of them had fancied.

'I didn't think that you'd come.' Josh flicked his cigarette butt into the canal and stood up to look at Annie.

'Of course I'd come, why wouldn't I? I never go back on my promises,' Annie said, meeting the gaze of the lad that she knew was going to get her into so much bother if her mother found out about their meeting.

'I just thought . . . you know, well, you are here now, so that's all that matters,' Josh said, looking awkward.

'Yes, I'm here, and as promised I'm going to show you York and perhaps we could have a drink of tea somewhere? There's a nice little tea room next to The Shambles and I have some money in my handbag.'

'We'll see, it will just be nice to walk and get to know you, anything else will be a bonus,' said Josh, putting his hands in his pockets as they strolled away from the canal and headed towards the Monk Bar, one of the main entrances into ancient York. 'So, tell me about yourself and your family. Have you any sisters or brothers?'

'Two sisters, Molly and Rose, I live with them and my mam. My father died quite a few years back. And you?'

'Just me and my ma, I never had a father around, he was a sailor and left my mother up the duff with me. She's had it hard because of him, so I understand if you don't want to be seen with me. Folk can judge you for what skin you are born in and are cruel to women who marry out of their class. My ma is white, by the way, I just inherited my father's good looks,' Josh grinned. 'She wasn't the only one, though. Liverpool is a port, sailors can get it where they will although my ma says she loved my father, it's just he never came back from one of his voyages.'

'I'm sorry, it must have been bad for you and your mother,' Annie said, ducking as they passed under the arch of the ancient Roman fortress that once defended York from attack.

'It is, right, but you get used to it. That's why I was surprised when you said you'd walk out with me. Your friend Joan, I don't think she was so enthralled with the idea.' Josh looked up at the mighty tower with loop holes for the firing of arrows and gun ports and murder holes where boiling liquids had been thrown on anybody trying to raid the mighty gate. 'This place is fantastic,

I've never seen anything like it,' he said, gazing up in amazement.

'We can walk around the walls if you want, they run all the way around old York and it's a good walk, it's about two miles altogether and there are different gates and towers along the way. Then I'll show you The Shambles, it's a lovely old street and it's got that nice tea shop I mentioned earlier, we could go there after we walk along the wall.' Annie smiled at Josh, she was glad that she had agreed to walk out with him, he was just a normal lad and nobody should have the right to judge him because of his colour, she thought, as they both climbed to the top of the sturdily built stone wall that surrounded the city.

'Lordy, you can see for miles from up here and look right down into York. Look at the minster, this is a beautiful city that you live in, Annie,' Josh said as they leaned back against the city walls and looked around them at the tall spires of the Minster rising above everything else.

'I suppose it is, but when you have lived here all your life and know no different you sometimes wonder what other cities are like. I'd love to travel the world and visit mysterious places. That's why I often sit on the canal bank and watch the barges unload their cargo. Sugar from the Caribbean, cocoa beans from South America; I like to think that sometime I will be able to visit those places, just sail around the world and never come back.' Annie spoke wistfully and looked into the distance.

'What, like my father? He never came back, but

everyone needs a home of some sorts,' Josh said, sliding his arm around Annie's waist.

Annie looked at him, wondering whether to permit this or not, but she found she liked it as he held her tight, and they continued their walk along the wall, ignoring the disapproving looks that they were given by some. They were enjoying each other's company and that was all that mattered.

'Isn't this lovely? Do you know, you could nearly shake someone's hand in the room opposite if you leant out of the bedroom windows,' Annie said as she took Josh's offered hand and walked with him down the medieval street called The Shambles. 'And have you noticed how small all the shops are? This is the tea room I told you about.' Annie turned and led him into the tea shop she had set her mind upon. It was built in Tudor style and above the doorway was a sign saying 'Ye Olde Tea Room'. Inside, the tables were covered with chintz rosy coverings and there was a divine smell of freshly baked cakes which felt heavenly as they both sat down at a table near the window.

'This is my treat for keeping me company all day. I'd have just been sitting in the cabin on the barge if you had not agreed to join me today,' Josh said, passing Annie the small menu to look at as the waitress walked over to serve them.

'I'll just have a cup of tea. I'm not hungry, my mam always insists we have a good breakfast on a Saturday morning, it makes up for the rest of the week when we are always in a rush.'

'Then I'll just have a cup of tea too, we can maybe have fish and chips on our way back home after the pictures, or is there a dance hall that we could go to? I love to dance,' Josh said as he looked across at Annie admiringly. He looked up at the waitress and spoke quietly. 'Two teas, please.'

'I can serve you two teas,' said the prim and proper waitress with her pad in her hand, 'but we will be closing in five minutes.'

'In five minutes? But it is only three o'clock, it's your busiest time,' Annie exclaimed, looking around at people eating cakes and drinking tea at their leisure.

'Well, I've been told to say we close in five minutes, so that's what I'm telling you,' the waitress said, glancing over at her boss behind the counter who was looking worriedly across at her.

'You are not closing are you? You just don't want our custom, is that it?' Annie said and looked across at Josh who was about to stand up and leave.

'Leave it, Annie, I often get this, we will just go. It's not worth the argument.' Josh shook his head and watched as Annie looked perplexed.

'No, it's not right, your money is as good as anybody else's,' Annie retorted, picking up her handbag from the floor as the owner came across to their table.

'Is there a problem here, May? Have you explained that we are to close shortly?'

'Yes, Mrs Walker, I have.' The waitress blushed.

'Don't worry, missus, we are going, there's no bother

here,' Josh said, taking Annie's arm. 'Come on, Annie, we will find somewhere more friendly.'

'Perhaps the eatery down the street will take your kind,' the owner said, pushing Annie's chair in as she got up and started to follow Josh towards the door.

But Annie stopped in her tracks at that. '*Our kind*, what do you mean by that?' she asked, standing her ground as Josh pulled on her arm.

'Annie, come on, I get it nearly everywhere I go, folk are just ignorant. Come on, I don't want any bother.'

'It's not right, Josh. She shouldn't be able to get away with it,' Annie said loudly, glaring at the people watching them or keeping their heads down as they ate their cake and sipped their tea. Then she followed Josh out of the shop. 'Is it always like that for you? How do you put up with it?'

'You get used to it. You learn where you can go and be made welcome and where you won't. In Liverpool back home, it's not too bad as it's a port, there's folk of my colour on most streets, but I knew I'd not be made welcome in there – it was too English!'

'It's disgusting, you should have warned me,' Annie said, linking her arm determinedly through Josh's. 'Come on, I know who will make you welcome and I bet you would rather have a pint of the best Yorkshire ale anyway. We will go and sit in the snug at the Olde Starre Inne, the landlord was a best friend of my father's. He'll not throw us out. He'll not be bothered where your money comes from just as long as he gets some of it.'

'I can't believe that you will still be seen with me. Most white girls don't give me the time of day,' Josh said as they made their way through the centre of York to Stonegate, one of the busiest streets in York.

'Then it's their loss, not yours. Now come on, we are here. Reg will serve us and we can stay there until we are hungry. I can take you home for some dinner if you want,' Annie said, bowing her head and hoping that he would say no, knowing how her mother would react to her new friend. 'Or, I can afford fish and chips if you don't mind buying your own.' Annie pulled open the engraved glass door at the entrance to the ancient pub. Her mother would have something to lecture her about, not only was she walking out with Josh, but she was also drinking in a pub. Something that her mother found common in a woman and never said a good word about. She held her breath and waited for Josh to reply.

'Nah, you are all right, gal, I'll not come home with you. Not until we get to know one another a little better, cause I know what your folks would say. I'll pay for fish and chips after a pint or two here. Can't have a lady paying the way, not after she's shown me all around York and nearly got into bother over me.' Josh watched as Annie went up to the busy bar and just waved at the burly man that was serving before walking to a quiet corner for them both to sit in.

Josh worried as one or two of the drinkers looked at him, but they seemed to decide that he made no difference to their enjoyment and carried on with their drinking. Annie looked at him and smiled. 'You'll be all right in here, Reg will make sure of that, look, he's coming over to see us.'

'Now then, young Annie, what brings you here and who's this lad that you've got in tow? He looks a bit far from home to me, has he come straight out of one of those magazines that you like reading about?' The big fella laughed and tucked his drying cloth into his apron and stood back and looked at Josh.

'This is Josh Ramsey. And no, Uncle Reg, he's not that far from home, he comes on the barges to Rowntree's with the cocoa and is from Liverpool.'

'Does he now, and is he finding York a welcoming place? It can sometimes be up its own arse, but you are welcome here, my lad,' Reg replied, holding his hand out to Josh who grabbed it and felt Reg's welcoming grip.

'Thank you, sir, I must say I've had my moments,' Josh said and knew that, whilst friendly, Reg could crush his hand as fast as shake it.

'Aye, well, you look after our Annie, no funny business and you will be all right here. Now what are you two having? The first ones are on the house. I remember how hard-up I used to be and anyway it is ages since I saw any of your family, young Annie. Are they all all right?' Reg stood and eyed the lad that Winnie would have plenty to say about if she ever found out about it.

'Yes, they are fine. Molly has just started at Rowntree's and Rose has just got engaged to Larry Battersby, so my mam will be planning a wedding with her shortly.'

'She's to wed Larry Battersby, then? I always thought Rose could do better than that. But love knows nowt about money or class and that's the way it should be. Your father would be proud of you all, he was a good man. Now, I'll send my lass over with your drinks. A pint of our best is it, Josh? And a very small sherry for you, Annie? No getting drunk, else your mother will be after me.' At that, Reg left the two of them together, shaking his head as he walked back to the bar. The Freeman girls certainly did things their way, he thought as he kept an eye on the young couple.

Annie and Josh sat back and drank their drinks slowly; neither had enough money to buy several more and though Annie was not keen on Reg's suggestion of sherry, it gave her a nice warm feeling as she sat next to Josh and listened to stories of his travels on the canals and his description of Liverpool and his life there. They were both comfortable there and didn't feel threatened in any way, until eventually both of them noticed the light dimming outside and the pubs' lamps being lit, and decided it was time to get something to eat before they parted.

'How come these fish and chips have never tasted as good as this before?' Annie said as they sat on a seat across from the minster shortly after. 'I've had them plenty of times, but they have never tasted like this.'

'It's because you've got some drink in you, everything always tastes better when you've had a drink or two,' Josh said as he licked his fingers free of the salt and vinegar before screwing the newspaper up into a ball. 'I've had a grand day, but I don't think it's over yet. Is that music I can hear, is there a dance hall nearby? I love to dance! Have we to go? Will your mother be worrying about you?' Josh stood up and looked at the lass who had been by his side all day and had shown him nothing but kindness, and threw his wrapper into a nearby waste bin.

'It will be coming from above Burton's shop, they are holding a dance upstairs in the big empty hall above it. I've never been but my workmate Susan says it's a lovely sprung floor, whatever that means. She was going with one of her friends, she has her eye on a boy that goes there, but I think he's got more sense than to go with her; she's a bit brash and has a terrible reputation.' Annie screwed her chip wrapper up and placed it in the bin before smoothing her skirt down. 'I can't dance, I've two left feet, I'll go home and leave you to it. Do you know your way back?' Annie said, hoping he would not decide to walk home her way.

'No, come on, Annie Freeman, let's finish our day off in style. Let us go to the dance, I'll learn you, just hold my hand and follow my feet.' Josh grabbed hold of Annie's hand and pulled hard on it and laughed at her protesting at the fact that she could not dance. 'Yes, you can, come on, let's dance and then I'll walk you home. I'll be gone in the morning, please let us end the day properly.' Josh smiled an irresistible smile and pulled her arm again. 'Come on, Annie,,you know you want to.'

Annie knew that half of the Rowntree's workforce

would be there in the hall. It had been all right going around York with Josh but dancing in his arms in front of everyone was a different matter. 'I don't know, I'm hopeless when it comes to dancing.'

'Come on, it will be all right, I'll teach you, we can have a real laugh. Please, because I won't be coming back for another week or two,' Josh pleaded, pulling on her arm again and urging her down the street. 'We will be fine, nobody will look at us, they will be too busy dancing.'

Annie felt her stomach churn and her heart beat fast, she wanted to go but she knew she would be the main topic of gossip in the decorating and packing department come Monday morning if she did, especially if Susan was there. Josh's smile won her over, though, and she finally agreed. 'Yes, all right then, but I'm not responsible for the state of your feet when the night is over.'

'Brilliant, come on, race you there.' Josh grinned and set off running down the street to the tall building with its upper windows letting the dance music sound down the street.

'Wait, wait, I can't run that fast,' Annie yelled, running as quickly as she could to keep up with Josh, finally catching him up at the doorway that led upstairs to the dance floor. She half expected someone on the door to turn Josh away as he felt in his pocket for the shilling that paid their entrance fee. However, nothing was said as the man stamped their hands from an ink pad and they both ran up the stairs to the room that was filled with people of all ages dancing to the four-piece band playing at the far end of the large wooden-floored dance hall.

Annie felt as if she wanted to hide in the nearest dark corner as a group of employees that she knew well all turned and looked at her and Josh as he took her hand and led her onto the dance floor. She could see the disapproving looks and read their lips as Josh put his hand around her waist and took her hand to dance to a lively foxtrot as he guided her around the ballroom. He looked to take no notice of the looks and gossip as he lost himself in the music and held her tight. He whispered in her ear.

'Take no notice, we are here to enjoy ourselves, and by the end of the night they will be jealous of you. Because we will show them what it is to dance.'

Annie looked at Josh, enjoying the feel of his arm around her and decided that he was right, she would enjoy herself; if they were troubled by her being with Josh then it was their problem not hers. Annie held Josh tightly and felt his body moving to the rhythm, she felt excited and knew she was flirting with danger.

They would dance until they both dropped, she decided, as St Bernard's Waltz began to play and she put her best foot forward, smiling at Josh, who was making her feel so special.

'What a hussy, just look at her . . . How could she?' Annie was disappointed, if not surprised, to overhear Susan cry as she stared and took the arm of Brian Mason. 'She'll be the talk of Rowntree's on Monday morning, everybody is staring at them both. I couldn't even put my hand in his! I'll tell her as much when I see her.'

'He can dance, I'll give him that,' said Brian as he watched them, until he noticed the look of disgust on the face of his date for the night. 'But never mind that, are we stepping out for a while?' he said, mesmerised by Susan's cleavage. 'I can think of better things to be doing than watching them two dancing all night.'

'Brian Mason, I don't know what you mean! But yes, I feel quite sick now I think about it, a quick breather outside might just make me feel a little better,' Susan said, putting her arm through Brian's. She glanced back at Annie and shook her head. Some women had no morals, she thought, as she stepped into a darkened alley with Brian.

The night went all too fast for Annie and Josh, they really did dance until they nearly dropped and Josh suggested they leave just before the last dance to reduce the chance of any comments as they walked out.

'Thank you. I just want to say thank you,' Josh said quietly as they reached the end of Annie's street after a companionable walk home. 'It takes some nerve to be seen with me, I know it does.'

'You've nothing to be thankful for. It's me who should be grateful for a wonderful day,' Annie whispered as they stood under the gas streetlight. 'When will I see you again?'

'I should be back again in a fortnight, but that's not for

certain, just depends if my boss gets a consignment,' Josh said, putting his arms around Annie.

'Well, I hope that he does, because I can't wait to see you again,' Annie said as she balanced on her tiptoes and kissed Josh on the cheek, blushing.

'Here, we can do better than that,' Josh said with a grin, leaning down to kiss her gently on the lips. 'I'll be back, now get yourself home, your mother will be worrying about you.' Josh let go of Annie and watched as she walked away into the darkness of her street, just waiting until he saw the light of her home as she opened her front door.

He would return and see Annie again, but she was going to have it hard, just like his mother had when she was with his father. People did not judge others equally and he doubted they ever would.

9

Molly had been waiting on the platform at the Rown-tree's stop and hoped that her friend Connie would be on the incoming train as a plume of steam filled the air. The chuffing black steam engine came around the bend and slowly came to a stop, letting a long, exhausted shot of steam out from its pistons as doors opened and pas-sengers climbed down from their coaches. Molly looked at all the people filing off the train, either to put in extra hours at Rowntree's or visiting friends and doing a bit of shopping. She stood there feeling glum as she looked for Connie and could see neither hide nor hair of her. Then, right at the back of the train, stepping out of the goods wagon, she appeared, waving her hand and smiling as the rest of the passengers cleared the platform and the station master blew his whistle for the train to continue to York's central station.

Molly waved and rushed up to her new friend. 'I thought that you weren't coming and that you weren't on this train. What were you doing in the goods wagon?'

'Sshh . . . Come on, quick, before the station master sees me. I hid in the goods wagon because I hadn't the money for a ticket. Let's get out of the station before he catches me.' Connie giggled, putting her arm through Molly's and quickly pulling her to the small gateway next to the turnstiles for those who were just there to await passengers. 'Quick, quick, he's waving the train off, hopefully he'll not see us for the steam.' Connie pulled Molly with her as she ran down the station yard in a panic and then slowed down as she realised that the station master was not interested in catching them. 'I could only get enough money for my ticket into the pictures, so I'd no option but to hide,' Connie gasped.

'You'll be locked up, I wouldn't dare to get on a train without a ticket,' Molly said, catching her breath and feeling her legs tremble as she thought about her friend getting caught and fined.

'Ah, I often do it, it's easy. I went to Scarborough the other weekend. I fancied going to the seaside, it was grand apart from having no money. Now, what are we going to do today? I've enough money to get myself into the pictures. I helped myself to what I dared from out of the fella's pocket when he was snoring like a pig in bed with my mam. He won't even realise that it's gone, both of them were that drunk last night.' Connie shrugged her shoulders.

'Oh, Connie, you'll get caught, and then you'll be for it. You shouldn't have come if you couldn't afford it. We could have gone next weekend when we both have a bit more money.'

'No, today is grand, now where are we off first?' Connie asked as they walked past the end of Molly's street.

'Mam says you've got to come and have a bite to eat before we go to the pictures and she wants to meet you, but don't tell her that you came on the train without a ticket,' Molly said quietly, still pleasantly surprised by her mother's talk of bringing the lass home for her to see, so that she could judge her for herself, rather than listen to what her girls were saying. 'Our Annie is skulking about; she went out yesterday and landed back late. She's a devil for keeping things to herself, Mam says she should join the secret service she is so secretive.'

'Sounds like a fella to me, that's the only reason I'd be acting that mysteriously. I'd nearly bet my last shilling it's a fella,' Connie said. 'That is if I had a shilling,' she grinned. 'Come on then, let's meet your mam and I'll act all proper and ladylike and not say a word out of place, I promise.' Connie winked and linked her arm through Molly's as they walked down the cobbled street towards the Freeman family's front door.

'Mam, I'm back and Connie is with me. We will just have some dinner and then we are off to the pictures,' Molly yelled, and smiled at Connie as she followed her up the hallway into the kitchen.

'Will you now, and what time will you be coming home at? Not near midnight, I hope, like someone I know,' Winnie said firmly before turning and smiling at Connie. 'Sorry, Connie, it's been one of those days so far, you sit down, my love. It's nice to meet you. There are some egg sandwiches and help yourself to a piece of my Victoria sponge. I made it fresh this morning.' Winnie looked Connie up and down and noticed how thin she was and that her cardigan was threadbare at the elbows. Connie did not have the same home life as her girls, she concluded as she watched the young lass sit at her kitchen table.

'Thank you, Mrs Freeman, it's very kind of you,' Connie said politely, waiting until she was passed the plate of sandwiches before eating one with relish.

'Well, I knew both of you have no brass, so I thought I'd feed you before you go out. So what film are you going to see?' Winnie sat down near the kitchen fire and sighed. She was worried about Annie; she was too quiet for her liking. And she was also worried about Rose. Although she was glad that she was to marry Larry it would be a fall in her household income and that would make a difference to what she could afford to spend on her remaining two girls.

'*Shall We Dance*, I hope,' said Connie quickly, looking across at Molly's face and clocking instantly that her friend hadn't that in mind.

'Rose went to see that the other night. I don't really fancy it. I thought we could go and see *Mutiny on the Bounty* at the Rialto? They have just changed all the seats and they say it is a real luxury to sit there and just look up at the screen.'

'Who's in it?' Connie asked as she helped herself to another egg sandwich and thanked Mrs Freeman for a cup of tea that she had passed her.

'Clark Gable, he's a much better actor than Fred

Astaire and I hate films with dancing in them,' Molly said, and hoped Connie would change her mind.

'Mmm, I suppose we could go to see *Mutiny on the Bounty*, go on then, we can always see Fred Astaire next weekend.' Connie wondered whether she dared take another sandwich or if it would seem too greedy.

'Tuck in, my love, I can always make some more when Annie shows her face. Our Rose has gone into town with Larry, so she'll not be needing any.' Winnie offered Connie another sandwich, she'd feed her up while she was under her roof, she decided. She and Molly seemed to be good friends, so she was thankful for that.

'Thank you, Mrs Freeman, I appreciate it,' Connie said, making sure she ate her fill. 'We'll go and see *Mutiny on the Bounty*, is it about pirates or something like that?'

'Yes, our Annie was talking about it, she fancied coming as well, and it's about some sailors that mutiny when they want to stay on an exotic island. Our Annie is always wanting to travel so it is right up her street. Mam, it's a pity she isn't here, else she could come with us.' Molly noticed her mother scowl.

'No, she's right, just you two go. Annie is doing what she wants to today, but Lord knows what that is.' Winnie spoke sharply.

'I don't know what our Annie is up to but my mam isn't happy with her,' Molly said as she and Connie queued outside the deco-looking picture house called the Rialto. It was busy as it was the latest release and all the women had found a new film star to swoon over in Clark Gable, plus everyone wanted to see the new furnishings that were said to be very plush.

'I don't think Annie likes me, she never says a lot to me at lunchtime,' Connie said, and put her hand in her pocket to find the little money she had to pay for her ticket.

'Don't be daft, she's just like that. Keeps herself to herself, does Annie, and she doesn't mix well. That's why we're wondering what she's doing, she never goes anywhere all dressed up.' Molly handed over the money that her mother had lent her.

'Well, we will see. It will come out in the wash, as they say,' Connie said, catching her breath as they walked through the door into the picture house and saw all the luxurious new seating that had replaced the rigid hard seats that had been there since the cinema had opened. 'Heavens, I'll fall asleep in these chairs, it had better be a good film to keep my attention.'

'It will be, I promise,' Molly said and smiled; she liked Connie and was glad that they had met on their first day at work together.

'Wasn't Clark Gable so handsome? And Charles Laughton played such a horrible character, no wonder his crew wanted to stay on Pitcairn. It was paradise!' gushed Connie a couple of blissful hours later.

'Yes, I knew that you'd like it, that was a lot better than folk dancing about the place,' Molly said as they walked down the street towards home and the station. 'Are you coming back home with me or are you catching the train? It's a good job my mam fed us as neither of us has the money for something to eat.'

'I'd better go home if I can without being caught. Don't you come to the station with me, two of us look more suspicious,' Connie said and looked down at her feet.

'Mam will lend you the money to get you home. It isn't that much, is it? She would rather do that than you get into bother, I'm sure,' Molly said, feeling sorry for Connie. She truly didn't have a penny to her name and she had no loving home, from what she had told her. She was just the opposite of Molly, whose family was so close.

'No, I'll be all right, I'll not get caught and anyway, I can always act my way out of it. So don't worry. There's nobody on the platform at Selby sometimes, he's usually asleep if he's there at all. I'll see you on Monday at work. We can go and watch that film with Fred Astaire next weekend and happen to afford fish and chips.' Connie smiled and gave Molly a quick hug. 'I'll be fine, don't worry, I've often blagged my way home on the train.'

'Well, just you mind, don't get yourself into bother. You could stay here for the night if you wanted to. There's room in my bed for two.' Molly looked worried as Connie started to walk away.

'Nah, got to look after my brother Billy. If I know my mam, she'll want her night on the town. Tell me on Monday what Annie's been up to, for her to be in such bother,' Connie shouted as she ran down the street to catch the five o'clock train home.

'I will. Take care and I'll see you later,' Molly replied as she walked down the street she loved to her home that she also loved, unlike poor Connie.

'That friend of yours looks a bit neglected, Molly, she's as thin as a rake and I noticed a bruise on her arm. But she's perky enough, I'll give her that.' Winnie watched as Molly took her shoes off and sat next to the fire.

'I don't think her mam looks after her and she seems to be looking after her younger brother all on her own. She had hardly any money today, I'm worried about her. Mam, I shouldn't tell you this, but she hadn't got a ticket for the train, she was going to hide and hope that she didn't get caught.'

'Oh, my Lord, that's no good, you should have come and asked, I know we are not rolling in money, but I'd have given her enough for her train ticket. She must be from a bad home, Molly, she'll need a friend.' Winnie put her arm around Molly. 'You just look after her,' she instructed firmly.

'You, young lady, are in a great deal of trouble.' The arresting officer held Connie tightly by her arm and marched her out of Selby station. 'Now, seeing you are so young and I think I know your mother, I'm going to walk you home and see if she'll pay for the ticket and make it right with the station.'

'Please, no, I'll pay the train fare tomorrow, please don't take me home. My mam will kill me,' Connie pleaded.

'Well, you should have thought of that before you got on the train without a ticket, the station master has had his eye on you for a while. What if everyone did what you do? We couldn't afford to have trains on the rails.' The officer tightened his grip as he turned into one of the poorest streets in Selby and stopped outside number two and knocked hard on the door with his spare fist as Connie tried to break free from his grip.

'Please, sir, don't tell me mother, she won't be able to afford to pay, she can't afford to feed us let alone pay for train tickets, please, I'll do anything, but don't tell my mother,' Connie cried and then went quiet as the door of her home opened.

'Too late, my lass,' Sergeant Wilson said as he looked up at the figure that had opened the door. From behind the man who stood in the doorway, dressed in a filthy vest with a belt keeping his corduroy trousers up, came a woman's voice.

'Who is it, Bill? Tell them to go away, we are busy.'

The man stood with his arm barring the way for the policeman and Connie. 'It's a copper, Flo, and your brat is with him, she's been up to something by the looks of it.'

'Are you Connie's father? Because we have caught her fare-dodging at the station,' Sergeant Wilson said, noticing the fear on Connie's face.

'No, nowt to do with that 'un. Thank the Lord, but she is Flo's and she'll have something to say about her bringing you to our door. Give us her here and we'll sort her,' Bill growled as he took hold of Connie's free arm with his rough tattooed hands, pushing her down the passageway.

'She owes the station threepence for a return ticket to York. Will you pay it for her or should they press charges?' Sergeant Wilson asked as he looked past the big man's shoulder, just glimpsing Connie's mother slapping her hard across the face.

'What do you think? We've not enough money to pay for us to be fed. Bollocks to the station, and she must go to court and jail hopefully and then we won't have to feed her,' Bill said and started to close the door.

'You've enough for a drink, I can smell it on your breath, and tell Connie's mother not to hit her or else she might be the one that stands in court,' Sergeant Wilson said, shaking his head. No wonder the lass left home frequently on the train, she had no real home, and she had no love shown to her. 'Take it as a warning this time, but if Connie is found on the train without a ticket again, then I will have to fine her. And no more slapping,' Sergeant Wilson yelled and stood back.

'Bugger off then and go and give somebody else some grief,' Bill said and slammed the door in the Sergeant's face.

Sergeant Wilson shook his head. Bill Tyler was a hard man, the police station knew him well, just as they knew Connie's mother and her way of making a living. He had hoped the lass Connie would rise above her lowly roots, but she was not making a good start, having been caught fare-dodging. He'd overlook it this time and make it right with the station, but if she kept getting into bother then he would have to do something about it.

Connie cowered in a corner, her face bruised and her back aching where Bill had taken his belt to her. She was left in the dark and filth of the terraced house that she knew as home. Upstairs her baby brother cried just as much as she used to do when she was his age. Now she just kept her head down and hoped that the beatings would soon stop. Bill and her mother had gone out on the drink, and with a bit of luck, they'd come back absolutely sozzled and forget about the Sergeant's call.

Monday couldn't come quick enough, but before then she had to find enough money to get a ticket for the train to work. At least there she would have a few hours of peace and a bit of normal time with caring people. Little did Molly know how much she envied her; she had everything if she did but know it. Connie wiped her eyes and blew her nose, the cries of her brother touching her heart as she climbed the stairs to where he lay in his cot. 'Sshh, my love, here, come to me, I'll love you and we'll make you something to eat.' Connie lifted her dirty-faced brother up from his cot and took the sodden, soiled nappy from his body and replaced it before taking him downstairs, where she warmed a small pan full of milk and put it in his unwashed bottle before sitting him on her knee and feeding him.

'We deserve a better life than this, my little one. I'm going to have to leave you, only for a little while, and then I'll come back for you, I promise. If I don't leave, Bill is going to kill me, I'm a nuisance just like you, but at least you are his son.' Connie looked down at the innocent baby in her arms; he was neglected by both his parents, just like she was. However, she had seen enough beatings and she was not about to share her wage or give it all to the bullying Bill. She would leave: where she would go, she had no idea, but leave she would!

10

Rose gazed into the window of Beautiful Brides on Coney Street and sighed.

'Just look at that dress, Larry, how I'd love it. Wouldn't it suit me? And Annie and Molly could wear these two bridesmaid's dresses, we would look so grand.' Rose decided she would go into the shop to see the price of all three beautiful dresses.

'Aye, and your bank would be short of a bob or two and all. Just look at the price. You want nowt like that, you just need a sensible two-piece suit anyway to be married at the register office, nothing flash. It's only one day, as my mother says. We would be better off saving the money towards a house and home. Although my mam says we can live with her until we get up onto our feet.'

Rose was startled. 'The register office! No, Larry, if I'm going to get married, I want a church do. It needn't be that posh, but I want to be walked down the aisle and have bridesmaids.' Rose unlinked her arm from Larry's and looked at him expectantly. 'I've always pictured myself in a long beautiful white dress, with a bouquet of red roses, my sisters by my side. It would be wonderful.' She beamed hopefully at Larry.

'But it's just a waste of money, a fancy frock and a big bash don't count in the scheme of things. We love one another and that's all that counts,' said Larry firmly. 'Besides, where are we going to get the money from? My lot don't have any and I know your mother must struggle.' Larry gazed at the love of his life; sometimes he couldn't understand what she saw in him and sometimes he worried she wanted so much more in life than he could give her.

'I've been putting some money aside for my wedding day, just a little once a week when I get paid. I've also started to buy a few odds and ends for our home. Because that's another thing, I've already said I don't want to live with your parents and brothers, there's enough of you in that small terrace as it is.' Rose felt the time had come to revisit what had been on her mind ever since the visit to Larry's home.

'But where are we going to live? We'll never be able to buy a home of our own and those houses down in the village at New Earswick will be far too expensive for the likes of me to rent. No matter what you think, I'd rather you stopped at home and kept house and looked after our children, once they come along, with my mam. She says that's where every good wife should be, looking after the house and home and her husband. She couldn't believe it when I told her you wanted to continue working when we were married.' Larry shook his head.

'Stop working and have no money and no life of my own, is that what you and your mother want?' Rose was indignant. 'Besides, I'm not marrying your mother, I'm marrying you, Larry Battersby.' Rose couldn't hide the annoyance from her voice: Larry's mother was always telling him what to do and what to think. She would have to put a stop to that once they were married.

'Aye, well, I'm telling you I don't want a big wedding and a fancy house, we are ordinary everyday workers, Rose. I sometimes think this new position that you've got has gone to your head. Having me sneaking around those posh houses down at Earswick, they are for the posh folk, not an engine stoker that was born in Foss Island.'

'We didn't sneak, we were just showing interest. If I hadn't been so busy with the launch of our new biscuit bar, I'd have gone to see the person in charge of housing to see if there would be one coming up for rent soon. Because believe me, I am not living under the same roof as your mother and brothers.' Rose wasn't going to mention that she had been shown around Ned Evans's home, in fact, she deliberately didn't mention him at all. She folded her arms and felt her cheeks reddening and her temper rising as she watched Larry start to walk farther down Coney Street, leaving her standing outside the bridal shop.

'Are you listening to me, Larry?' Rose yelled and walked quickly to catch him up.

'I'm listening to you and I'm thinking happen my mother's right. Happen you are too up your own arse and happen I have been a bit rash by putting that ring on your finger!' he blurted out. 'I can't give you what you

143

want and you'll never be happy with me. If it's like this now, what is it going to be like when we are wed?' Larry turned to Rose, his heart breaking.

'Well, if that's how you feel, take your ring back,' Rose cried, pulling at the engagement ring that had been on her finger for not more than forty-eight hours. 'Happen your mother *is* right,' she said tearfully as she pushed it into Larry's hand. 'There, you go home to her and I'll go on my way. Let's see what your mother says now!' With that, Rose turned and walked away.

'Rose, Rose, don't be so daft, don't be so bloody head-strong,' Larry shouted, starting to catch her up before deciding to leave her to her temper. She'd come running back to him when she had calmed down, she always did.

Rose sat in the chair next to the fire back home and sobbed to her mother.

'It's *my mother* this, *my mother* that, *my mother* says. That's all he can say, and when he said we were to have a register office wedding, that was it, Mam. I'm not expect-ing, there's no rush to get married, everyone would think that, wouldn't they? I want to get married in a lovely dress and have bridesmaids and the lot. But, no, his mam says it's a waste of money.' Rose gazed at her mother through the tears. 'Oh, Mam, what have I done, I gave him the ring back!'

'Oh, our Rose, I don't know. He's a nice enough lad but on the quiet I'm a bit relieved, I always thought that he's not right for you. He will always be happy just being an engine stoker, he's not got much ambition. And his family, well, we all know what they are like: glass-backed and idle and a bit dodgy from what I hear. Happen you are best out of it, although it must be the shortest engagement I've ever known.' Winnie sat on the armchair and put her arm around her weeping daughter, holding her tight and kissing the top of her head. 'It'll be all right, my lass, things always work out one way or another. It's better finding out what he's like now, before he had put a wedding ring on your finger.'

'But I think I love him, Mam, I shouldn't have given him the ring back. I was so angry,' Rose wailed.

'You only said "think", you have to know, to feel it in every beat of your heart; and you have to miss him every minute you are apart. Just like I still miss your father; I'm lost without him some days. Happen it's a good job you have had this tiff, if that's how you feel. I admit, I was looking forward to buying myself a new hat and actually seeing our Annie smile for once at your wedding,' she said with a rueful smile. 'But never mind, my love, what will be, will be, it's happened for a reason. That Maude Battersby is a tartar and has a sharp tongue in her head. You'd have killed one another in the first week if you had lived with them. It'll be all right, my lass, you'll see.'

Rose couldn't stop the tears even when she was in bed, making Annie cover her head with her pillow and lose patience with her sister.

Rose kept thinking about everyone saying that they weren't suited; she had felt that once wed she would be able to change him. But the more he talked about what his mother said, the more she knew her love was a lost cause. And besides, in the back of her mind was the image of a smiling Ned Evans and the promise of a walk out with him the following morning. Perhaps it was the thought of him that had made her act so rashly; she still couldn't believe she'd actually been to meet him at his own home. Before that she had been happy with her Larry. A wave of guilt swept over her: poor Larry, perhaps she should go back and apologise and ask for the ring back. Or, then again, perhaps she would just see how the walk with Ned Evans went? After all, she was now suddenly free and single and folk had been telling her for so long that she could do better for herself. Tomorrow she would find out where her heart lay, she thought as she hugged her pillow.

'So, for once in your life, lad, you are taking my advice and actually having a walk out with a girl. It's not before time, mind.' Ivy Evans smiled as she gazed up at her son who was brushing his suit down with a clothes brush and slicking his hair back with some Brylcreem, checking his appearance in the hallway mirror as his mother talked to him from her armchair.

'I'm only going to have a walk with her, Mother, and perhaps stop for a tea or coffee. You are not going to get rid of me that easily or that fast.' Ned smiled affection-ately at his mother through the front-room doorway. 'Now, have you got everything you need while I'm out?

Glasses, book, biscuits? And do you need another cup of tea before I go?'

'No, I'm all right, I can usually look after myself, you know I can. You go and enjoy your time with that lass. She seemed a grand 'un and bonny as well. You could do a lot worse.' Ivy smiled. It was time her lad was doing something for himself rather than worrying about her all the time.

'Right then, I won't be long. I'll be back before you need to pull the curtains, so don't you get up and try it yourself.' At that, Ned walked over and kissed his mother on her cheek.

'Keep those for your lass. Now, go on and stop fussing, I'm going to have forty winks while you are away.' Ivy smiled, she had never known her lad to look so handsome; he usually dressed well but that afternoon he looked just like a film star as he walked down the garden path and through the gate.

Ned stood outside the large medieval tower of Monkgate and checked his watch, it was five past one. Rose was late; perhaps she had thought better of walking out with him. After all, he had asked her completely out of the blue and he already knew she had a boyfriend; but he assumed it was not that serious, or she wouldn't have agreed to walk with him. He looked up from his watch and his heart leapt as he spotted Rose walking quickly towards him with a smile on her face.

'I'm sorry, my mam would have us all sit around the table together for our Sunday dinner; she is a stickler when it comes to Sunday dinner. We all have to be there as a family else it's more than our lives are worth.' Rose stopped to catch her breath and hoped that she looked as smart as the man that stood in front of her.

'I understand, my mother likes just us two to sit together for an evening meal, it's where we discuss the day and make sure that we are both all right,' Ned replied with a warm smile, holding his arm out for her to link in his and smiling at the rosy cheeks that made Rose so suit her name. 'I didn't think you were going to come, but I'm so glad you did; I'm looking forward to our walk out together. We might see each other every day at work but we hardly know one another, and I'd like that to change.'

'I know, it isn't encouraged to fraternise at work with the other sex, although there have been plenty of marriages and relationships between Rowntree's staff. It can't be helped,' Rose said quietly, worrying she might have overstepped the mark with her comment.

'As you say, it happens, and seeing Rowntree's expects their workforce to work long hours, where else are they to find a partner?' Ned said with a grin. 'Now, how about we walk down to Ouse Bridge and along the river way? There's a nice tea room at the end of Coney Street if we come back that way. I'm sure we can both fit in a cup of coffee or tea with a cream cake, that is if it is open on a Sunday.'

'That sounds a lovely idea,' Rose replied with a beaming smile, linking her arm tightly with Ned's; she felt special and cared for and her heart was beating fast as they began to stroll, Ned talking away about his mother and his past and how he had come to work in such a good position at Rowntree's. Like her, he had started at the bottom but had worked his way up in life and he was full of ambition; just the opposite of Larry. However, she still felt a pang of guilt as she looked across to Foss Island where Larry had previously lived. In winter the area was always flooded due to the Ouse overflowing and it was one of the poorest areas of York. Perhaps she should be a bit more understanding when it came to Larry, he was only being careful with his money, like he had been all his life.

'There's a lot of people walking out, even though the shops are all closed today. I thought it would be quieter than it is. However, the weather is still mild and the walk on the riverbank has brought some colour to our cheeks. Another few months and that way might well be flooded,' Ned said as they both walked down the main shopping area of Coney Street.

'Yes, York always floods in winter,' Rose said as she glanced at the wedding shop window, recalling the tiff that she and Larry had had just the day before. Feeling a mixture of hurt and guilt she took one glance up at Ned and told herself her decision had been right. Ned was far more attractive and a better catch, and even though she hardly knew him at the moment, she had a feeling that they would grow to know one another very well over the coming weeks. Ned opened the tea-room door, the bell ringing and making them both welcome as he asked her to choose a seat with a smile on his face that made her legs feel weak. Yes, she was with the right man, he was a gentleman, and knew how to treat her.

'Well, you look a different lass to the one that was bawling her eyes out last night,' Winnie said as she stirred the cup of Ovaltine she had made herself before bed. 'What have you been up to? Have you made up with Larry?'

Rose smiled. 'No, I haven't made up with Larry and I don't think I ever will do because I'm pretty sure I have found someone better.' She sighed with happiness, a warm feeling in her heart. 'I've had a lovely day out with Ned Evans, we walked along the riverbank and then down Coney Street. Oh, Mam, he's just the perfect gentleman. He even bought us tea at that posh tea shop on the corner.'

'Blinking heck, lass! One day you are broken-hearted about breaking it off with Larry and the next you are off with another man. It's a damn good job you did give him his ring back if you are so fickle,' Winnie retorted, warming her hands on her mug of cocoa, her hair in curling rags and her drab dressing gown making her look like a bag of potatoes. 'Now, he's that boss of yours from Rowntree's, isn't he? Well, at least you'll have plenty in common and he'll not be short of a bob or two, unlike Larry. Poor lad, he did love you.'

'He might have loved me, but we would never be free of his mother interfering and, to be honest, Mam, he was beginning to bore me. We had nothing in common. Ned might live with his mother too, but she's lovely, right down to earth, just like us. They were originally from up Durham way, too, but his mam is no way near as hard as Ivy.'

'Aye, well, you've only walked out with him the once, see what you think of him in another few weeks when the excitement has calmed down. And make sure you are sure about Larry, because he did love you, no matter what. You lasses will send me to my grave with all your comings and goings, I don't know what your father would make of it all.' At this, Winnie made her way to the bottom of the stairs. 'Don't be long before you get yourself to bed, else you'll be late up for work, and I hope our Annie gets up in a better mood than she's been in all weekend. I still don't know what's been wrong with that lass.'

'Night, Mam, love you,' Rose soothed, as she sat down at the kitchen table feeling warm and content. She had just had the best afternoon in her life and she hoped it wouldn't be the last.

11

Winnie smiled at Molly as her daughter chatted about her coming day at work. She patted her on her back and told her to look after herself and Connie and then went quiet as she turned to see Annie coming down the stairs.

'She's common, Mam. She looks at men and tries to get everything for nothing, from what I can see.' Annie spoke sharply, hoping that she could deflect any attention from herself after being late in on Saturday night and not telling her mother what she had been up to.

'Well, you, young lady, can't say anything. I don't know where you had been until the unearthly hour that you came back at, but I'll find out, believe me.' Winnie glared at her daughter. 'As for that lass Connie, you make her welcome; not everyone is as lucky as you three. It's only because your father left us with enough brass that we have managed this long. Now, the next few years I don't know how we will fare, but you could so easily have been her if we were less fortunate.'

'No, we couldn't, we would never be as low as where she comes from,' Annie said as she helped herself to a cup of tea.

'Well, I don't care, she's a good friend to me and that

is all that matters,' Molly said, puzzled by Annie who seemed even more outspoken than usual.

'Well, I hope that you are right, I've known her sort before and they are only friends for what they can get out of people. You always take people at face value,' Annie said tartly before gulping her tea down and looking at herself in the mirror.

'I don't know what gets into your head sometimes. Your father would have words if he was still alive. Connie is welcome here anytime, Molly; if she's a good friend to you then she will always be welcome.'

'Yes, she seems all right, Annie, cut her some slack, as long as she is good with Molly that's all that matters.' Rose looked over her sister's shoulder and pulled a face in the mirror. 'Come on, you beautiful growler, it's work and we are going to be late as usual.'

'Bugger off, our Rose, you often moan and growl, so I'm not on my own,' Annie said back and hit her sister gently.

'Out, the lot of you, give your old mother some peace and I'll see you tonight,' Winnie said as she pushed her three daughters out of the kitchen and sighed with the relief of the silence they left behind them.

The three sisters walked to work together as usual and, also, as usual, they were running late, with Annie still eating her slice of toast as she clocked herself in. She was dreading working across from Susan that morning, she knew that she had seen her dance with Josh and she also knew what she was going to face in the way of jibes and snide comments. She had overstepped the line for many, dancing with a black man all night, and she knew it.

'Mam says you've got to come back home in a better mood tonight, else there will be words. And you know what that means when it comes to our mam,' Rose said as she waited in the middle of the yard before all three went off in their own directions.

Rose was in a hurry to get to her part of the factory, not wanting to miss a minute of being around Ned, but knowing that she would have to treat him as nothing more than her boss whilst at work. She always loved going to work, but this morning she felt an extra spring in her step as she neared the production line and the workers producing the chocolate crisp bar.

'Morning, morning,' Rose said cheerfully to everybody as she walked past familiar faces that she worked with every day, but she kept one eye upon the open-windowed office, hoping to see Ned as the production line was set in motion for another day of never-ending bars of chocolate-covered biscuits to be made and packed. Never had she wanted to see him as much as she did that morning.

And when she saw her bosses gathering together and noticed Ned's dark hair as he sat down at the office table, obviously about to attend a meeting about the new product, her heart beat so fast she almost needed to sit down.

'I don't think this batch is right, the wrappings are loose.' She had to pull herself together as one of the workers came up to Rose, her face a picture of concern. It wasn't like Rose to miss a mistake, especially with the first batch of the day.

'What, oh Lord, yes, that's no good. Something is caught in the folding machine. Stop it now and I'll come and look. Sorry, Bessie, I should have noticed.' Rose was annoyed with herself, she must keep her mind on her work and not be distracted by her new feelings for Ned Evans, she scolded herself as she followed the lass that thankfully had had the sense to approach her with the problem. This was exactly why she should not be swayed by someone who worked at Rowntree's. She must keep her mind on her job, she determined, as she stopped production and sorted the problem with the wrapping machine. When she was finished, she was startled to hear a familiar voice.

'Have we got a problem here, Miss Freeman?' Ned said quietly.

'No, not any more, Mr Evans, it is in hand, just a Monday morning glitch,' Rose reassured him, watching as he picked up one of the newly wrapped wafers and inspected it.

'Good, I'm glad. May I just give you this?' he added, handing her a piece of paper. 'We have just had a meeting and this is the number of bars that we sold last week.' Ned grinned at her. 'Thank you, it's going well,' he added with a smile before walking away, leaving Rose unfolding the paper and wondering why she was privy to sales figures.

She then read what was on the note and smiled.

*I enjoyed our stroll yesterday, Rose, we must do it
again next weekend. However, are you able to come
around on Thursday evening for tea? Mother insists
that she would like to see you again and she is not
alone in that.*

Ned

Rose looked back up to the glass windows of the office
where Ned was standing watching her. She smiled shyly
and nodded her head. Thursday could not come soon
enough.

Annie said nothing as she stood at her position and
started her work.

'Well, you looked to be having a good time with
your new *friend* on Saturday night. He could dance,
I'll give him that, but how on earth could you be seen
with him?' Susan exclaimed, in between packing chocolates and watching Annie decorating them. 'I mean . . .
he's . . .'

'What is he, Susan?' Annie fumed. 'You mean he's
black? Does it matter what colour he is as long as he's
a nice lad? And that, I can assure you, he is. He's a lot
nicer than some of the lads that work here, he's polite and
understanding and that's all that matters,' Annie snapped.

'You must be the talk of Rowntree's this morning,
are you not bothered? You just don't go out with one of
them,' Susan said haughtily. 'I thought that you would

have more sense. Your mother must have had something to say?'

Annie didn't respond and just got on with her job.

'She doesn't know, does she?' Susan's eyes widened. 'My Lord, you are going to be in for it when she finds out, and she *will* find out. In fact, I bet she knows already because Sheila Bridges saw you dancing with him and she only lives at the end of your street. All your neighbours will be gossiping about you this morning, believe me.' Susan sounded right proud of herself for saying it as she thought it was as she watched Annie get on with her job. 'He's that lad that comes with the cocoa beans, isn't he? Joan said you were keen on him, but I didn't think that you'd got that far.'

'Just keep quiet and get on with your work. What is it to you anyway? You can't talk, I saw you getting far too friendly with Brian Mason. Now he is somebody you should avoid, he's been with half of York already and what's more he's ugly,' Annie bit back.

'He is not, and he's not got that bad a reputation. Anyway, at least he's the right colour. How could you, Annie?'

'Just shut up and mind your own business, at least I didn't drop my drawers. I saw you go out with that Brian and come back half an hour later, I know what you'd got up to,' Annie retorted, cursing as her piping bag burst, spilling chocolate all over her hands.

'That serves you right, and you can just take that back

because I'm not that sort of girl!' Susan glared at Annie, outraged.

'Just keep your mouth shut, poodlehead, that new perm looks awful and it's too blonde,' Annie said waspishly, as she wiped the chocolate from her hands and walked away from her station to find a washbasin and calm down. Susan was right, she knew everyone was looking at her and whispering under their breath about her. But frankly, she didn't care, if they were that narrow-minded it was their problem.

Annie walked out of the toilets and her supervisor made a beeline for her, looking more than annoyed.

'You have only just started work, you should have gone to the toilet before you started,' she scolded, noticing the mess that Annie had left behind and the number of chocolates building up at her station to be decorated and finished. 'Well, this is a nice mess that you've left behind. What do you think you were doing this morning?' she asked, and started to help Annie tidy her workspace.

Susan looked up from her post and spoke quietly. 'She likes chocolate, it's her favourite colour.' She sniggered at her own words whilst packing the finished chocolates.

'Just shut up, you!' Annie said fiercely, cleaning down her station and watching carefully as her supervisor stood back, clearly unsure what to say.

'That's enough of that, I've heard the rumours this morning already. If it's nothing to do with work then I don't want to know about it. Just get on with your jobs. But, Annie, I'd be careful who you walk out with; barge people, no matter what colour skin they have, are – let's say – a bit more free and easy with their ways. Not that I should interfere.'

'Water gipsies, that's what they are,' Susan said as she lifted her head and looked across at Annie. 'Sorry, Annie, just be careful. I wouldn't give my heart to him anyway.'

'All right, I hear you both, and thank you, Miss Fraser, I'll take more care now, I wasn't concentrating,' Annie said, thinking to herself she would do whatever she thought fit, regardless of anyone's interference, and as Susan said, if her mother hadn't found out what she had been up to over the weekend, she would by the end of the day and she would have to face that.

Molly watched her sisters go to their work and waited next to the Blick machine for Connie as the stream of workers from the Selby train filed in through the main gates. Right at the back of the line, looking forlorn and dragging her feet, Connie eventually appeared. She didn't look as perky as usual and as she came closer, Molly noticed a bruise on her cheek and a look of despair about her.

'Morning, Connie, are you all right? We had a good day on Saturday, didn't we? I really enjoyed the film,' she said, trying not to stare at Connie's bruise.

'Don't say a thing, I walked into a door, that's all,' Connie said, trying to make light of her bruise. 'I never have any balance when it's dark, stupid idiot me. Yes, the film was good, I enjoyed it.' Connie dropped her head. 'I don't know if I'll be able to make it next weekend though, my mam needs all my money and the bloody station master reported me to the coppers for not paying my fare.'

'Oh, Connie, I knew you'd get caught if you didn't take care. How did you manage to get to work today and what did the copper do?' Molly asked as the girls quickly walked across to their work.

'The copper, Sergeant Wilson, was lovely, to be honest. He has even paid my train fare at the station until Thursday, I found out this morning, when the ticket office didn't charge me for my ticket. My mother and her fella weren't quite so caring.' Connie hung her head and for once in her life let her true feelings show. 'I hate him, he doesn't care about anybody else but himself. He's a right bastard, no matter what my mother says.'

'He's all right with you though, is he? It wasn't him that gave you that bruise, was it?' Molly looked and instantly knew the answer even though Connie denied it.

'No, I tell you, I walked into a door, I'm just clumsy,' Connie said sharply before changing the subject. 'We'd better get back to chocolate-box-making, you seem to be getting the hang of it better than me. Towards the end of the week, your boxes were perfect, you really have the knack. I get my fingers in a knot when I put the paper lining in, but they are getting better.'

'Yes, it seems to make more sense to me now, I quite enjoy it. Although I wish we didn't have to fill the glue pots. I hate that job. Talking of that, my stomach hasn't churned this morning as we've walked into the factory, I must be getting used to it.' Molly smiled as she went to her first job of the day filling the worktops with chocolate box cut-outs. She'd actually found herself looking forward to going back to work this morning, unlike most of the Rowntree's employees.

The girls worked steadily all morning, but just before their lunch break, the supervisor Mrs Beaumont stood up on her chair and asked for everyone's attention. Molly and Connie stood at their stations and wondered what she was going to say as everyone stopped work and listened.

'Next week we will be having visitors to our department. As usual, those who have been employed with us for a while will be helping us to entertain local businesses that stock our products, as well as those who look to doing so in the future.' Mrs Beaumont stopped for a second to steady her balance and tried to ignore the usual groans from the workers, who knew visitors would interfere with their work day and would involve the appearance of their hated chaperone. 'Now, I expect every courtesy to be given to our visitors; if they ask any questions, you must answer to the best of your ability, and if they ask you to do something then that is what you must do. I know that it will interfere with our production schedule but these people are the ones who give us our work so they must be pampered. Thank you for your cooperation; I know that you will not let me down.' At that, she stepped down from her stool and announced lunchtime.

'They shouldn't come near us two, we are only just

learning,' Connie said as she and Molly walked to the dining hall.

'I hope not, I'll be all fingers and thumbs if somebody watches what I'm doing. What are you having for dinner? I think I might try the mince pie, I feel like eating well today,' Molly said as they both stood in line to be served.

'I'm not hungry, I'll just have a cup of tea, besides I've no money for anything, I couldn't get my hands on any spare this weekend,' Connie said, trying to smile.

Molly ached for her friend. 'I've got a spare tuppence, I'll buy you something or you can share my dinner,' she said warmly, reaching in her pocket for her change. 'Here, it'll buy you a sandwich if nothing else, or some soup. I can recommend the soup, I lived on it all last week.' Molly watched as Connie's mouth watered, she was clearly hungry and she looked so tired. 'Here, take it, get some soup and have a mouthful or two of my dinner too, it's always a good helping.'

'Are you sure? I'll pay you back,' Connie said, looking so thankful as Molly placed the tuppence in her hand. 'I feel guilty because I had big dinners last week and you didn't eat hardly at all.'

'That's because I couldn't afford to but Mam has raided the family pot for all our dinners this week. We are all skint and she's playing heck with all of us for spending too much this last weekend. Get what you can with it, and don't feel guilty,' Molly said as she appreciatively watched her plate being filled with mince pie, potatoes and cabbage. She was hungry and going to enjoy her dinner, she thought, as she made sure Connie got what she could with her money before walking across to Annie who was sitting on her own.

'What are you doing sitting on your own? Where's Rose?' Molly said, and shuffled up next to Annie, making sure there was room for Connie.

'She's busy with something to do with her work, I saw her walking outside with Ned Evans,' Annie said, noticing the bruise on Connie's cheek. 'What have you been doing, has somebody belted you one?'

'No, of course not, I walked into a door in the dark,' Connie said and knew instantly that Annie didn't believe her.

'Aye, well, I can't talk, I'm being shunned by all my so-called friends today and I'm sure you two will know, as I'm the talk of Rowntree's seemingly.' Annie looked near to tears. 'Look at them, they are all looking at us and whispering about me.'

'Don't be daft, nobody's looking at you and what are they saying anyway?' Molly said and looked at her sister with concern. She already had a friend feeling sorry for herself and now her sister was sounding paranoid.

'They are all saying how low could I go to date a black man I know nothing about, and one that delivers cocoa beans in a barge to boot. But it wasn't like that and they don't know him. My mam is going to play hell with me and all tonight because she will have found out from gobby Sheila Bridges when they meet for their donkey stones and penny blue from off the rag 'n' bone man.'

Annie gasped as she finished her outburst and hung her head.

'You didn't! And I thought *I* had problems,' exclaimed Connie, nearly missing her mouth with her spoonful of soup. 'Not that it bothers me,' she hastened to add, kindly.

'Oh, our Annie, is that what all the fuss was about when you were late home on Saturday?' Molly said, her face creased with concern. 'And my mam still doesn't know? You should have told her, it would have been better coming from you than any gossiping neighbours.' Molly shook her head as she ate her dinner.

'You didn't do anything with him, you know . . . did you?' Connie asked, looking coy.

'She must have done something, she was with him nearly all day,' Molly said, not understanding Connie's full meaning.

'No, I did not, I wasn't brought up that way. He was a gentleman, despite what anybody thinks of him,' Annie replied and blushed along with Molly as she suddenly realised what had been meant.

'Well, you are all right then. Just don't see him again. This lot will soon find something else to gossip about and you will be old news by this time next week,' Connie replied as she made quick work of her dinner.

'That won't stop my mam from playing hell with me tonight, I'm dreading going home,' Annie said, looking at Molly for support. 'I want to see him again, no matter what anyone says.'

'Mam will be all right, but our Rose might think

differently, you know how snobby she's gone of late,' Molly said as she pushed her empty plate to one side.

'Your home sounds lovely compared to mine, I'd swap any day.' Connie sighed and wondered what she was going to do after her day's work as she couldn't face home and Bill Tyler, who had beaten her and her brother that weekend just to make himself look big. He was a bully and she hated him.

'I don't know, our mam has one hell of a temper when she loses it. Even our father was frightened when she went off on one,' Annie said, close to tears.

'It will be all right, our Annie, after all, he's only a fella and our Rose has been walking out with Larry for months and he's not got a brain cell in his head.' Annie looked at Molly: she might not be the brightest in the family, but she was certainly the most observant and was totally right about Larry. However, Molly, bless her, hadn't taken into account the colour of Josh's skin and her mother definitely would.

It was pouring down when the three sisters walked home later that day, hardly a word said between them, given each had worries of their own. As they walked through the front door, there was no smell of cooking coming from the kitchen and all three remembered instantly that, as it was washday, it would be a plate of whatever their mother had deemed fit if she had been busy and had nothing left from the previous day's Sunday dinner. However, Annie's mind was more on the tongue-lashing she anticipated from her mother than having to eat any cold unappetising tongue placed on a plate.

'We are home, Mam,' Rose shouted. 'It's pouring down out there, we have got absolutely sodden.' The three girls shook their coats and hung them up on the hallway stand before walking into the kitchen and jostling one another for the warmth of the kitchen fire. 'I know it's not yet autumn, but it is cold today,' Rose said as she looked at the already laid table with cooked meats on each plate and a dish of lettuce and tomatoes in the centre. 'I fancied something warm to eat.'

'Well, you'll have to make do with what's on the table tonight,' said Winnie as she bustled into the room, bringing a loaf of already sliced bread with her and putting it on a breadboard that had been her mother's. 'I'm always busy with the washing on a Monday, but today I seem to have got absolutely nothing else done,' she added, taking in the sight of her three girls.

'Before we sit down, I need to talk to Annie, there's something I need to clear up rather than have it linger over our supper. You two lasses get yourselves upstairs and dry your hair,' she instructed Rose and Molly, who needed no prompting to make for the staircase, leaving a pensive-looking Annie standing by the fire.

Molly and Rose got halfway up the stairs and sat on adjoining steps, both wanting to hear what was going to be said. Rose had heard the rumours all day, but it wasn't until now she realised that the rumours about her sister must be true.

Back downstairs, Winnie folded her arms and stared at her daughter. She, out of all her daughters, was the one that shared her looks, with her dark hair and ice-blue eyes, and they shared character traits too, such as a way of saying what they each thought. She was, however, also the most stubborn of the bunch and Winnie had learnt over the years just how to handle her if guidance were needed.

'I had an interesting conversation when I was waiting for the rag 'n' bone man. Sheila Bridges never shut her babbling mouth. Sometimes she just doesn't know when to shut up,' Winnie said sternly, looking at her daughter, who she could see was near to tears.

'Well, is it right, what she told me? That you were carrying on with a lad from the barges and that he's black?'

'I'm sorry, Mam, it is. I'm sorry, but you'd really like him if you knew him,' Annie sobbed.

'Why didn't you tell me? Were you ashamed, or did you think I'd be angry? If you'd said, I could have shut that old gasbag Sheila Bridges up good and proper.' Winnie uncrossed her arms.

'No, I'm not ashamed, but I thought that you'd be angry and you are looking like you are,' Annie said and started crying.

At this, Winnie softened even further. 'I'm only mad because you told me nowt about him. He could be blue, green or pink with yellow spots on for me. I think nothing of these signs that state No Irish, No Blacks and No Dogs, nothing would get done in this country without all three of them and folk want something better to talk about than what colour a man's skin is. Folk like gasbag Sheila are ignorant,' Winnie finished carefully as she watched Annie lift her head and wipe away her tears.

'I thought you'd be so mad, Mam, I didn't want to tell you,' she said, dumbfounded by her mother's reaction. 'But when he asked me to dance with him above Burton's rooms, I've never been so happy,' she added, blushing.

'Aye, I heard he can dance, I think that's half the problem, he put some of the local lads to shame and their girlfriends were envious of you, no matter what they say about the colour of his skin.' Winnie sighed. 'Now, what are you going to do about him? Are you meeting up with him again?'

'I think so, Mam, he comes back and forward regularly with deliveries to Rowntree's and we said we would.'

'Then next time he's here bring him home for tea, I can get a look at him then and it will give some of the nosy buggers something to talk about. If he makes you happy, that's the main thing. Besides, it's better than spending at least eighteen months walking out with a fella that has the spine of a jellyfish when it comes to standing up to his mother,' Winnie said loudly. 'Don't you think so, Rose? Because I know you are both listening out there on the stairs, the top step never creaked as you went up them.'

Both Molly and Rose came down and put their arms around Annie. 'See, Mam is always right behind us, she's right with folk if they are right with us. And no, I'll not say anything about you walking out with him. But perhaps you could do a little better for yourself. After all, he's on the canals,' Rose said, wrinkling her nose.

'Aye, and you were engaged to a man who cleans engine boilers out until the weekend when you realised you could do better,' Winnie retorted, giving her eldest daughter a warning glance.

Rose sighed. 'All right, I'll tell you both,' she said to her sisters. 'I've finished with Larry, I gave him the engagement ring back. And before anyone else tells you, I walked out with Ned Evans on Sunday, and like you, Annie, I had a wonderful day.' Rose beamed, relieved to have it out in the open.

'He's management, Rose, how come you get to walk out with management? Now, that will cause a scandal at work!' Annie exclaimed, feeling a weight lift from her heart at the thought of talk shifting to another member of the family.

'Yes, that's why you won't say a word to anybody, not yet anyway. It wouldn't be fair to Larry, I don't want to hurt him too much and anyway, we have only started to know one another, just like you and this lad on the barges,' Rose said.

'He's called Josh Ramsey, his mother is English from Liverpool and his dad was a sailor from Jamaica,' Annie said, relieved beyond belief by the reaction from her family.

'Well, it seems we are giving the neighbours something to talk about. You had better keep your nose clean, our Molly. Thank heavens you are a bit too young for lads yet,' Winnie smiled, hugging each of her daughters to her. 'Come on, let us have supper, and yes, I can tell by all your faces you're not looking forward to it, but it's all you are getting tonight, so hard luck!'

12

Connie trailed behind the workers who were making their way to catch the train back to Selby; she didn't want to go back home but she had nowhere else to go. The bruise on her face still hurt and there were cigarette burns on the top of her arms where Bill had stubbed his cigarettes out on her as punishment for bringing a copper to their door. She couldn't go back home, she just couldn't, she thought, as she watched the train pull into the station and heard the guard call for everyone to climb on board. She thought of baby Billy, the child that was called after the monster that had fathered him; he would be left at the mercy of her mother and Bill and neither of them would bother with him if she was not there to fend for him. She couldn't leave him to their devices, she decided as she suddenly ran for the train, showing the guard her ticket as he blew his whistle and shook his head at her lateness, slamming the door closed behind her and whistling the train out of the station. Once in her seat, Connie felt sick at what she was going home to, but it would be the best for Billy and she would survive somehow, she mused, as the train brought her nearer and nearer to the home that she hated.

'Ssssh, sssh, Billy, please be quiet,' Connie soothed as she dressed her nine-month-old brother in the cleanest clothes he had the following morning after changing his nappy. 'Sssh . . . I'm doing this for the both of us, else one of us will end up dead,' she whispered as she pinned the note she'd written to his cardigan, hoping that he would go to sleep as she pushed him into the battered pram on their early morning escape. Their mother and Bill lay sozzled and snoring in their bedroom, both smelling of drink and cigarettes after their night in the Red Dragon with their cronies. Connie took a last look around the tip that she had called home all her life and vowed that she would never return as she lowered the ancient pram out of the front door with Billy inside wrapped warmly in a blanket. She hurried along the dark streets. It was four o'clock in the morning; another hour and the streets would become awake with early workers. She had to get across to the other side of Selby and leave Billy on the orphanage steps before anybody could see her. In the orphanage, he would be safer than left with her uncaring mother and her lover. She never saw to his needs and his father often slapped him when he cried. She pushed the pram with fervour and to her relief, Billy slipped back to sleep and Connie found herself worrying that she was doing the wrong thing. Wedged between the pram body and springs were her few precious belongings; she was going to go to work as usual and then that evening she didn't know where she was going, but even sleeping on a bench in York would be better than living as she and Billy did.

A tear ran down her face as she neared the orphanage driveway, the wheels of the pram on the stone shingle making it harder to push as she hoped that the noise of her approach would not be heard. She looked down on the peaceful Billy who she reassured herself was content and warm, and looked at her note pinned to his cardigan. '*Please look after me, my mother doesn't want me and my father hits me. My name is Billy.*'

Gently, Connie bent down and kissed her little brother on his cheek. 'I love you, Billy, our older sisters have abandoned us both, our mother doesn't love us, and I'm trying to do my best to keep you safe. Forgive me, my love.' She wiped her nose and eyes, pulled her bag of things from below the pram and put it under her arm. 'God bless, my little brother.' And with that she ran as fast as she could before her courage left her, leaving the pram and Billy directly outside the orphanage doors. She knew he would be quickly found and she had to get across to the other side of Selby to catch the train to York. She also had to keep herself together, for nobody must ever know what had happened to Billy, especially her mother and Bill. She knew that if Bill had his way her mother wouldn't be allowed to find either Billy or her. That he would be glad to see the back of them both. However, she hoped her mother would shed at least a few tears at the realisation that they had both disappeared from her life. For a brief moment she felt pain for her mother; she was weak and used but had at one time shown both her and Billy love.

Connie made her way to the station and waited for her fellow workers to arrive, trying not to look suspicious as she boarded the train with an extra large bag perched on her knee. On arrival in York, Connie walked into the station's waiting room, hiding her bag of goods behind a tall cupboard in the far corner, making sure nobody saw her before running to catch up with the rest of the workers.

'I was beginning to worry you had not made it today, you are one of the last here,' Molly said as Connie walked quickly to her station in the Card Box Mill, straightening her turban and trying to look calm.

'I just got held up, the station master had a quick word with me and apologised for getting me into trouble,' Connie lied and smiled at Molly. 'He's a nice fella really, we are good friends now.'

'That's all right then, I thought that you must be poorly or something. My mother said you looked white when she met you on Saturday, I feel guilty for not noticing it myself.'

'No, I'm perfectly well. Now, did your Annie get into bother with your mam last night? I could see she was fair dreading going home,' Connie asked and started to stir her glue pot in readiness for making the boxes; each one she made was an improvement on her previous efforts and she was getting to the point that not many were rejected.

'We were all dreading her being told off, but my mam just took it in her stride. We should have known she would, we have always been brought up to treat people the same, no matter what colour their skin is, or where they are from, until you really get to know them. Then it is up to you if you keep them as friends, Mam says. Anyway, the long and short of it is that Annie is to bring him home to tea. So, I don't know how that's going to go, but we'll see,' Molly said cheerfully but keeping her eyes on her friend. She felt concern as she noticed Connie put her hand to her head, seeming almost to swoon for a second or two until she pulled herself back and was able to concentrate on the job at hand.

'Are you sure you are all right, Connie, you don't look at all well?' Molly said, concerned.

'I'm fine, just don't keep asking me! I'm just a bit hungry, I never got any breakfast this morning, I was busy looking after my baby brother before I came to work. That's all.'

'Oh, have you got any money for your dinner today? Because I'll share mine with you again, I don't mind. Our Rose said she would bring some of the new wafer biscuit rejects for us this lunchtime too. That is, if she's not too busy with Ned Evans, which is my other news, by the way. She and he are courting by the sounds of it, she's finished with Larry, although I'm not supposed to say anything . . .' Molly pulled herself up, feeling guilty for breaking her promise so quickly as she carried on making her chocolate boxes. Thankfully she didn't have to think too hard about what she was doing these days, it had started to come automatically to her in the last day or two and now she had got making the boxes off to a fine art.

'Lord, you can talk and gossip, Molly, do you never think of piping down? My head is aching and everybody is talking and this bloody glue stinks.' Molly was shocked to hear Connie sounding just the opposite of how she usually did. All lightness in her voice had gone, and Molly could have no idea that all her friend could think about was having left baby Billy on the orphanage steps and where she was going to sleep tonight, never mind how she was going to afford to eat until payday.

'I'm sorry, I talk too much, my mam always says I babble on too much,' she replied, shocked and a little hurt. 'But we usually have a natter in the morning. Are you sure you are all right?' Seeing the look on her friend's face, Molly quickly wished she hadn't asked.

'For Lord's sake, yes, Molly. Now let's get on with our work. Hopefully this week someone else will fill the glue pots up after dinner because I don't want to,' Connie snapped, looking away from Molly. She didn't want to talk to her for fear of telling her what she had done that morning; she had such a longing to share her worries with someone, but she knew she couldn't.

Molly and Connie worked in silence all morning, the sound of everyone's chatter all around them seeming louder than ever to both of them, and as the hooter sounded for lunchtime they looked anxiously at the number of boxes they had both produced and hoped that they were up to standard.

'Dinnertime, are you coming or would you rather be on your own today?' Molly asked quietly, glancing at her friend who did look as if she had the worries of the world on her shoulders.

'I'll just go to the toilet and then I'll join you. Do you think I could borrow a little of your money for my dinner until Thursday and then I'll pay you back?' Connie asked, a look of shame on her face.

'Yes, you know you can, you don't have to even ask,' Molly said warmly, smiling at her friend and wishing she knew what was wrong. Connie never acted like she had done that morning.

'Thank you, I'll catch up with you in a short while.' Connie felt terrible as she walked to the main toilets and closed the door behind her in one of the cubicles. She had been unkind to Molly, and yet the girl was somehow still there for her. As she sat on the toilet seat and cried her heart out in anguish and pain for leaving Billy all on his own, she had no idea that it was Rose who was in the cubicle next door.

Rose listened to the sobs and decided that whoever it was crying obviously needed help or at least somebody to talk to, so after washing her hands she waited patiently for the cubicle door to open.

After a while, out came Connie, her eyes dark and her face pale, no longer looking the confident cocky lass that the sisters had first met on her first day.

'Connie, I hope you don't think that I'm prying, but what is wrong? I heard you crying and sobbing,' Rose said gently, saddened to see it was the girl whom Molly had befriended. 'Is there anything I can do? Are you not liking your job?'

'No, no, it's not my work, I love it, even though I'm still learning. Please don't say anything to the bosses, I love my job,' Connie wailed and wiped her eyes. 'I can't say, you wouldn't understand, but you and your sisters have a lovely home and mine is just the opposite.'

Rose, even though she had previously not been exactly fond of Connie, put her arm around her. 'We would understand, we have all felt despair at some point, especially when our father died. Now, come and get your dinner and talk to Annie, Molly and me, I promise we will not judge you,' Rose said tenderly, putting her arm around her and feeling Connie's body shaking as another sob came over her. 'Heavens, there's nothing to you, you need a good meal in you before anything else,' Rose said kindly. 'Go and sit with Molly and Annie and I'll bring you something over. What would you like?'

'I've no money, so anything would be wonderful.' Connie bowed her head and felt so vulnerable as she stood next to the tall, good-looking Rose, who had her entire future planned out in front of her.

'I'll get you the same as me, will that be all right? Now go and sit next to Molly and tell us all your worries. We all look after one another here at Rowntree's, no matter what your problem.' Rose watched as Connie walked with her head bowed between the full tables and benches to where her sisters sat, seeing both of their faces crease with concern as they spotted Connie coming towards them.

'Connie, I knew something was wrong. Please tell me what you are crying about, I'm here to help,' Molly cried, grabbing Connie's hand as she sat down next to her and Annie.

'I can't, I really can't,' Connie sobbed.

'Yes, you can, we are here for you, all of us,' Molly said, looking hard at Annie to indicate she should also offer her some comfort, and then putting her arm around Connie and hugging her close.

Connie gave in, giving a big sigh as she started to tell her story. She would tell them she had left home, but telling them what she had done with her baby brother was another matter. She daren't say a word about that yet. 'I've left home, I've nowhere to go and no money. I might as well throw myself into the Ouse and be done with it because I'm no good to anybody. I can't even stick paper and cardboard together right this morning, my hands have been shaking so much.' Connie exploded into tears again and the workers on the neighbouring tables looked at her and shook their heads, wondering what was wrong.

Annie and Molly looked at one another and didn't know quite what to say for the best.

'Has your mother thrown you out? Surely not,' Molly asked gently, putting her arm around her friend.

'No, I've left of my own accord, I can't take it any more.

This bruise on my face was from Bill, my mother's fella, just for not making him a cup of tea when he got up on Sunday. And my mother doesn't give a damn about either me or Billy, all she wants to do is go to the pub with him. I never have any money, Billy is always crying and hungry and is soiled if I'm not there to change him, and we live like paupers.' Connie wept uncontrollably and took big, shuddering breaths. 'I had to leave and I had to take Billy somewhere safe. But I know now I can never go home again.' Connie folded her arms onto the table and put her head upon them and just sobbed and sobbed while Annie and Molly wondered what to do for the best.

Rose came across carrying two dinners on her tray and spoke firmly. 'Connie, here, love, I got you corned beef hash, is that all right? And a sponge pudding and a cup of tea. You didn't look as if you had eaten all day. It will do you good.'

Connie raised her head and wiped her nose on the sleeve of her overall, which made Annie utter a quick warning, 'Don't let the bosses see you do that . . .' but she was stopped from saying more by Molly kicking her.

'Thank you, that's more than kind, I'll pay you back on Thursday when I get paid, I promise,' Connie murmured, looking gratefully at the three girls who were trying to eat their own dinners but were too concerned by the state she was in. 'I'm all right, I'll sort myself out.'

Rose looked at her sisters, wanting to know what had been said.

'She's left home, her father brays her and is a bastard

and her mother is a drunk and her poor baby brother is uncared for except by her,' Annie said in her no-nonsense way, shooting a glance at Molly as she patted Connie on the back and encouraged her to eat between sobs.

'There's nothing like telling it as it is, our Annie,' said Molly and pulled a face at her middle sister.

'So, have you got anywhere to go and is your brother safe?' Rose asked as Connie pushed her food around her plate. She was hungry but she felt sick with worry and her nose wouldn't stop running.

Connie felt her worries well up inside of her; she had to share her troubles, even though she had vowed to keep them to herself. 'I've nowhere and I can't forgive myself, but I took my brother to the orphanage this morning and left him on the doorstep with a note attached to him giving his name and why he had been left there. If I hadn't left him there, Bill would have killed him and my mother would have starved him to death. Once I find a place of my own, I'll go back for him.' Connie sobbed.

'Then we must do something. Mam will help, you can come back with us tonight. You can't sleep on the streets, it's not safe,' Rose said matter-of-factly and looked at her sisters. 'Molly, you could fit Connie in your bed for a night or two. Or she could sleep on the sofa in the front room.' Rose patted Connie's hand. 'We will fit you in somewhere, don't you worry. As for baby Billy, you have done right, you couldn't look after him and he wouldn't be safe staying with your mam. The orphanage will look after him until you return and explain the situation that you were in.'

Connie looked up with tear-filled eyes and managed a watery smile. 'You'd do that for me? You hardly know me,' she whispered.

'You've become friends with our Molly, that's good enough for us,' Rose replied firmly.

'Yes, you can share my bedroom and bed although there may not be a lot of room, happen the front-room sofa might be more comfortable. We very rarely go in there anyway. We live in the kitchen mostly and Mam won't mind once she finds out what you've been going through.'

Connie smiled at her generous friend, and finally felt more like eating.

'Mam will take it in her stride, she always does, no matter what any of us do. It'll be right but I don't think I could leave my baby brother in an orphanage,' Annie said and looked hard at Connie; she hadn't liked her when she had first seen her and she still wasn't that sure, to be honest.

'I'd no option, I couldn't bring him into work with me and yesterday when I was changing him after work I noticed bruises on both his arms where Bill had got hold of him and shaken him. He's got such a temper,' Connie said, catching her breath as she remembered all the times he'd lashed out at her.

'Of course you couldn't,' Rose said, giving Annie a stern look as she heard her swear under her breath. 'Now stop crying, eat your dinner and know that you are both going to be safe. Do you think that you will be all right at work this afternoon or do you want me to go and have a word and get you excused?' she added, putting her management hat on.

'No, please, no! I have to earn every penny I can now and then I can save up for somewhere to live for me and perhaps Billy. He might be only my half-brother but I do love him.' Connie looked anxiously at her three saviours. 'I'll be fine now, honestly, I just didn't know what I was going to do.'

'All right, we will all walk home tonight together after work and ask Mam, I know she won't say no,' Rose said.

'No, she won't, because she said you looked ill when you came to tea and I couldn't help but wonder why you didn't stay the night with me after the pictures. Was it because of your brother?' Molly asked, feeling so sorry for her friend and the worries that she had been carrying until things had got too bad.

'Yes, I knew he'd need feeding, he's been getting thinner and thinner since I started here. He's left by himself to cry a lot. My mam never was the best mother, but since she met Bill, she doesn't care about anybody or anything.'

'Then you have done right and we will stand by you,' Annie blurted out, smiling at Connie, ashamed of her initial reaction. 'We might be a bit squashed and you might be the last one to have the bath water on a Friday night, but we will all manage. And Mam will be the first to say that.'

'Yes, you will be fine, we will all look after you. It's

183

what we do, look after one another,' Rose said and looked at Connie and her sisters.

'Have you seen the bruises and cigarette burns on that frail body of hers?' Winnie said a few hours later, sitting down on the edge of Molly's bed. 'I just took her a night-dress of yours, not thinking to knock before I went into the front room and saw them all over her arms. She's done right to get away from that home, although you can't call it a home when they have treated her like that.' Winnie looked at her precious youngest daughter, tutting. 'The things that she brought with her all need washing and mending too, her mam has never lifted a finger to help her, you can tell.' Winnie sighed. 'I don't know how long she can stay with us, but we will figure something out, I won't be the one that throws her onto the street. And when I think of the poor wee mite of her brother, without any family in an orphanage, it makes my heart bleed. Some folk just shouldn't have children, you can be poor but rich in love, but she seems to be neither. It's a sin, that's what it is, just a sin.' At that, Winnie left her daughter lying in her warm bed, loved and cared for.

13

It was Wednesday evening and Rose put her coat on as she prepared to see Mary. She was worried about her, she was struggling in her work in the Melangeur Block given her condition; it was hard work for someone carrying a baby. Her department was where the cocoa liquor was mixed with sugar, vanilla and some of the cocoa butter. Before they reached her, Rose knew that the ten-ton bags would have been hoisted up into the northeast corner of the factory called the Gables where the beans were then poured down a chute to be cleaned, to remove any dirt and dust before they being passed through drums to be roasted and winnowed with fans blowing away the husks, leaving the cocoa nibs that were then ground into a fine paste. It was then passed over to Mary and her colleagues in the Melangeur Block to be stirred and mixed continuously, whilst being heated to allow any acids within the chocolate liquor to rise to the top. This was then called conched chocolate.

The chocolate took two long days to reach perfection, stirred by huge paddles in vats before being carried in huge tubs all over the factory to whichever department it was destined for. It was the department where you had to have muscles and Mary was one of only a few women that worked there. Unfortunately, it was also the part of the factory where the chocolate smelt the strongest and Mary's delicate stomach was finding it hard to cope with the heavy, rich smells.

'I'll not be long, just going to catch up with Mary and see if she is feeling any better. I never get a chance to talk to her nowadays, we are so busy making the chocolate wafer bar, which seems to be selling really well,' Rose said as she tightened the belt around her coat and noticed the snigger between Annie and Molly. 'What are you three sniggering at, I am only going to see Mary,' Rose said sharply.

'Aye, because you haven't time to see her at work because of your new fella.' Annie winked at Molly and Connie.

'Just be quiet, you, and mind your own business. Anyway, it's to your advantage for me to visit her, Annie, because she will be able to tell me when that fella of yours will be next in with his load of cocoa. She knows which barge is coming and when, so I'll ask her for you if you can keep your mouth closed about Ned and me,' Rose said sharply before grinning at Connie. 'We love one another really, it's just banter.'

'I know, it's nice to hear, compared to the constant yelling back at home and Billy crying,' Connie said with a smile.

'Right, well, I'll see you all later. I'm glad that you are

safe with us now,' Rose said kindly to Connie, and closed the door behind her.

Mary opened the door to her good friend and smiled. 'I'm so glad that you've come around tonight, I've so much to tell you.'

'You sound a lot brighter than you did the last time I knocked on your door. Are you feeling better now, and have you heard from Joe?' Rose asked as she walked up the hallway and into the kitchen where she had spent many an hour over the years. Saying hello to Mr Entwistle as he stirred the coals in the fire with a metal poker, she sat down.

'She is feeling better, because she took me as a fool. I might be old and I might have bad eyesight but I can tell when a woman is carrying a child. So, I told her so and that it was no good hiding it from me,' Mary's father said and looked across fondly at his daughter, who blushed at her father talking so openly. 'It's our flesh and blood and we will take care of it, and anyway, my help might not be needed now the father is coming home,' he added, at which news Rose's eyes lit up.

'I'm so glad that you know, Mr Entwistle, and that you are standing by her.'

'Aye, well, I wouldn't be much of a father if I didn't. Now, no doubt I'll be in the way of you two talking. I know when I'm not wanted, I'll get myself into the front room and read my book and then you can talk.' Mary's father rose from his chair and reached for his walking stick, glancing at Rose. 'Folk might think I should be ashamed of her, but she's my lass and it won't be the first time a baby is born out of wedlock. It was only a matter of luck that I didn't put her mother in the same position at her age.'

'Father, please! You are making Rose and me blush,' Mary cried.

'Nay, it's too late for your blushes now. You know what there is to know and there's no taking it back.' Rose watched as Mary's father put his newspaper under one arm, and with his walking stick in the other began to walk down the passage to the front room, leaving the girls in peace.

'Sorry, I haven't had a chance to tell you, my father and I had a long talk this last weekend. He'd seemingly known that I was expecting but had not said anything, hoping that I would have the courage to tell him. Anyway, I was sick when I was frying some bacon for supper and he just came out with it, asking when did I think the baby was due and when was I going to actually tell him and did the father know?' Mary sat down next to Rose, who looked at her friend expectantly, longing to hear the news about the baby's father.

'He seems to be taking it in his stride, especially now that I have heard back from Joe saying he will be home as soon as he can and has received one of my letters, which in itself is a miracle. He also sounds as if he is going to stand by me.' Mary sighed and, for the first time, put her hands on her stomach and patted it with a touch of love. Rose was so glad that things were working out for her friend and said as much, giving her friend a hug.

'Rowntree's have been wonderful too, I thought with me not being married they would wash their hands of me, but my supervisor has told me that I can work until the baby is nearly due as long as I feel well enough. However, I might have to change my department because I can't do any heavy lifting and the smell of the conchie has been making me feel so sick, as you know, although that is easing off now.' Mary paused, and for the first time in a long time, she looked happy.

'I'm so glad for you, Mary, I knew things would work out.' Rose breathed in and looked at her best friend with utter delight before sharing her own news. 'Have you heard that I have finished with Larry? We were engaged just for a few days, only for me to find out after all those years of courting that he wasn't the one for me. What do you think of that?' she asked nervously.

'I had heard, but I wasn't going to say anything until you told me. You know what the gossip is like at work.' Mary hesitated. 'To be honest, Rose, I think that you've done right, you can do so much better than Larry Battersby. Perhaps at one time he was right for you, but I never felt you were head over heels for him like you should be. And you have worked your way up in Rowntree's, you need somebody with brains and ambition to match yours,' Mary said, hoping that she was not offending her best friend.

'I feel bad, but sometimes things happen for a reason. I've not seen him since we split up and to be honest, I haven't missed him.' Rose smiled and looked at Mary. 'Promise you won't say anything if I tell you a secret?'

'I promise. You know me, I won't say a word.'

'Well, I know this is quick, but the truth is I'm walking out with Ned Evans. I can't believe it myself, I still don't know how it happened, but it did. Straight after I had finished with Larry, would you believe it? Oh, Mary, he is so nice, he smells lovely too, not of engine oil and soot, and he is so polite and we have so much in common.'

'Blinking heck! Lord above, how have you managed that? He's the darling of Rowntree's. Every woman just wants him to glance at them, let alone walk out with them,' Mary exclaimed excitedly. 'When you decide to change your fella you don't hang around,' she teased, rubbing her hand on her stomach and smiling at her best friend.

'I told him I'd been looking around the empty house not far from where he lives and he asked me down to look around his and meet his mother. We just get on, I really can't believe it: me and Ned Evans, who would have thought it?'

'Well, I'm glad, you will make the perfect couple. Now, tell me, is it true about your Annie and all? Has she been seen out with the lad that comes with the cocoa beans? I mean he's a nice enough lad, but . . . is it worth the looks and the words said behind her back?'

'I know, but she doesn't think like that and Mam says

if he's a nice lad then there's no harm in it. But I doubt she is doing herself any favours, you know what I mean . . . not everyone is as liberal-minded as our mam.'

Mary shook her head. 'I don't think I'd like to be seen with him, not like that anyway. I couldn't be as brave as your Annie.'

'That's not the only thing that's going on at our house. Molly has brought back a waif and stray to live with us, a lass she works with who's from a bad home, so it is all going on at the moment.' Rose sighed and watched as Mary made a cup of tea; it was good to have a natter with her best friend and get things off her chest, and now Mary was more settled she could tell her troubles to her.

It was dark by the time Rose finally left Mary, the nights would soon be starting to draw in and autumn would be on its way, a touch of frost in the air. Soon parts of York could well be flooded with the winter's heavy rainfall, when the mighty Ouse burst its banks on a regular basis, leaving some of York cut off. Rose was going to enjoy the late summer sun, but right now she was glad that she had put her warmer coat on as she rushed home, walking past terraced rows and ginnels that were the backstreets of York. All of a sudden she felt an arm reach for her, pulling her into a darkened alley, and recognised the smell of a man that she was all too familiar with.

'I thought if I waited long enough you'd walk back this way,' Larry said, pinning her against an outhouse wall and putting his hand over her mouth, telling her to be quiet if he was to let go of her. 'You nearly always visit Mary on a Wednesday, and I wasn't going to show my face at your house and be ridiculed by you and your family.'

'What do you mean, ridiculed? And let go of me, Larry, what do you think you are doing?' Rose gasped as she tried to move out of his grip.

'I'm doing what, perhaps, I should have done a long time ago and I'm going to prove to you who the boss is between us. You've had too much your own way, that's what my mother says. So I'm here to show you that I am the man you want and to make you come back to me.' Larry pinned her to the wall with his body and kissed her hard.

Rose turned her head and tried to avert his advances, horrified as he started to undo the belt on his trousers and fumble with her skirts. He opened her coat and pulled the buttons off in his frustration.

'Stop it, stop it, Larry, there's no need to do this. You never have acted like this before. What's wrong with you? Stop it, stop it!' Rose shouted, and freeing one of her hands she slapped him across the face.

'Is this what you wanted from me? To show you that I'm a man, not a poodle for your pleasure? Perhaps I should have been doing this all along.' Larry leaned against her and tried to undo his flies while he kept Rose pinned to the wall.

'Don't be stupid, let me go.' Rose lifted her leg and kneed him in the crotch and then slapped him again as he swore and winced. 'I loved you because you were a gentle man, not an animal like your brothers. Now leave me be,' Rose said firmly as she kicked his shins and freed herself from his grip. 'Go home, Larry, go home to your mother and let me get on with my life,' Rose said, catching her breath and wiping away a tear that was falling down her face. She pulled her coat back around her shoulders and watched as she saw Larry crumple in a heap on the stone-paved ginnel entry.

'I love you, Rose, you might not love me, but I still love you,' Larry shouted after her.

'No, you don't, Larry, you just need someone to look after you and pander to your needs, just like your mother, and I'm not that person. Now go home and forget this ever happened.' Rose felt her heart beating fast as she walked away, turning the corner to the next terrace before she started to run. She feared that she was still going to be raped by Larry, she'd nearly even feared for her life, but at the same time, she was sure he was not a man who would ultimately go through with either. Nevertheless, she ran like she had never run before, tears streaming down her face, her lungs struggling for breath. Listening for any sign of Larry following her, she turned the corner into Belgrave Street and let her fear out as she pushed open the door of her home and burst into the brightness of the kitchen to a set of surprised faces.

'What on earth is wrong, Rose, what's with all the tears, and look at your coat!' Winnie gasped, pushing her chair back and putting her arm around her daughter.

'It was Larry, Mam, he was waiting for me on my way

back from Mary's. He tried to . . . he tried to . . .' Rose gasped and felt her legs go weak as her mother held her up and guided her to a chair.

'He didn't touch you, did he? I'll go and get the coppers,' Winnie raged. 'Annie get my coat, we'll have him jailed, he can't be doing things like this.' Connie and Molly just looked on, wondering what best to do.

'No, Annie, don't get Mam's coat, there's no need for all that. Look, I've not a scratch on me and he never got his way. I'm just shaken up, he came off worse, Mam, because I kneed him in his bits. You should have heard him groan.' Rose struggled to smile as she tried to calm down and stop shaking as Annie, instead of going for the coat, passed her a cup of tea.

'The bastard, I'd have thought better of Larry. His brothers, now, that wouldn't shock me, but I always thought Larry was different. None of them will ever make anything of themselves, their mother will always make sure of that. A vile woman, she is, I'm glad that we are not going to have owt no more to do with them,' Winnie said, searching her daughter's face. 'You are sure he didn't do anything, you are not lying to me?'

'No, Mam, he didn't get the chance, now stop worrying and don't say anything to anybody about tonight.' Rose looked around at her sisters' and Connie's shocked faces. 'He was just angry at being stood up but I know now more than ever that I'm better off without Larry Battersby if he's got that side to him.' Rose sipped her tea and looked wistfully into the fire. She had had a narrow escape from a marriage from hell and could have been in a worse position than the now-happy Mary. But she wasn't going to be the talk of Rowntree's by reporting him for attempted rape, she had more pride than that and didn't want the shame of people perhaps thinking that she had asked for it after calling off her engagement. She was better than Larry Battersby and she was going to prove it.

14

It was payday at Rowntree's and Molly and Connie watched with excitement as the clerk with the pay trolley came around and handed out brown envelopes filled with the money they had earned the previous week.

'It seems like I have been here a lifetime already,' said Connie as she watched the trolley approach. 'I've never had any money of my own. It will be my first time ever. I wouldn't have any of it if I was still at home, Bill would take every penny from me. Although of course your mam and I have come to an arrangement that I pay her for my board while I'm living with you, it's only right.'

'I think she would have let you stay for nothing if she could afford to, she was saying so the other night when you had gone to bed. She was quite chuffed that you are already looking a lot better than when you came to us the other night. She was really worried about you,' Molly replied, feeling herself getting properly excited about taking home her first pay packet.

'I'm hoping that I will have enough money to take a train ride back to Selby on Saturday. I don't know how I'm going to do it, but I just want to check on Billy at the orphanage. I'll have to make up a story or something or just watch for him in the gardens. Do you want to come with me?' Connie asked.

'Do you want me to? I didn't think that you would ever want to go back there.' Molly held her breath as the pay clerk came closer.

'I do, please come with me! I don't know if I can do it on my own,' Connie said. 'I need to make sure I have done the right thing and then I can rest easy.'

'Then I will, we will go together, I'll tell Mam I need some train fare out of my wages if nothing else.' Molly stood and gave the wage clerk her name and beamed as the clerk ticked her off the list and passed her the most-treasured wage; Connie received hers just after.

'Oh, look at it, a little brown packet of money!' Molly cried, tearing back the sellotape on the top and looking inside at the few folded notes and the change at the bottom of the packet before checking the total on the front which the pay clerk had calculated once tax had been paid. 'My mam said they would take tax off me, but I didn't think it would be this much,' she said, moment-arily disappointed. 'I think I must be working for next to nothing.'

'You'll have to get used to that, the government will be wanting more and more money off us after this coming election,' Connie soothed. 'I saw it on the newspaper the man that inspects the Bunson burners had under his arm. And it sounds like there's a war on the way, those Germans are running riot in Europe. Just not what we want, but we have to do our bit,' she said passionately.

197

'They'll not bother with us. So I'm not worried, I'm just glad that I've got a job and some money of my own, even if the taxman and my mam take most of it. Although Mam says I'm allowed to keep a little for myself.

'Now, you will be all right, won't you? You'll both take care, won't you? I can understand that you want to see your brother, but don't go near that Bill, you are just beginning to look well, Connie,' Winnie said with concern as she stood on the doorstep and watched both girls walk down the street arm in arm on their way to catch the train to Selby.

'Your mother does worry, I'm not used to being fussed over. She needn't fret, I'm not going anywhere near my home if I can help it. I only want to see Billy and make sure he's well. I don't need to talk to him or pick him up, just see him and make sure he's all right,' Connie said as they walked briskly to the station together.

The ticket man gave Connie an amused smile as she approached the small office at the station. 'I haven't seen you for a while, I hope that you've both got money for your ticket, wherever you are going? I know the station at Selby has got their eye on you. We'll have none of this travelling for nowt if I have my way,' he teased.

Molly blushed; she had never ever been talked to like that before, but Connie just laughed. 'I've turned over a new leaf now. I'm working and have got a good caring home, I don't need to duck and dive, but at least you have remembered me,' she said cheekily before passing a few pence through the hatch. 'Return to Selby, please, I don't aim to stay long, though.'

'Well, you keep your nose clean, you are too likeable to end up in trouble. Now you, young lady, is it the same for you? Return to Selby, is it?' The ticket man smiled at Molly.

'Yes, please, I know it's only twelve miles away, but I've never been there,' Molly said, checking the ticket that he gave her and the tuppence ha'penny change that she put in her pocket.

'It's a pit village, lass, as well as a market town, but there's a bonny abbey in the centre – not as good as ours though. Nobody can beat our marvellous cathedral,' the ticket man said with pride. 'You'd better get a move on if you are to catch this one, the guard is about to blow his whistle.'

Both girls ran through the ticket hall archway and quickly jumped onto the steam train just before the guard closed the carriage door behind them, blowing his whistle and waving the train out of the station.

'Are you all right, Connie? You look a bit worried,' Molly said as her friend looked out of the window.

'I need to see my brother, but I'm frightened I'll bump into my mam or Bill, Lord knows what they would do to me if they caught me,' Connie said, her gaze still fixed on the passing countryside through the window.

'We won't see them, don't worry, we will just make our way to the orphanage and get back straight away. Anyway, what can they do to you?'

'You don't know Bill, Molly. He'd break your neck as

soon as he looked at you if he thought that you had done him wrong. We must not see him or go near him, else I'm done for.' Connie's voice faltered; she was clearly having second thoughts about taking the train to ease her conscience over her baby brother. Selby might be a reasonably large market town, but everyone knew one another and word would soon get around if somebody spotted you.

'Come on, we will go straight to the orphanage, you need to know that Billy is safe and cared for,' Molly soothed as the pair alighted from the train and made their way out into the town of Selby.

Molly took in the stalls as they made their way through the busy marketplace; she would have liked to have looked at the goods for sale but Connie pulled her past them all and past the square-towered abbey that dominated the town.

'Come on, don't dawdle, we've got to see if Billy is all right and then you can perhaps do a bit of shopping if you must.' Connie urged Molly down a backstreet that led to the orphanage.

Once there she stood by the side of the main gates and memories flooded back to the morning she had left Billy on its steps.

'I've got to check on Billy, please let me see him,' Connie murmured under her breath, hiding behind the ivy-clad gatepost with Molly standing behind her.

'I don't know what we can do, neither of us is old enough to say we are looking for a child to adopt. I don't know how we can gain access to the orphanage,' Molly said, pulling on Connie's arm.

Then the girls couldn't believe their luck. 'Wait, the doors are opening, some people are coming out pushing prams, it must be time for their after-lunch stroll. Be quiet, Molly, just a minute longer and we might see Billy,' Connie urged. 'Come on, we will sit over there on the bench and wait for them to pass, I hope our Billy will be there, please let Billy be there.' Connie held her breath as they both made their way to the green-painted bench by the side of the road leading down into the town.

Connie could feel her heart beating fast. 'Please let him be there, please let him be there,' she whispered as the parade of prams and their occupants passed them, with matronly women pushing them. She stood up and took as careful a look as she dared into each pram but eventually she got to the very last one and there was no sign of Billy. Then she spotted him, propped up by pillows, his hair blonder than she had ever seen it and his cheeks looking red and rosy. His nurse was rushing to catch up with the rest of the prams as she walked briskly towards them. Connie caught her breath, she had done right, and Billy for once was being cared for and fed. She could rest easy, she decided, as she tugged on Molly's sleeve and stepped forward to peer into the pram as his nurse wheeled him past.

'Do you like babies? You are a bit too young yet to become a mother, give yourself time,' the young woman said as she stopped for a brief second, letting Billy smile at his sister, recognising her face.

'He likes you, bless him, just look at him smiling, he's one of our newest children to be left with us. Just abandoned, can you imagine that? He's such a darling as well.' The nurse smiled as Connie sat back down with Molly. 'Anyway, I must catch up with the others,' the nurse said, and walked away quickly without giving the two girls a second look.

'Thank heavens, Molly, he is well and looked after, I need not worry any more. Didn't he look so sweet? I'm so glad that he's being cared for,' Connie gushed, wiping a tear away and putting her arm through Molly's. 'I'm so glad, but now let's go home. Did you want to have a look around the market? We do have time if you want, the train doesn't go for another half-hour.'

'I'm so glad for you, Connie, he does look a bonny baby and he looks happy. You definitely did do the right thing.' Molly smiled. 'If we could have just a quick look around the stalls, I have a bit of spending money on me and I noticed a stall that was selling knitting wool. I'd like to knit some gloves for my mam and sisters' Christmas presents. I know it is a few months away, but I'm a slow knitter. It will be the first time I have had some money of my own to buy or make something for them and I thought gloves would be welcomed by them all and I already have a pattern that was my mam's.'

'I don't know, Molly, you and your family are just the opposite of mine. You spend time and money on one another and you always put yourself last. I don't know where mine went wrong, it's everyone for themselves with mine,' Connie said sadly.

'We always have looked after one another, isn't that what a family does?' Molly said, genuinely puzzled as they walked back down into the market square.

'Everyone's but mine. My mam used to love me and my sisters before Bill came along and my dad left. It's all gone downhill since then and that was about eight years ago now. I'd forgotten what family life was about until these last few days I've spent with you.'

'Mam stepped into my dad's shoes when he died. She worked at all sorts until Rose and Annie started to work themselves and even now she will take in mending from folk if she's asked to and needs a bit more money. I hope that she doesn't have to now I'm bringing money in as well,' Molly replied as she spotted the wool stall that had caught her eye earlier. 'I'll not be long, I promise, I just need a few ounces and then I can make a start.'

Connie went and sat on the steps of the fountain and watched as Molly picked the wool that she was going to knit into gloves with love. She also kept her eyes peeled, dreading either her stepfather or her mother spotting her back in Selby. Concentrating on watching the busy market, Connie jumped up in surprise as a hand grabbed her shoulder from behind.

'Connie Whitehead, are you still living here? I thought that all your family had flit from Selby.'

Connie turned and looked at her old next-door

neighbour, who never missed a thing going on in the street. He had often asked if she was all right but had never dared to interfere when he had heard her crying in the night.

'The tallyman's been knocking on your door every day and this morning the landlord came and has thrown everything out onto the street. Not that there was a lot! You'd better make yourself scarce, else he'll be after you for their rent.' Michael Lambert looked at her with concern. 'I've not seen you or your brother for nearly a fortnight, but I know your mam and that brute were still there on Wednesday; I spotted them when I went out into the back-yard lavvy for a pee, they were loading their things up and clearly doing a moonlight flit.'

Connie decided she could trust this kind man, and told him the truth. 'I left, and our Billy is safe at the moment, it was time to leave home,' she said, breathing deeply, not wanting to tell him the whole truth. 'I didn't know my mam and Bill have left, I wish my mam would leave him.'

'Aye, lass, he's not a good 'un and he has dragged your mother down to his level. I'm glad that you are standing on your own two feet. You owe neither of them anything, I know how you have been treated over the years and I'm just sorry I never intervened. But that Bill is a brute and he'd have minced my bones as soon as he looked at me,' Michael said, patting Connie on her back. 'You keep yourself safe and don't fret over them two, just look after yourself and Billy. That's all that matters.'

'I will, Mr Lambert, I'm sorry if we were bad neigh-bours, I know that you heard what was going on in our house many a time,' Connie said, relieved to see Molly making her way back to her with a bag full of wool.

'It wasn't your fault, lass, nor your mother's, it was the bugger she was married to. I'll not lie, I'm glad they have cleared off, but you'll need to know where they have gone and on that I can't help,' Michael Lambert said. 'You take care of yourself, lass.' At that he shook his head before walking away from the girl he knew had been brought up by her bootstraps but who nevertheless was always polite.

'Who was that? Are you all right?' Molly asked, noting the worry on Connie's face.

'It was our next-door neighbour. He's just been telling me that my mam and Bill have done a moonlight flit and he doesn't know where they have gone. That's typical, that as soon as me and Billy have gone, Bill couldn't wait to take my mam away. I only hope that she will be safe with him.' Connie sighed. 'By the looks of that bag, you've bought yourself some wool.'

'Yes, just a few ounces. It looks like you will be staying with us for a while if you don't have a home at all now. I think maybe we should make room for you in my bedroom, I don't mind sharing, at least not with you. My sisters are a different matter,' Molly said with a smile. 'Hope you like blue because I'll add you to my Christmas mitten list – that is, if I ever get a stitch cast.'

'Blue will be just lovely, thank heavens I found you as a

friend and the rest of your family. I'd be out on the streets by now,' Connie said gravely and with tears in her eyes, giving her friend a grateful hug. She truly was thankfulfor everything the Freeman family was doing for her.

'We'd never let that happen to you. Come on, let's go back to York; that is your home now and will be as long as you want it to be,' Molly answered with a reassuring smile.

15

The following Friday, Molly spotted a welcome sight.

'Hey look, two new girls are coming around our section, they are being shown what we were shown when we started, which hopefully means it will be their job now to fill the glue pots. No more glue pots, now today is a good day.' She grinned and nudged Connie. 'The poor devils, they don't know what they are letting themselves in for.' It was as if she had been working at Rowntree's for years, not a matter of weeks.

Connie and Molly watched as the two new girls were given their stations and Mrs Beaumont stood over them just like she had done with Connie and Molly. They both smiled a knowing smile when they saw one of the new girls hold her nose and nearly retch at the smell of the glue; she would soon get used to it just like they had. It hadn't taken long and now both Molly and Connie were getting quite adept at the process of making chocolate boxes, especially Molly, who had been given the job when other box-makers were too busy of decorating and finishing the special gift boxes with bows of ribbon. She had the knack, and as her mother had said to her, 'God gives you the skills he thinks that will see you through life.' It seemed that Molly's was one of chocolate-box-making.

All the workers looked up when the group of visitors that their supervisor had warned them about the previous week arrived. There was a noticeable hush as the group walked into the room and everyone concentrated even more on the job at hand.

Molly heard the woman next to her whisper to her fellow workmate quite loudly, '*Oh, God, it's him!*' and then continue with her work, not bothering to look up at the group of well-to-do business people and shop owners who had come to see how Rowntree's made and boxed their chocolates.

Molly looked at Connie, whose hands were shaking as the group came nearer to them, stopping to talk to Vera Cockell who had been working in the box factory since she had left school over twenty years ago, and was usually chosen to display her skills and speed in box-making. Molly caught Connie's eye, they were only folk as her mam would say, they all sat on the toilet of a morning just like her. In her mam's eyes, nobody was better or worse than anyone else.

A portly man in a cream-striped suit approached Molly, smoking a cigar, the smell wafting over her as he watched her fold and glue her box's corners down and stretch the lining paper into each corner neatly. Her hands trembled and she wished he would go and watch somebody else. Then a woman dressed in a tight red suit came and watched, holding a handkerchief to her nose.

Obviously bothered by the smell of the glue, she passed quickly and went to wait for the rest of the group as they talked and viewed the workers on the factory floor.

The Rowntree's colleague in charge of the visit came and talked to Molly, watching her and smiling as she tried to concentrate on her work.

'I don't think I've met you before, you must be fairly new here. You definitely were not here the last time I showed a group around.'

'I started work here a few weeks ago, sir,' Molly replied, worried that she wasn't able to concentrate on lining the box as it should be done.

'I thought as much, I would have remembered such a pretty face and you seem to have learnt your job well. I'm Mr Robert Jones, I arrange the visits and promote Rowntree's as best I can. I think that you will find that my name is known throughout the firm.'

Molly nearly missed hearing the woman working next to her as she glanced at the pompous man and shook her head, whispering, 'Aye, for all the wrong reasons.'

'It's nice to meet you, Mr Jones, I'm honoured, I'm sure,' Molly said politely.

'Erm, I was just wondering, do you know how much of that grade of cardboard is in stock in the warehouse? I was thinking of perhaps letting the visitors have a go at making their own boxes, just to prove to them that it is a complicated job. I wonder, would you come along and show me whereabouts it is kept and then I can see for myself?' Robert Jones was smiling such a beguiling smile that Molly knew that she had no option but to do as she was asked. The words of her supervisor echoing in her ears that she should do whatever was asked of her by the visitors, she wiped her hands on her tunic and smiled nervously as she stepped away from her workspace. She noticed Beatrice who worked next to her shaking her head and looking concerned as she did as she was asked.

'This way please, sir,' Molly said and walked down the production line as every pair of eyes watched her with the suited middle-aged Robert Jones.

'This is so kind of you, Molly, I will tell your bosses that I am very much impressed with your eagerness to please me. It is to be commended,' Robert Jones said as Molly opened the door into the warehouse that was usually empty at that time of the morning, with all the production lines already full.

'Thank you, sir. Now this is the cardboard I was using. There are all the different ones that we use stacked in here and they all have a different purpose depending on which chocolate box you are making,' Molly said and felt nervous as the middle-aged man looked at her and smiled.

'What's that one in the corner over there? I think I have used that in the past,' Robert Jones replied and closed the warehouse door behind them both, putting the latch on as Molly headed to the furthest corner of the highly stacked warehouse. The smell of the cardboard reminded Molly of school as she started to unwrap a pack of pre-cut boxes for his use. She felt nervous and wondered why the door had been closed behind them both.

'Now, there's no rush, is there, Molly? I'm sure your supervisor has told you that no matter what you do you have to please me,' Robert Jones said and walked right up to Molly, grabbing hold of her as she leaned over to untie the pack. 'Let's start with a kiss and then we will see how far we can go without interruption.'

Molly felt her legs turn to jelly as the man pushed her back into a stacked pile of cardboard boxes and forced himself upon her. Holding her arms down by her side, he kissed her hard on the lips and forced his tongue into her mouth.

'Please, sir, let go of me. I don't like this,' Molly said and felt tears come to her eyes as she felt his body next to hers and realised that his free hand was undoing the buttons of his trousers.

'Quiet now, Molly, you know you have to please me, now it will all be over and done within a minute or two and then you will know your job is secure. I have the power to make or break you while working in Rowntree's, and don't you forget it.'

Molly tried to cry out but Robert Jones put his mouth over hers as he tried to pull her knickers down and force himself into her. 'Shut up, you silly bitch, give in else it will be the worse for you. I'll get you sacked and tell everyone that you offered your body to me. I'm well respected, you are just another penniless nobody who's come to work here like half of York does.'

Molly felt his hands where no man's hands should go uninvited and she froze for a minute. This is what her mother had always warned her of and she wasn't going to let this horrible man get away with it. Whether she was to lose her job or not she didn't care and she reached for a pack of cardboard boxes and hit him over the head with it as he tried to push her onto the hard concrete floor to have his way with her.

'You stay away from me,' she gasped and moved her face at the last minute to bite him on the nose as he persisted, drawing blood that trickled down his face.

He put his hand to his face in shock and looked at the blood on his fingers. 'You bitch, you little bitch!' he yelled, and for a crucial second let go of Molly, giving her just time to pull her knickers up and rush to the warehouse door as he pulled his handkerchief out of his pocket to wipe his nose and quickly fastened his trousers.

Molly could feel tears running down her cheeks as she fumbled with the latch and opened the door onto the main factory floor, where she looked around her and tried to compose herself before approaching her supervisor Mrs Beaumont with as much decorum as she could. Not looking back for a second at Robert Jones as he walked back onto the factory floor, she couldn't see that he was acting as if nothing had happened, other than holding his handkerchief to the end of his nose.

'What do you want, Molly Freeman? I hope that you saw to Mr Jones's needs,' Mrs Beaumont said sternly, her eyes on the man that could make or break any of her workers.

'I have a complaint, Mrs Beaumont,' Molly said quietly. 'He tried to do things to me that good girls don't do. He tried to . . . he tried to . . .' Molly sobbed and felt faint.

'Hold your noise, girl, Mr Jones is a gentleman, he would never do anything like that. Go back to your station and get on with your job and I want to hear no more of it. I hope that you didn't blacken the name of this department,' Mrs Beaumont said crossly, looking back at Robert Jones who was blowing his nose on a blood-stained handkerchief and looking flushed as he made his way towards her.

Molly hung her head, she was going to lose her job, the job she needed so badly, if he told everybody what she had done. After all, Mrs Beaumont had said that she had to do whatever he wanted, but no matter what happened she wasn't going to do that. She walked with unsteady legs back to her station and wiped the tears from her cheeks, unable to bear looking at Connie or her other work colleagues who were keeping their heads down.

'Are you all right, Mr Jones? I hope Molly showed you what you wanted,' Mrs Beaumont enquired as Robert Jones walked past her.

'Yes, but she's not the brightest worker that you have, Mrs Beaumont, I'd keep my eye on her, in fact I'd think twice about keeping her employed.' He snuffled through his handkerchief. 'I'm afraid I'm having a nose bleed, would you mind taking the visiting guests to the next stage until I can compose myself?'

'Of course, Mr Jones, whatever you say, and I will

indeed keep an eye on Molly Freeman,' Mrs Beaumont said, looking daggers across to Molly's station. She was as much in fear of her job as Molly was; everyone did as Robert Jones said, he held a lot of influence with Seebohm Rowntree and it made for a quiet life if he was kept satisfied.

'Are you all right, Molly? You look like you've seen a ghost, and what are you crying for?' Connie whispered as she watched her friend try and compose herself and blow her nose.

'I'm fine, just a bit upset,' Molly whispered, not daring to look at Connie, knowing that Mrs Beaumont was watching her.

'She'll not be all right, that bastard Jones will have tried to have his way with her, he always does pick on one of the new ones when he comes around with his toffee-nosed visitors,' said Beatrice, who was the other side of Molly, in a low voice, patting Molly reassuringly on the back. '"Show me the cardboard," he always asks, and it's more like, "Let me show you my cock"! We all know him!'

'He doesn't, does he? Oh Lord, Molly, are you all right? He needs to be taught a lesson. That is, if you haven't already, did you hit his nose? It's bleeding,' Connie said quietly, trying to concentrate on making her chocolate box and not get caught talking.

'I'm all right, he tried to pull my knickers down,' Molly said in between tears and wiping her eyes. 'Mam said I'd to keep my knickers pulled up no matter what. So I bit him on the nose and then ran out. But I'm frightened of him, he looks really cross with me and so does Mrs Beaumont.'

'You did nothing wrong, Molly, but somebody wants to tell on him. He shouldn't be able to get away with it,' Connie fumed and glared at Mrs Beaumont as she returned to her post and got on with her job.

'He said I'd lose my job if I said anything to anybody, please don't say anything,' Molly said, and tried to concentrate on her work.

'We'll see, he's a bully and a coward. I've just left home because of one of those, I'm not doing that only for him to think he can get away with it.' Connie breathed in deeply, she remembered the nights when Bill would rattle her bedroom door and swear at not being able to get into her after she had locked it for her safety. She remembered his beer-laden breath and the letching touches that he had given her when her mother wasn't watching. Robert Jones was no better than Bill, he was just better dressed and in a position of trust, which made it even worse.

16

'You look miserable, our Molly, what's up? Has the cat got your tongue?' Annie asked as they sat around the supper table and discussed their day.

'She'll just be tired, like you used to get, Annie. They are long days compared to school days,' Winnie soothed, but she also sensed that there was something wrong with her youngest.

'Yes, I've just had a long day at work. Visitors were looking around the factory and we all had to be on our best behaviour.' Molly poked at her supper of scrambled eggs and didn't feel like eating them.

'Yes, that creep Jones brought them around. I couldn't help but laugh at him, he had blood on the end of his nose. Somebody must have punched him, I hope, he is a horrible little man,' Annie said, without connecting anything to her sister, and Connie wondered whether she should say something about Molly's run-in with Robert Jones. But she thought better of it as Molly shook her head at her from across the table.

'Mam, is it all right if I go and have a walk up to the canal? I just want to see if there's any sign of Josh, I know I'm perhaps a little early, but I can't wait for him to return,

I'm sure he said he'd be back in a fortnight and that's today. Although I'm not going to take Joan with me tonight, she's done nothing but make fun of me since I spent the day with Josh,' Annie sighed.

'Then she's not much of a friend, is she? Go tomorrow and I'll keep your supper warm. It's dark now, I don't want you wandering up there alone. You never know who's about nowadays,' Winnie said and looked at the table surrounded by her girls who were all growing into young women. Even Molly seemed to have blossomed of late, what with working and having Connie as a friend. She had been dubious about the friendship at the start but Connie seemed to be good for her. She was bringing Molly out of her shell and teaching her things that a growing lass should know. Molly would be fine with Connie by her side, although tonight she and Connie were strangely quiet. Something was afoot, she couldn't help but think.

'Oh, Mam, can't I go now? He might have been and gone by then,' Annie moaned. 'Then I'll have missed him and he'll think I'm not interested in him any more.'

'Stop moaning, Annie, there's no delivery of cocoa booked in until next week, Ned was saying so at lunch-time and Mary said that the one you'll be interested in is due next Wednesday or Friday, depending if all goes well at the docks,' Rose said, though she quickly wished she hadn't as all heads turned her way.

'Ned, Ned, Ned! That is all the workers ever talk about, you and him, especially now. They know that it is more than business that's being talked about between you and Ned Evans! Susan even thought she had seen you holding hands with him out in the garden. She's always gossiping!' Annie sat with her mouth open wide. She was still finding it hard to believe that her sister was really courting the sexiest man in Rowntree's. And management to boot!

'We are still only friends, we won't be seen together in work time. Don't you say anything to anyone, especially you, Annie Freeman, do you hear?' Rose said sharply.

'Blinking heck! I know she has mentioned him to us all, but I didn't know it was that serious,' Annie said, looking at Molly and Connie.

'I'd a good idea, but like Rose says, keep it to yourself. He can't be showing any favouritism to his staff and that's all Rose is to him through the working day. Just keep it to yourself, no gossiping!' Winnie couldn't help but notice the look between Molly and Connie as they were reminded that Rose had the ear of one of the bosses. 'He doesn't have much to do with the rest of you from what I understand anyway. He's more on the new product ranges from what Rose has told me.'

'He's a boss, blinking heck, Rose, and he's only the one that everyone swoons over when he walks by. How have you managed that, he never says boo to a goose?' Annie said and sat back in her chair.

'He's quiet and keeps himself to himself. So keep your mouth shut. We are, as I said, only friends,' Rose said again and looked hard at her middle sister.

'Yes, friends, I've heard that one before . . .' Annie grinned.

'Does he have anything to do with Robert Jones?' Connie asked, not daring to look at Molly.

'Sometimes, it depends which product he's working on. Robert Jones came around with his group today and we showed them how the biscuit crisp was being made. I must admit I agree with Annie, he's an obnoxious man.'

'You can say that again,' Connie said quietly, watching as Molly left the table and went to her room without saying anything to anyone.

'Has our Molly been all right at work today, she seems very quiet to me?' Winnie said, and looked worriedly at Connie.

'She's not had the best of days, she didn't like the visitors watching her, nor Robert Jones,' Connie said, but refrained from saying more.

'Nobody likes him,' Annie said, though she was distracted at the thought of missing a night with Josh.

'He's good at promoting the firm and that's what we need. We have Craven's breathing down our neck, they keep trying new products in the shops we supply, we have to keep one step ahead,' Rose said.

'Whooo . . . listen to her, management already!' Annie said and laughed.

'Oh well, as long as that's all that's up with Molly, she usually likes this time with us all together, she's probably just tired.' Winnie leaned on the kitchen table. 'I'll be moving her bedroom about at the weekend. There's enough room for an extra bed if I put the chest of drawers out onto the landing. The rag 'n' bone man is bringing me one he's been promised on Monday. We can't have you sleeping on the settee for ever, Connie, Christmas will be with us before we know it. We always entertain visitors in the front room.'

'Are you sure that's all right, Mrs Freeman? I don't want to be a nuisance,' Connie said, watching Annie and Rose closely to see their reaction to the news that Connie was going to be a permanent fixture in their home.

'Well, we can't throw you out upon the streets now, can we, and Molly thinks a lot of you. It'll do her good to share her bedroom. These two have to, even though they argue like cat and dog.' Winnie rose from the table. 'Your rent money is a grand help and you can stop with us as long as you need to, it's only right that you do.'

'Thank you, I'm so grateful,' Connie sighed.

'Just look after my Molly, that's all I ask. She's the most vulnerable one of all my lasses and her sisters cannot always be there for her,' Winnie asked, smiling at her daughters.

'I will, Mrs Freeman, I'll not let anyone hurt her, I promise,' Connie said and looked at Rose. She was going to have to put her faith in Molly's big sister and her connections to management at Rowntree's.

'This is comfy, Molly, I hope I'm not going to be in your way, am I?' Connie said as she sat on the edge of her bed in Molly's cramped but homely bedroom on Monday evening.

'No, I never wanted to share with one of my sisters but you are different. You don't argue with me like they do,' Molly said and sighed as she lay back in her bed and looked up at the ceiling.

Connie bounced on her bed and laughed as every spring made a noise and the mattress went down in the middle with her weight on it. 'I don't think that your mother got the best bargain when she bought this, but it doesn't matter, I'm not complaining. I'm just so thankful that your mam has taken me in, you really have no idea how bad things were at home.' Connie hesitated for a moment. 'You know that Robert Jones reminds me of Bill. He thinks he can take what he wants and that nobody will stop him. He doesn't care if he wrecks people's lives just as long as he gets what he wants.'

'I don't want to talk about him, please don't mention it to me. I feel ashamed and embarrassed,' Molly said and turned her face to the wall, not wanting Connie to see the tears that at any moment could well up in her eyes at the memory of her ordeal.

'Oh, Molly!' Connie left her bed and sat on the edge of Molly's to put her arm around her friend. 'Sorry, but you know somebody should tell on him. Perhaps if you said something to your Rose then she could confide in Ned Evans and he could see that he's sacked. You wouldn't want another girl to feel like you do. You've not been yourself all weekend,' Connie said softly.

'I'm not telling anybody. They would all say it was my own fault and I'd lose my job. Don't mention him again and don't tell anybody anything. I'm all right, just tired like my mam says.' Molly pulled her pillow down over her head and went quiet and wished just for once that Connie would go away.

'Oh, all right then, as long as you are fine,' Connie said and left Molly's side. She knew she was anything but fine, but she would bide her time or talk to Rose herself, although she didn't want to put her friendship with Molly in danger, it was too precious. 'I just care, Mol, that's all.'

Annie wandered along the canal towpath. For the others in the family the weekend had not been long enough but she had been counting the days till Wednesday evening when Rose had said that the next delivery of cocoa was to be brought in by the canal barge that Josh worked on. She pulled her coat around her; the leaves were starting to change colour. If there was no sign of the barge in the next half-hour, Annie decided that she would return home. It was too damp to remain sitting on her usual seat for too long and as she had not invited Joan along with her she felt uneasy, sitting on her own with all the world passing her by as they made their way home or walked their dog or lived their lives in their barges. She stamped her feet to keep them warm. Another ten minutes and she would return home, she thought, and felt her heart sink at the thought of not seeing the lad that she had befriended despite everyone saying she was a fool. She was about to go home when in the darkening gloom a stoutly built man came walking along the

222

towpath with a cap on his head, a reefer coat on and a muffler around his neck. He waved a piece of paper in his hand and cried out.

'Annie, is it Annie? I hope it bloody is cause I'm not wasting any more time running around after that little bugger,' the rough-talking fella said.

'I'm Annie, yes, why?' Annie said, recognising the man now as the owner of the barge that Josh usually worked on.

'Cause I'm playing Cupid for that bloody little bugger called Josh. He's sent me to give you this. He said you'd be sitting waiting for him where we berthed, but I'm a bit further up the canal today and he was right seemingly. Here, Lord knows what he's written to you, but he's not with me any more, the silly little bugger has joined the Merchant Navy, all because I wouldn't give him a pay rise. He'll regret that when them Jerries decide to take us into their war again.' The man passed over an envelope to a crestfallen Annie. 'I hope that you've not lost your heart to him because you'll not be seeing him for a long time now. He'll have gone with one of the Arctic convoys out of Liverpool, protecting the fishing fleets. He'll be lucky if he comes back into port for six months or more. Anyway, he must think something of you, else he wouldn't write. I've done my job now, so I'll be on my way.'

Annie watched as the man disappeared, following the canal path to where, in the distance, she could just make out the shape of the barge that had brought her and Josh together. What for, she wondered, if she was never going to see him again? She could have cried as she looked at the letter but could not read the writing in the dim evening's light. It was going to have to wait until she got home, she thought, as she placed it into her coat pocket. Did she mean so little to him, after all? She must do if he had joined the Merchant Navy. He could be sent anywhere in the world and she may not ever see him again, just like Rose's friend Mary's fella, though she had heard he was on his way back for her. You should never fall in love with a sailor, but Josh had been different, he was on the barges and his voyages were back and forward on the canals with his loads of cocoa. Just when she thought she had found somebody he had disappeared and after all the jibes and digs that she had put up with about his colour! She walked home feeling miserable; she felt like the weather: gloomy, dark and sad, and she had a feeling that worse times were to come as she thought about the news headlines and what Josh's captain had said. There was perhaps the making of a war coming and Josh would be right in the middle of it now he had joined the Merchant Navy.

'You are back early, Annie, has he not shown up?' Winnie said as she paused her knitting and looked up at her daughter as she came in and sat down.

'No, he hasn't, Mam, but he's sent me a letter. His captain passed it to me and told me that he's left him and gone to work for the Merchant Navy. I'll never see him again, will I, Mam?' Annie said as she looked at the letter she had taken out of her pocket and put onto the kitchen table.

'I don't know, my love, see what he says in his letter. I'm sure from what you said he's not that callous,' Winnie soothed, hoping in one sense that he would not be back because that would make for an easier life, but in another, she knew Annie had lost her heart to the lad.

'I'll go and read it in my bedroom. Is Rose up there? I don't want her being nosy and looking at what he says.' Annie sighed.

'No, she's gone out, she didn't say where she was going but she is probably visiting Mary.' Winnie shook her head as she had to pull back the stitch that she had just dropped. 'The other two are in the front room, playing a game of draughts, so there is no one upstairs at all.'

'Right, I'll go and see what he's written. I wish I had never met him if I'm never going to see him again,' Annie replied, taking hold of the letter whose contents she was dreading; she just knew it would read *sorry but I'll not be seeing you again.*

She looked at herself in the dressing-table mirror as she sat on the chair with the letter in her hand. She was not the best-looking girl, she knew that, her nose was too long and when she smiled it looked as if she was in pain, she always thought. She couldn't blame him for not feeling she was enough to stay here for. Finally, she ran her finger under the envelope's seal and pulled out the letter written on paper that looked like it had been torn out of a school exercise book.

Dear Annie,

*I'm sorry that I have had to write this letter and
ask my old boss to give it to you. It was the only
way I knew that you'd get to know what I'm doing.
I couldn't remember the street that I said goodbye
to you on.*

*Anyway, I needed you to know that I want so
badly to keep in touch with you and for you not
to think I've deserted you. I was nineteen last week
and I need to start earning a better wage than being
a skivvy on board the Freespirit. My mother is struggling with what money comes into the house and I
need to start saving for my future plans. I applied
to join the Merchant Navy and they started me in
a job going back and forward to America. I'm not
up in the Arctic like I know my old boss will have
told you out of badness. I'll be back home regularly,
so don't worry. This is my address so that we can
keep in touch with one another. My mother knows
you will be writing to me, so she will keep the letters
until my return. At least I hope that you will keep in
touch with me. I understand if you have had second
thoughts, I know it won't be the easiest of friendships.
My address is:*

Mr Joshua Abebe
49 Toxteth Street
Liverpool

Thank you for that lovely day around York, I never will forget it. I am hoping more than anything that we can still keep in touch.

Yours faithfully,

Josh

Annie held the letter in her hand and smiled. She had his address and she knew where he was going and that he wanted to keep in touch with her. Of course she would write to him, she would write every day if she needed to and nobody was going to stop her.

17

Winnie Freeman sat down in her chair and sipped her tea. She had finished Monday's wash and now she was going to have ten minutes to herself with her own thoughts. She had always thought that when her girls got older her life would be easier, but it didn't seem to be going that way. Plus, she had taken on the added responsibility of Connie, but she had been left with no option, she couldn't have seen the lass on the streets.

She sighed and closed her eyes; it was pouring down, a typical autumn washing day, where everything was going to be hung on the washing line in the outhouse until it was semi-dry and then she'd bring it in to hang above the kitchen fire on the clothes rack. Life was hard and some days she felt like giving up on it all. If it hadn't have been for her three young daughters when her husband died she would have done just that. At that time she had felt lost and abandoned, with the weight of the world upon her shoulders, but she had made the best of it, taking in washing and ironing until her eldest, Rose, had been old enough to go to work and start bringing a little well-earned income into the home. Then Annie eighteen months later and now finally the baby of the family was employed by Rowntree's. Thank heavens for Rowntree's, it had been the saviour of many a family in York and long may it continue, she thought, as she sighed and decided to stir her shanks and make sure that there was enough cold meat left for the girls' supper. It was always left-over cold meat on a Monday, it was the easiest after a hard washday. Although she knew that Annie and Molly would pull a face at the cold platter of meat with pickled onions and bread and butter on a cold, wet day. They'd have to take it or leave it, they would have probably have eaten well at dinnertime anyway. Rowntree meals were always wholesome and warm so that they could get the best out of their workers. Winnie looked at the cold leg of mutton; she could just make it feed them all, or perhaps she could mince it up with an onion and put some mashed potatoes on the top, make it into a shepherd's pie? That would be more appealing to Molly and warmer for the cold day.

Her thoughts turned to Molly as she fastened the metal mincer's screw to the wooden kitchen table, securing it tightly and then feeding chunks of cold mutton through the top as she turned the handle to rotate the mincer, making the meat come out finely ground onto a plate directly underneath. That looks better, she thought, as she peeled an onion and found the acid from it stinging her eyes, before she also minced it and then put a pan of potatoes on the cooker to boil. She stood and looked out of the window and thought again about Molly; something was not quite right. She was still too quiet and she was picking at her food. It might be that she was just tired or that she had suddenly realised that work was more of a chore than enjoyment. But it was more than that, she had heard her crying a morning or two when she was in the outside lavvy. However, when she had asked what was wrong, her daughter had shaken her head and said it was nothing; but there was something and eventually she would have to say, she'd not be able to keep it to herself for much longer. Whatever it was, she would put it right for her girl. Nothing would be allowed to hurt a Freeman lass, Winnie thought as she checked her potatoes and put the oven on.

'Molly, you can't go on not sleeping like this. You are on edge whenever Mrs Beaumont announces anything at work, you are not eating and you even turned down going to the pictures at the weekend,' Connie said, putting her arm around her best friend as she sat knitting on the edge of her bed. 'It's all because of that Robert Jones and what he did. You know you are not the first girl he's tried it on with, Beatrice says if you went and complained to one of the bosses, there would be a queue as long as your arm standing behind you and backing you up.'

'I don't want to talk about it. In fact, I wish that you'd go back downstairs, I'm fed up of having to talk to you and you not minding your business,' Molly said coldly, completely out of character for the easy-going happy lass that she had been a few weeks ago.

'Don't be like that, Mol, I'm only trying to help. I can go and sleep back downstairs if you want but that's not going to mend anything. You need to talk to your mam, even if you are not going to say anything to the bosses,' Connie urged, knowing she was on a hiding to nothing as Molly did not even reply.

'I'm going downstairs for a drink of water. Do you want anything brought back up?' Molly just shook her head as Connie took one of the small paraffin lamps that they used in the evenings in the bedroom and left.

Connie, in her winceyette nightdress that had once been Annie's, made her way down the stairs and walked barefoot across the cold kitchen flags to the cupboard where the cups were kept and ran herself some cold water from the sink. She leaned back and looked around the homely kitchen; she had always dreamed of a home like this. It was everything a home should be, she thought as she watched the flame of her lamp flicker on the walls. The smell of paraffin filled the air and it reminded her of when she was small and everything was right in her world when her father was still with them. She was suddenly brought back into the real world as she heard the front door open and close and the electric light turn on as Rose returned from visiting Mary.

'What you doing down here without the electric light on, are you all right?' Rose asked and looked at Connie as she pulled off her coat and removed her head-square.

'Yes, I just came down for a drink of water and didn't want to waken anyone else up so I brought the paraffin lamp down with me.' Connie hesitated. 'I also thought I'd let Molly have some time to herself, she's knitting in the lamplight, but I think she's dropping more stitches than knitting,' Connie said, looking at Rose.

'She's in a right way with herself. Mam was saying she's hardly eating supper and she looks really upset some mornings. Do you know what's up with her? She doesn't usually act like this, I thought she would enjoy sharing her bedroom with you as you are as thick as thieves.' Rose looked at the young lass that she still wasn't all that keen on, but she knew Molly could not have a truer friend.

Connie hung her head, she didn't know what to say. She wanted to be true to Molly but at the same time, she knew something had to be done about the abusive Robert Jones. 'I think I know what's wrong, but I don't want to lose Molly's friendship. Please, if I tell you, can I ask you not to say anything until you know what can be done?' Connie asked, hoping Rose might have an inkling of what she was going to be told.

'Yes, of course, all I want to see is my little sister happy, and if I can help, I will. Come and tell me what it is that's worrying her in the front room where nobody can hear us talking. I knew there was something,' Rose said and walked down the corridor to the front of the house with Connie following in her footsteps.

'Now, what do you think is wrong with our Molly? None of us can understand what is going on in her life at the moment, one minute she was happy and the next it was as if a cloud had just crossed over the sun and left her in the dark.'

'Well, she's not going to like me for telling you, so

perhaps we could keep it as our secret, or at least share it only with those that matter.' Connie sat down, feeling as if she was sneaking behind her best friend's back. However, she knew it would be for the good of not just Molly, but also other girls that might be future prey for Robert Jones.

Connie sat and cupped her hands together and started to tell Rose about Molly's experience with Robert Jones, or as much as Molly had dared to tell her. Then she went on to say it was common knowledge that he preyed on the newest starters, especially in the Card Box Mill, and had done so for some time. She also added that she thought Mrs Beaumont was making Molly's life hard by picking fault in her work for no reason.

Rose's face told of her anger and disgust that anybody in a position of power would take advantage of young naive girls, especially when it came to her sister.

'Poor Molly, she should say something, she should feel she can talk to us and our mam. It isn't her fault, it's that disgusting excuse of a man. I'll go and talk to her,' Rose said angrily and got up from her seat.

'Rose, before you do, think about the other girls that he's picked on and has done the same thing to, and I need to keep my promise of secrecy to Molly. He needs stopping first. Do you think you should talk to the bosses at Rowntree's? Get him caught out maybe, or get them to talk to some of the other girls that he's done this to, too?' Connie went silent for a moment. 'I don't want Molly to think I've been telling tales about her. Big Beatrice who works next to Molly knows it goes on and she might have actually been used by him herself. She's listened to by a lot of the lasses, I'm sure she would help.'

'The last thing I want is for Molly to lose her friendship with you. I'll be honest, when both Annie and I first saw you we thought that you were not right for her. However, now I know she couldn't have a better friend.' Rose sat back down. 'I'll talk to Ned, he's got influence, and I'll speak to Mrs Beaumont, surely she realises what's going on under her very nose?'

'No! Don't talk to Mrs Beaumont, I think she knows all too well what's going on in the box room. I think she's as frightened of losing her job as the rest of the girls. She tells the girls that they must do whatever the visitors or Mr Jones ask them to do, as they control their jobs with Rowntree's.'

'What a load of rubbish. I never did like Bessie Beaumont. Tomorrow morning I will talk to Ned and he will go straight to the top. This is everything that the Rowntree family does not stand for. Robert Jones's days will be numbered if everyone has the courage to speak up about him and his disgusting deeds. Don't worry, it will be stopped, but can you promise me you'll look after Molly until it is? Once girls come forward, hopefully she will speak up, especially if she knows we will think none the worse of her. Men can be bastards and I don't often swear, but of late I'm seeing a different side to them.'

'You don't have to tell me, I've lived with a version of Robert Jones for the last eight years, my stepfather, who was abusive. But to have it going on in the workplace and for Molly to hate going to work because of one man has to be stopped.' Connie sat and felt tears in her eyes and then breathed in deeply. 'Thank you, Rose, I feel better now I've spoken to somebody. I'll look after Molly, I think a great deal of her, she's a good friend.'

'Right, well, leave it with me. Ned will listen to me, I hope, and he will get it sorted.' Rose sighed and looked at Connie. 'Give Molly a hug from me but don't let on. We will all talk to her when the time is right.'

Connie quietly walked back up to her bedroom and looked at Molly who was still knitting in the dim light of her lamp.

'You've been a long time. I thought that you had fallen out with me. I wouldn't blame you if you had, I was really rude to you,' Molly said as she put her knitting down and pulled the cover back on her bed, then took a sip of the water Connie had brought upstairs with her.

'Don't be silly, I've not fallen out with you. I know you are worried about one thing or another. You know a trouble shared is a trouble halved, as my mam used to say. I'm sure if you spoke to your mam she would listen and understand,' Connie said, and then sat down on Molly's bed next to her and hugged her.

'My mam would go mad with me and then stamp off down the road to Rowntree's and make me lose my job. That's the last thing that I want. She may take most things in her stride, but when she loses her temper, she's a different woman. I daren't tell her anything and besides you don't talk about things like that,' Molly said and hugged Connie back.

'It will all get sorted, and you stop worrying about Robert Jones, forget about him, and hold your head high. You are really doing well making the boxes and soon we start making boxes for Christmas, they will be ever so special. Have you seen the ribbons and the paper they are to be wrapped in? I saw it all being delivered to the warehouse yesterday,' Connie said and saw a slight smile come to Molly's face.

'Yes, I saw it, I can't wait to see what they are going to look like. I love Christmas.' Molly sighed. 'Sorry, Connie, I can't stop thinking about what would have happened if I hadn't bitten Robert Jones. Mam should have told me straight what men like him are after, instead of just saying keep your knickers up.'

'Not all men, Molly, just some. He is just a wrong 'un and his days are numbered. Of that, you have my word. Now go to sleep and think how bonny those Christmas boxes are going to look when you've finished with them. Rowntree's will not sack you, Mol, you have the knack of folding and an eye for detail.'

'I hope so, Connie, and thank you for being my friend. Night, night. Sorry for being a grump,' Molly said, watching Connie climb into her bed as she curled under the covers herself. She dreaded every minute at work, just waiting for Robert Jones to show his face in the Card Box Mill; no matter how much she loved her job, he was ruining it for her and she wished she had never set her eyes on him.

'Well, I can't believe that, why on earth has nobody said anything before? Has it been going on a long time?' Ned was horrified as Rose told him of the conversation between her and Connie the previous evening.

'It's true, Connie would not make anything like that up and our Molly looks as if she is about to slit her wrists. You've got to do something, Ned, he can't be allowed to do things like that, he needs stopping. If you don't say something or get to the bottom of it, then I will. I'll go and see Seebohm Rowntree myself if I have to.' Rose could see that Ned didn't know what best to do and felt frustrated.

'No, leave it to me, I've never liked the man anyway, but I didn't realise he was up to anything like that. I'll have a word with Seebohm; if this got out it could damage the reputation of the whole of Rowntree's. He is taking advantage of the new young workers and he needs stopping. It goes against everything that the Rowntree family believe in.'

18

'Do sit down, Mrs Beaumont,' said Seebohm Rowntree the following day. 'What we are about to discuss is very important and I want you to give me a true and honest answer. I also assure you that what you tell me will not endanger your employment with us. That is, if you yourself have not gained by the dirty business that we have just become aware of.'

Bessie Beaumont sat down and felt herself shaking and feeling faint as Seebohm Rowntree addressed her, with Ned Evans standing behind him and the company secretary poised on a chair taking note of every word said. She had known it would eventually come to this, ever since Robert Jones had left with his nose bleeding; she also knew that her treatment of Molly had not been fair, she was ashamed to admit she had picked on every little mistake, but the girl had persevered and had even become one of the best box-makers that she had ever known.

'Sir, before you say anything, may I ask, is this about Robert Jones? If so, I will tell you everything I know. It is the least I can do as I have turned a blind eye to his practices and have been used by him as much as the girls.' Bessie pulled her handkerchief from out of her sleeve and twiddled it in her hands as Seebohm looked at Ned and shook his head.

'You sit in front of me now, when this despicable man's exploits have been found out, but you didn't have the strength of character to tell me beforehand? Good grief, woman, how long have his terrible ways been affecting people, and how many of my workers are involved?' The owner of Rowntree's glared at the woman he had, until now, thought to be a good, hard-working employee, despite being too frightened of Robert Jones to come and see him.

'It's not been going on too long . . . for about three years now. He told me that I would lose my job just like the girls if I told anyone.' Bessie felt herself near to tears.

'Three years! Good God, I can't believe it. I need a list of all the girls that you think he might have forced himself upon, I think that is the least you can do. Then I will have to speak to each one individually and assure them that I had no idea what was going on within the firm. It stops today. I will inform the police of Mr Jones's actions and I am sure they will be pressing charges and wanting to see you and whoever he had his wicked way with. As for your position in the firm, I will seriously have to consider if I wish to keep you in my employment.' Seebohm Rowntree looked at the woman who was close to tears, but felt no pity for her.

'Go into the next room and compose me a list of girls you think were involved, and Mr Evans and Rose Freeman from our new product department will sit and interview them and give them our reassurances that nothing like this will happen again. You truly do disgust me.'

'Please, not Rose Freeman, Mr Rowntree, sir, could your secretary not interview them,' Bessie Beaumont said as she sat up from her chair.

'No, Mrs Beaumont, it will be Rose Freeman because we know that her youngest sister, and a new starter to Rowntree's, was one of the girls he forced himself upon. Yet you turned a blind eye and even made her life harder in my employment. She is a bag of nerves from what I understand. Now go, write the list and await my decision on your future within Rowntree's.' Seebohm Rowntree watched as Bessie Beaumont left, her head down and looking dejected. He had already alerted the police about Robert Jones and a policeman was also going to sit in on the interviews with the young girls. There was no room for such behaviour in his firm and those guilty were going to pay.

There was an uneasiness in the Card Box Mill as, individually, girls' names started to be read out an hour or so later by Ned Evans, and they were asked to go upstairs one by one to the main offices. Everybody wondered what was going on when they didn't return to their stations and Mrs Beaumont said nothing about what was happening.

Connie looked at Molly; should she tell her what this was about or should she remain silent? At least her conversation with Rose had come to fruition and somebody in higher management was sorting it. She only hoped that Molly would forgive them both.

Big Beatrice stopped working for a moment and came over to stand next to both Connie and Molly. 'I've figured out what's going on. Them that are going upstairs have all been in the warehouse with Robert Jones. That's what this is all about. You'll have to tell him how you bit his nose, it will make them laugh if nothing else.' Beatrice folded her arms and looked across at Bessie Beaumont. 'She'll be for the chop and all because she's known about it from the very beginning. I should have said something, but I don't mix with management.'

'They aren't getting the sack, are they? It isn't their fault. I don't want to lose my job, I'll not say anything about what went on,' Molly said, and a look of panic crossed her face. She had been trying to forget all about it and now everyone would know what had been going on in the warehouse.

'Nobody is going to get the sack. Everybody on the floor knows, Molly. They just don't talk about it. Just like you don't. Now's the time to tell them what they need to know and then they can get rid of him – and her, because she's as bad,' Connie said and glared at Bessie Beaumont. 'You say what he did and that she's been watching you and finding fault with your work ever since. Do you hear? You get going now.'

'Aye, tell it as it is, Molly. I would do if he'd ever have picked on me, but there was a bit too much of me for him to push around. Sometimes it pays to be fat and ugly,' Beatrice said, not attempting to move back to her work as Bessie Beaumont looked at the three of them talking.

'She knows – look, she's not so bloody bossy now, the cow,' Beatrice said and fished a packet of Victory Vs out of the pocket of her uniform, put one in her mouth and sucked on it with attitude.

'I don't want to go, perhaps they will forget about me,' Molly said and felt her stomach churn at just the thought of having to walk past her work colleagues and everybody thinking the same as Beatrice.

'Can Molly Freeman please make her way to the main office,' Ned called from the top of the stairs, and Connie smiled and looked at her friend as Beatrice patted her on her back. 'Say it like it was. Somebody needs to tell the truth about pervert Jones. You'll be all right, I know you will.' Connie wished that she could go with her as she watched Molly walk past all the lines of workers, looking like her legs were made of jelly as she mounted the stairs to the top offices.

'The poor devil. I hope there's somebody who will be kind to her and all the other girls. I also hope that they cut off Robert Jones's bits for what he's done,' Beatrice said loudly, so that Bessie Beaumont could hear. 'It's disgusting what some folk can get away with.'

Molly swore she was going to be sick as she knocked on the glass window of the main office and waited to be told to enter. Her legs really did feel like jelly, she was near tears and if she had dared run she would have done so. The door opened and Molly walked in with her head down, like a lamb to the slaughter.

'Ah, Molly, now come and sit down, we just want to

have a talk to you in private, and the officer here is going to take a few notes.'

Molly looked across the desk at Ned Evans and saw a policeman sitting next to him with his notebook open. But to her relief, sitting on a chair at the other side of the desk was her big sister Rose.

'It's all right, Molly, we all know what you've been through. We just want to hear it from you in your own words,' Rose said quietly. 'You should have told me, Molly, we could have sorted it out a lot sooner.' She leaned across the desk and held her young sister's hand and felt her shaking. 'It's all right, love, just tell them what he wanted to do with you. The other girls already have. There will be no more visits from Robert Jones, and Mrs Beaumont is due for a reprimand.'

'I couldn't tell you. I'd have lost my job and I've never let anybody do anything like he did. Our mam would disown me,' Molly sobbed.

'It's not your fault, now you just take your time and say what went on and then that will be the last of it.' Ned Evans smiled reassuringly at the young lass who looked so innocent. 'The policeman here is just going to ask you some questions and make a note of your answers and then you are free to go home for the day. Your sister Rose can go home with you if you wish, I'm afraid we have left you until the last so that she can do so.'

'I'm not going to lose my job?' Molly asked, and tried to smile.

'No, of course not, none of this is yours or the other

girls' fault. If anything, it is ours for being conned by that dreadful man. We had no idea what his game was besides inviting rich and wealthy businessmen to look around our firm. Now, when you are ready, take a deep breath and tell us what happened.' Ned looked at Rose and then smiled warmly at Molly. 'Your sister and I are here for you, no matter what.'

'Lord above, you two, what are you both doing at home at this time of day? Has there been an accident at Rowntree's? And where are Annie and Connie?' Winnie woke up from her five-minute snooze after her lunch in her chair and looked at Rose and Molly standing in front of her. 'I was just having my usual cat nap.'

'Nothing's happened at Rowntree's, Mam. Not that you need worry about anyway,' Rose said, and put her arm around Molly.

'What do you mean? What should I have been worrying about? Have I missed something? Why does our Molly look like she's been crying?' Winnie stood up and looked at her youngest. 'Are you all right, Molly, what's up? I've been worrying about you for a while now.'

'I'm fine, Mam. Sorry, I should have told you, but I couldn't, I was frightened and worried, I didn't know what to do.' Molly stepped forward to her mother and wrapped her arms around her waist. It felt so much better now that a weight had been lifted and Rose had assured her that her mother would not be angry and that she was valued at her work. 'I hated him, I never asked him to do what he did.'

Winnie looked questioningly at Rose, who shook her head and then said, 'Molly and a few more girls have been targeted by a man in a high position, he's abused his position at work and led them to believe if they didn't do what he wanted they would lose their jobs. He only went so far with Molly here. In fact, she used her head and managed to bite his nose and escape. That served the devil right, but it was still a horrible ordeal for her to go through. It only came to light because somebody told me in secret, that's how I became involved.'

'Oh, Molly my love, are you all right? I knew something was wrong. You weren't acting like yourself but we all told ourselves you were just tired.' Winnie held her daughter tight and kissed her. 'So, you bit his nose, did you? That would serve the devil right.' She wiped Molly's tears from her eyes and kissed her again.

'I knew I had to keep my knickers up, Mam, I knew he was doing wrong but I couldn't stop him, so I bit him and ran,' Molly said in between tears.

'You did right, my love,' Winnie said and held her tight as she mouthed, 'He didn't do anything else?' to Rose. To which Rose shook her head.

'Nobody must ever do anything like that to you, do you hear? You should have told us all. What's happened to him and who was it?'

'He's in the nick, Mam. It was Robert Jones, you'll have seen him, he likes to think he is somebody, knows everybody and anybody,' Rose said, and started to make herself a cup of tea.

'Well, he will get to know a whole lot of new people when he's locked up. And I'd like to get my hands on him, it wouldn't be his nose that was hurting, I can tell you that if I did,' Winnie said and hugged Molly to her.

'There will be a few mothers saying that when they find out what's been going on. I feel so sorry for Rowntree's, they had no idea that it was happening. If it hadn't been for Connie telling me everything the other night because she was so worried about Molly, it would never have come to light. You've got a true friend there, Molly, she was really concerned about you and terrified that she would lose you as a friend if she told me or one of the bosses. There's quite a few that should be glad that she spoke up,' Rose said as she poured hot water into the teapot.

'Aye, that lass, he didn't touch her and all, did he?' Winnie sighed and hugged Molly closer. 'She's been through enough already.'

'No, but she was adamant that Robert Jones had to be stopped, I think her stepfather was rather like him, from what she said,' Rose said.

'Thank the Lord she's your friend, Molly, she can stop here for as long as she wants. Now, how about you have forty winks, I know you haven't slept lately, I can tell by the shadows under your eyes. You forget all about Robert Jones because as far as I'm concerned I hope the key is going to be thrown away. His life will be made hell once the other prisoners find out he's been preying on young girls.' Winnie kissed her daughter again and couldn't stop hugging her.

'I feel so much better now that you all know. It was like a dark secret and I knew what he had done was so wrong but I was frightened of losing my job.'

'You'll not lose your job, but I think Bessie Beaumont will. She's known about it all going on and not lifted a finger. Ned says he's going to make sure she's sacked,' Rose said as she sipped her tea.

'I like your Ned, he's kind and so good-looking,' Molly said with a smile.

'He is just the opposite of Robert Jones, he is a true gentleman. Now you go to bed and get some sleep before Connie and Annie come home, because they will be full of gossip and will want to know everything. You did well today, little sis. Don't you ever keep anything like that to yourself again! That's how people like Robert Jones thrive. And remember to thank Connie, she was worried to death about you.'

'I will. Love you, Rose,' Molly said and felt a cloak of relief fall over her. She would go to bed and sleep. She had a loving family, the best friend she could have, and was valued in her job. She could sleep easy.

'Well, that was a day and a half! Connie's just been telling me what's been going on. Is Molly all right?' Annie said a few hours later as soon as she walked into the house with Connie a few steps behind her.

'Shh, she's asleep. Worn out with the worry of keeping this to herself. Thank heavens you had the sense to tell one of us, Connie. I've been worrying about that lass for weeks now. I knew there was something wrong.' Winnie smiled gratefully at Connie.

'I knew I had to do something, he couldn't be let loose on the new girls that have just started and Molly was in such a state. I owed it to her, and Rose did the rest,' Connie replied, feeling for the family that the scandal had hit without being invited.

'Everybody's talking about it. They all knew what he got up to but nobody dared say,' Annie said, helping herself to a slice of buttered bread from the kitchen table. 'Anyway, he's in the clink now and the bosses are trying to keep the scandal quiet. Our poor Molly, bless her. Is it right she bit his nose? It should have been something else she bit, he'd have learnt then!' she giggled.

'Annie Freeman, don't talk so dirty, there's no need to stoop to his level,' Winnie said, looking disgusted at her daughter.

'Well, the lasses that work in the Card Box Mill are glad it happened because Bessie Beaumont has got the sack. She was sent packing halfway through the last shift. But Molly never will believe who's got her job, just on trial at the moment, though,' Connie said, smiling as she saw Molly come quietly down the stairs and stand in the doorway. 'Are you all right, Mol? I was just telling everybody the good news that we have a new supervisor and that you'll never believe who she is!'

'I'm all right, feel a little stupid and that I should have told you all what was going on, but we don't talk about such things in this family.' Molly sighed and wiped her eyes. 'Go on then, tell me who the new supervisor is, she can't be any worse than Bessie Beaumont,' she said as her mother put her arm around her and kissed her forehead.

'It's Beatrice, Big Beatrice that works next to us. She will be completely different to Bessie Beaumont; the one thing she will be is fair and she will speak her mind and show no favouritism.' Connie smiled and looked happy with her news.

'Yes, she will be good, she's always straight with the two of us and she's worked there a long time,' Molly said, looking relieved. 'Thank heavens Bessie Beaumont has left, she couldn't possibly have stayed. But she'll never get a job if folk find out about her.' Molly seemed worried at the thought.

'Never you mind about that, she's made her own bed and she must lie in it. You just look after yourself for a while and we will all hold our heads up high and look after one another. Us Freeman girls look after each other and that includes you, Connie,' Rose said, putting her arm around Connie. It had been a long day, but things were now getting sorted for the better.

19

Rose sat outside in the Rowntree garden; even though the autumn winds were turning much colder now, she and Ned still chose to meet there when they could.

The ordeal with Robert Jones had brought them even closer, daft as it sounded, she thought, as she waited for him and thought about the conversation that had taken place between Ned, Robert Jones, Seebohm Rowntree and herself. Never in past years would she have dared to even look at Seebohm Rowntree, let alone talk to him. And the conversation that she had shared with her seniors would have made her blush and feel foolish not that long ago. As for poor Molly, she was being spoilt and cared for by the family, but occasionally Rose would catch her gazing into space, remembering and thinking about the ordeal that she had gone through along with the other girls. It was just as well that Robert Jones was locked up and no longer welcome anywhere near the grounds of Rowntree's ever again. How the mighty did fall, she thought, and whispered the words her mother always said: 'Those that make the most noise are the emptiest vessels.' A quote from Plato, so Ned had told her.

'Hello, penny for your thoughts,' Ned said quietly as he

sat down beside her with the lunchbox that his mother had made him up that morning. 'Mother insisted that she made me my lunch today after hearing I missed mine yesterday as I was too busy to eat. Fancy a fish paste sandwich?' Ned asked, pulling a face at the contents.

'No, I think I'm fine, thank you. I'll just sit ten minutes with you and then I'll join my sisters.' Rose smiled as he bit into the paste sandwich and then wrapped it quickly back up again in the greaseproof paper that his mother had lovingly wrapped around it.

'I was just thinking about what went on the other day. How the young girls must have felt when they were in that stockroom with Robert Jones. They must have been petrified. No wonder Molly could not sleep or eat or stop thinking about him for worrying that it could happen again if he came back.' Rose sighed. 'I'm glad they all decided to tell on him.'

'So am I, and Bessie Beaumont has decided to tell us more about him as well. Which I am only too glad about. It means that younger girls like your Molly need not give evidence against him in court. That would have been dreadful for them. Bessie Beaumont returned this morning to the offices, I don't suppose you saw her? To ask, if she gave damning evidence and proof against him, could she have her job back.'

Rose shook her head, she'd not been up into the offices that morning, she had been too busy keeping her eye on the growing numbers of the new wafer biscuits being made.

'Anyway, she is willing to stand trial to say what she

knew he got up to, despite damaging her own reputation. She has been given a job with Rowntree's but not the one she had previously. She has obviously lost the respect of anyone who worked beneath her. We thought it only fitting that she was put in charge of the team working on the cardboard templates and keeping the glue pots filled up. Quite a downfall for a woman of her standing. However, she should be grateful for that because we had dismissed her without so much as a by your leave.' Ned sighed and looked at a piece of cake that his mother had made at the beginning of the previous week, which was obviously no longer fit to eat, given the green mould on it.

'That's worse than being sacked! She'll not enjoy doing that,' Rose said and smiled slightly.

'It's more than she deserves in my eyes,' he agreed. 'But that's Rowntree's for you, always ready to forgive. They have also paid to keep the scandal out of the papers, everyone agreed that it would be bad publicity for the firm. So Seebohm has pulled a few strings and is keeping a lid on it. It will be better for the girls involved anyway.' Ned closed the lid of his lunchbox and looked at Rose.

'Why don't you come and have some lunch with me and my sisters?' she suggested. 'Surely it can't be that bad to have your lunch with your fellow work colleagues even though you are higher up the ladder than us. Besides, I'm sure people have seen us sitting out here for a while now and put two and two together; anyway, if you don't, either your mother is going to poison you or we are going to freeze to death.' Rose grinned and pulled her coat around her.

'I shouldn't, we have the ruling of not fraternising with the factory floor workers, they tell us it undermines our authority. However, you are a supervisor so I think I will risk it, and what the hell, I do my job well! Why shouldn't I sit with the woman I love and have lunch with her?' Ned said, and grinned as he saw Rose's face light up.

'Did you just say what I thought you said?' Rose whispered, and felt her heart miss a beat.

'I certainly did, Rose Freeman, and every word is true, I think I do love you. When you were talking to the girls with so much concern and so much commitment, I realised what an honest, caring person you are. So, Rose, I do love you, and it's time everyone knew that we are courting instead of hiding away like two lepers.'

'Oh, Ned, it is early days yet, but yes, I think I love you too. I just can't believe it has happened so quickly, although I have admired you for some time, but never thought that you would give me the time of day,' Rose said quietly.

'And why did you think that? After all, you are the most beautiful woman in Rowntree's and I feel so lucky to have you next to me.' Ned squeezed Rose's hand and quickly kissed her on the cheek. 'Come on, my lunch is not fit for anywhere but the bin. Let me break a few rules and I'll come and sit with you and your sisters for my dinner, just don't tell my mother.' Ned took Rose's hand as she stood up from the bench. 'Mentioning which, I think she would like to meet your mother and has asked me if you would like to bring her around for tea?'

'Your mother wants to meet mine? Heavens, that will put my mother in a tizz. She'll be worrying about what to wear, what to say and if she's drinking her tea correctly. She soon gets worked up about things,' Rose replied, and felt a blush come to her cheeks as they walked into the dining room together and made their way to the table where the Freeman family were sitting. Everyone glanced at Ned Evans as he walked beside Rose and there was a noticeable murmur as he pulled up a chair to sit next to Annie and patted the one next to him for Rose.

'Right, girls, what do you recommend? I've decided to join you for my lunch, although by the look on your Annie's face, she is a little bit worried.' Ned smiled as the two sisters stopped eating their lunch and Connie couldn't believe her eyes that a boss was actually sitting at their table.

'I've got the shepherd's pie and it is really good,' Molly said, distracted only for a moment from eating her steaming-hot meal. She looked at the man that Rose seemed to be more than friends with, even though he was from upstairs.

'And I've got the liver and onions, but it's a bit tough,' Connie said as Annie started to eat her shepherd's pie without a word said to either Ned or Rose.

'Shepherd's pie it is, then. I'll get two portions, hey, Rose? They won't charge me, you might as well save yourself some money.' Ned got up from his seat and walked over to the queue, waiting in line instead of going to the head of it like he was entitled to.

Everyone was staring at Rose. 'What have you brought him over for? We always have a good natter and catch up at dinnertime and the other workers will think we are sucking up to management if he sits with us,' Annie said between mouthfuls of mince and potato.

'Don't be so daft, Annie. Everyone knows that he's the one who saved any more young girls from being used. That's why they are all looking at him, it's nothing to do with him sitting with us,' Rose said quietly, and looked across at the man she was starting to lose her heart to. He looked so handsome and she couldn't believe that she was the one he had chosen to walk out with. 'You'll have to get used to him joining us because that's what he will be doing from now on.'

'Huh, you and your men, you've gone from the gutter to the rooftop! I don't know if that's a good thing or not,' Annie said, and looked across at her sister.

'You can't say anything, Annie, and well you know it, now be decent and get to know him, he's all right,' Rose said quickly, smiling at them all as Ned made his way back to join them.

'That's wonderful, thank you, Ned,' Rose said with pride in her eyes as he sat next to her and every jealous woman in the dining hall looked at her and wished that they were her.

'Do you really think that it is wise to sit and eat your lunch with the workers, Ned? We have to look as if we are a little superior,' Seebohm Rowntree said with a frown as he washed his hands in the washroom that afternoon, having seized the opportunity to show his feelings towards management and workers mixing.

'I can see no wrong in it, sir, it keeps me in touch with what is happening on our busy floors. You should hear the conversations that are had between our workers, they are proud that they work for you, sir,' Ned replied before drying his hands on an embroidered towel and looking at the man who was feared by so many people.

'That's what we have supervisors for, as go-betweens. As well as the suggestion boxes which we encourage our employees to put their views into. The supervisors are there to report what they see going on and give advice to our workforce. I may be seeing this wrong, Ned, but it seems to me that a certain supervisor has caught your eye of late. Am I right?' Seebohm looked at Ned and knew all too well that he was indeed right.

'I can't lie, sir – yes, I do have feelings for Rose Freeman, we have become quite close,' Ned said, looking straight at Seebohm.

'All I ask is that you don't flaunt it when at work. It just causes bad feelings for the other workers.' Seebohm reached for the washroom door handle. 'Oh, and Ned, I expect you back in the small dining room for lunch with the other management. We have to set a good example.'

Ned didn't reply; some things he did not agree with when it came to the running of Rowntree's. He finished drying his hands on the towel and went back to his work, annoyed that he would have to abide by what his boss had told him, if he wanted to stay in his employment.

'Oh, heavens, Rose, what am I going to wear? None of this stuff I have is posh enough.' Winnie looked at the one or two posher outfits that were hung up behind her bedroom door and sighed.

'You know they are not royalty, Mam, they are just an ordinary family. Ned's mam dresses just the same as you, she's no airs or graces and she talks with a slight Geordie twang. They are not posh by any standards. Just be yourself, they don't judge you by how you dress.'

'I know, but I have to look half decent. You might end up marrying this lad. In fact, I hope that you do, he's obviously got brains and brass, and from what I've heard Molly and Connie saying, looks as well. I've got to impress for your sake.'

Rose shook her head, Ned was not one bit like that, nor his mother. 'That blue one, it's a nice skirt and jacket and you have a good pair of navy shoes that match it well. But honestly, if you went with what you have got on it would be right.' Rose held up the suit that she had only seen her mother wear once, at a cousin's christening. Her mam never dressed up if she didn't have to.

'I couldn't go looking like I am with a mucky pinny on and a ladder in my stockings, our Rose. I couldn't put my head out of the front door as I stand, so don't give me that flannel, but yes, I look partly respectable in that blue suit. Can I borrow some of your face powder and a squirt of some scent? I think I have a lipstick that I bought a year or two back.' Winnie looked flustered as she started to undress in front of her daughter. The last thing she wanted to do was let her daughter down by looking rough and ready in front of her new fella's mother. It was bad enough she had been invited, that meant that she would have to have them back at some point and theirs was just a humble terraced house compared to the posh houses down in the Rowntree village.

'Of course you can, Mam, and there's no rush, we don't have to be there until three and it's only half one. So stop flapping.' Rose smiled. All the years that she had been courting Larry Battersby her mother had never once been invited to tea there. This was definitely a different sort of a family. One that she knew her mother was taking pride in meeting. She was lucky to have Ned in her life, she thought, as she went into her room and changed into a matching knitted two-piece and skirt that she had laid on her bed in readiness for her visit and tea. She was just as nervous as her mother as she dressed in her brown tweed skirt and pulled the Fair Isle short-sleeved jumper over her head before putting her set of faux pearls around her neck and inspecting herself in the wardrobe mirror. Was she smartly dressed enough to walk next to and date the best-looking man in Rowntree's? Even she was worried as she powdered her nose and added rouge to her cheeks. She ran her fingers through her lightly permed blonde hair and smiled. Of course she was, anyway, it wasn't all about the looks, there was something special between them, that was for sure. And at that, she went and gave her mother her face powder and scent.

'Lord, Rose, I've never been in one of these houses before, they are a bit posh. Everyone looks alike and all the gardens are so well tended. There's no need to scrub your step with a donkey stone here, it's tiled, and it will always be clean,' Winnie said as they both stood on the doorstep and rang the doorbell.

'Now remember, Mam, not to worry, they are just like us. Ned's family come from the North-East and are working class just like us. You'll soon find out anyway because his mother is lovely.' Rose then saw the shadow of Ned coming to open the door through the stained-glass window.

'Rose, Mrs Freeman, don't stand on ceremony, please do come in. My mother has been waiting for you, she says she is going to look forward to a right good natter and catch-up.' Ned took Winnie and Rose's coats and hung them up in the hallway, kissing Rose lightly on her cheek before guiding them into the living room where his mother sat with a shawl around her shoulders despite the house being nice and warm.

'Mother, Rose and her mother are here to see us as I said. I'll let them get comfortable and then I'll bring some tea for us all.' Ned glanced at his visitors and then said to his mother, 'Don't get up, both our guests will understand that you are not so good on your legs.'

'No, don't get up, sit yourself down, it's only us two.

259

'Some days my legs ache and all I want to do is sit and be comfortable, it's no joy isn't this getting old,' Winnie said warmly as she walked into the living room and looked down at the grey-haired old lady who smiled up at her.

'No, it isn't, I tell my lad that many a day. But do these young 'uns listen? No, they don't. Now, you must be Winnie, my lad tells me. Well, I can tell you this, my lad thinks a lot of your lass, so that's why I thought it was best that we met.' Ivy smiled. 'I'm Ivy, called after the creeper, and that's what I do in my old age now, just creep along.'

'As long as you keep creeping, that's the main thing,' Winnie said with a grin as she sat down at the end of the settee next to Ivy. 'And yes, I'm glad that you have asked us both down today, it will be good for us to get to know each other.' Winnie instantly knew that Rose was right, Ivy Evans was just like her; a few years older and in worse health, but she had the same outlook on life.

'That's what I thought. Now, you young'uns, don't sit in here with us two while we get to know one another. I'm sure you can both find something to do that's more interesting than listening to us two talking about our aches and pains.' Ivy patted Rose's hand. 'And if you can't then you don't deserve to be young.'

'Mother!' Ned said sharply.

'Oh, go on, stop being huffy, pass Winnie and me the sherry and two glasses and leave us to it, until you want to serve tea.' Ivy winked at Winnie. 'Take him into the kitchen, Rose, and keep him busy.'

Winnie looked at her daughter as Ned got out two

small glasses and a bottle of cream sherry from a cupboard and placed it on the table in front of Winnie and Ivy. Rose had been right, Ivy definitely didn't put on airs and graces, she was going to enjoy her afternoon. They both might live in a posh house and he might have a job in management, but they were normal everyday folk, just like them.

'Lord, listen to them two laughing and carrying on,' Rose said as she sat on Ned's knee with her arms around his neck.

'I hoped that they would hit it off, your mam will be company for mine, now they have found one another.' Ned held Rose tight and then looked seriously at her. 'I don't know if I want to work for Rowntree's much longer, some of their rules are a little outdated, they haven't moved with the times,' he blurted out, shocking Rose.

'What are you talking about, Ned? They are always going forward with new ideas and products. You have a brilliant job, and they handled Robert Jones brilliantly once they knew about the issue!' Rose couldn't believe what he was saying.

'Seebohm Rowntree had words with me the other day, only casually when we were passing. But he told me, if I was wise, not to sit with you girls at dinnertime. It is seemingly not company policy.' Ned sighed.

'Then stop sitting with us and go back to management dining. I don't mind, we can see each other of an evening and I have a feeling that your mam and my mam will be living in one another's pockets, given half a chance. Besides, I think I might just last the day without you

looking at me over shepherd's pie, even if it will be hard.'
Rose smiled and kissed him on the forehead.

'It's not just that, Rose, I have become restless at Rowntree's, I don't want to be making chocolates in a factory all
my life. I would like to join the Royal Air Force and learn
to fly, or at least become an engineer, which is just what
Rowntree's, being Quaker-owned, is against. It would definitely not fit in with my views, if war ever happened again,
especially in the management canteen where I will have to
listen to everyone's views of turning the other cheek. I feel
I could do so much more. My religion is a bit lapsed and
my urge to join my friend Peter in flying is tempting me.'

'You don't think a war is going to come again? Mary's
father keeps saying it will. But no one ever listens to him
because he always thinks the worst of everything.' Rose
looked into his eyes.

'I don't know, Rose, and to be honest I don't really
know what to do. Whatever happens, things are changing and we will have to change with them or not survive.'

Rose lay back in Ned's arms. 'I don't want you to ever
go away and I don't want you to learn to fly, I think even
after these few brief weeks I really do love you.'

'I love you too and as you say, it hasn't come to that
yet, but I thought that I would tell you my thoughts and
be fair to you. We were made for one another, Rose, and
no matter what happens, I will always love you.'

20

'Your family knows how to cause a stir, I'll give you that,' Joan said to Annie while they both sat at their usual meeting place on the seat next to the canal and shared a bag of roasted chestnuts that were so warm they had to juggle them in their hands.

'What do you mean by that? We don't, we are just like anybody else,' Annie said, licking her fingers as she peeled the hot outer shell from her chestnut.

'You are not, you are all up to something. You with this lad from Liverpool, dancing and making a scene. Then there's your Molly biting Robert Jones on the nose and then getting him sacked and putting him in the nick, and now there's your Rose setting her cap at Ned Evans. You do know they are the talk of Rowntree's, both sitting together at lunchtime looking at one another and nearly dribbling over one another,' Joan said between mouthfuls.

'You are always saying somebody is the talk of Rowntree's; besides, if they are talking about us then they are leaving somebody else alone. Plus Robert Jones deserves all that he gets and it wasn't just Molly he was a letch with, there's a lot more he's had his way with over the last few years. It's just that her friend Connie had the sense to say something. And as for Ned Evans, he's back to having his lunch with the toffs,' Annie replied and threw the hard skin of her chestnut to the ducks that fought and splashed madly for the worthless shell.

'Well, that Connie, what I've heard about her is un-believable. It's a wonder your mother lets her sleep under your roof. I could tell as soon as I met her that she was from a rough home.' Joan looked out over the freezing waters of the canal.

'She might come from a rough home but she's a good friend to Molly and her heart is in the right place once you get to know her. She's had a terrible life over at Selby, my heart goes out to her,' Annie said sharply, somehow managing to keep her cool as she listened to Joan, who sometimes could be quite cutting with her remarks. 'I didn't like her at first but she's all right, you should get to know her.'

'I don't think so, it is bad enough that I have had to defend my friendship with you to my other friends after you showed yourself up with that Josh from Liverpool. Thank heavens he's not been back. I hope he never shows his face again.' Joan spoke sharply and screwed the empty bag of chestnuts into her pocket along with her hands. 'Is there nothing else we can do but sit here freezing on this canalside? You need to learn to mix with people more, Annie.'

'And you need to learn some manners. I don't say anything about what you get up to or comment about your family. If you don't like me or mine, then go and find another friend,' Annie replied firmly. She had had enough of Joan Smith saying what she thought. She stood up and pulled her knitted woollen hat over her ears. 'I'm going home. You can suit yourself.' Annie walked away quickly, she was in no mood to be told how she should act, and besides, Joan couldn't talk, her father was having an affair with the landlady at the Black Bull. Everyone knew it except Joan, and Annie was not going to be the one to tell her.

'Annie, Annie, come back, I'm sorry, I shouldn't have said . . . ' Joan called after her friend, but it was too late, Annie was on her way home with her head down, and nothing would stop her. She was loyal to her family and she would let Joan stew for a while.

'You are soon back, Annie, I thought you'd be out at least another hour. I was just sitting down and having a few minutes to myself, while the house was quiet,' Winnie said in surprise. 'Rose is round at Mary's and the other two have gone window shopping, seeing what they fancy for Christmas, so I thought I'd have a cup of tea and a warm-up next to the fire while you were all out. The days are so cold now that we are in November. I don't like this month, it's always damp and miserable.' Winnie stopped, noticing a dark look on Annie's face. 'What's up, is something wrong?'

'Nah, it's just Joan, I've had enough of her gossiping and moaning, so I came home. Besides, like you say, it is cold.' Annie slumped in the chair next to the fire.

'Well, I think I have something that will cheer you up.

This came in the post just after you had gone. I was nosy and looked at the postmark, it looks like a word from your friend in Liverpool. I must say it's a miracle the letter has ever found us, his handwriting is not that good, Winnie reached for the white envelope that was propped up next to the milk jug on the kitchen table. 'He's written back to you then, I noticed that you have been writing to him of late?'

Annie smiled and looked at the letter. 'Yes, I didn't know if I would hear back. He must be back in port somewhere or else he wouldn't have had the chance.' She took it and wondered whether to read it while she was with her mother or when she was alone.

'Go on then, read what he has to say, I'll not look. I am glad that he's corresponding with you, it shows that he does care,' Winnie said quietly and went about her business in the kitchen while Annie opened her letter and read it.

Dear Annie,

The days are going so fast now I am working for the Merchant Navy, they all run into one because the hours I work are so long. We have just docked back into Liverpool, I have never been so cold in all my life after sailing up to Greenland to deliver goods to a town called Qaqortaq with some supplies for winter. If you think it's cold in this country, you should have been with me. I could hardly feel my fingers and there

*was ice in my hair. The older men were telling me all
the time to keep warm and not get frostbite. They are
a good lot and they all look after one another. I've seen
some wonderful things, huge whales that come out of
the sea and spout water out of their bodies, and por-
poises that follow the boat. There's icebergs that glare
and nearly blind you in the sun's light and are as big
as houses sticking out of the sea but with a lot more
under the water. Our lookout is always watching for
them because they would sink our ship if we got too
close. It's a long way from doing the canals with ingredients for Rowntree's, where it was a lot warmer but
not half as exciting. I hope that you are keeping well,
I lie in my bunk and think of you a lot and when I
came home Ma gave me all the letters that you have
sent. I loved reading them. I hope Molly is all right
and it sounds like Rose is doing well for herself with
her new fella. I'm hoping that our next trip will be a
short one and that I will be at home for Christmas.
I'll try and get across country to see you then if I can.
Keep writing to me, I keep thinking about you all
the time.*

Josh xx

Annie smiled as she folded the letter up and placed it back
in its envelope. She couldn't stop thinking of him either.
It didn't matter what Joan Smith thought of Josh, he was
a friend and hopefully, in time, more than a friend.

'Is he all right then?' Winnie asked her daughter as she started to set the table for supper.

'Yes, Mam, he's been to Greenland and seen whales and all sorts.' Annie held her letter tight. 'He hopes to come and visit us this Christmas – will that be all right, Mam?'

'Of course it will, love, you know it will. If anybody makes my girls happy, they will always be welcome at this house.' Winnie smiled, she admired her middle daughter; if she decided to stand by somebody, she would, come hell or high water, no matter who they were or what their background. That was more than could be said of her friend Joan.

Rose stood on the doorstep of Mary's home and knocked on the door. They had spoken only briefly at work when taking delivery of chocolate for their departments. Mary had looked tired and her belly was growing under her tunic. She had been put on light duties by the management, but even so, the work looked to be taking a toll on her. Rose pulled her coat around her as she heard feet coming to the door and it opened.

Rose took in the tall, dark-haired, handsome man dressed in his naval uniform and smiled with delight. 'Joe, you are here! When did you get home?'

'I got special discharge as soon as I could, once I heard the news. I couldn't have Mary facing the world on her own and worrying if I was going to do the right thing for her. So, here I am. And we have some news, but I'll let

Mary tell you, she will be so glad that you are here.' Joe grinned. 'Come on in, we are celebrating.'

'Celebrating! Now, what are you celebrating?' Rose asked, though she had a fair idea, and followed Joe into the small living room where Mary and her father sat.

'Oh, Rose, I'm so glad that you have come round today. I so much want to tell you our news.' Mary got up from the sofa with a helping hand from Joe and smiled and hugged her friend. 'Joe's been to the town hall and we are to be wed before he goes home. Saturday the thirtieth of November at noon in the register office. I know it's short notice, but will you be my bridesmaid? I'd love you to be my bridesmaid, although it's not a fancy affair with this one showing.' Mary patted her stomach.

'It's a good job it isn't because I couldn't have afforded to give you a big wedding.' Mary's father sighed. 'But I'm glad the baby is going to have a father and you a husband.'

'Oh, Mary, that is wonderful news!' Rose hugged her friend tightly and rubbed tears away from her eyes, utterly delighted for Mary. 'I would love to be your bridesmaid. You just try and keep me away.'

'And father says we can live here with him, so we need not look for a home and Joe, bless him, is happy to live here when he's not at sea. You should have seen my face when he was standing at the door and waving a register office form in my face. I just couldn't believe it. I also panicked slightly as it only gives us fifteen days before our big day, and Joe has to go back to sea the very next day,' Mary fretted, but she smiled as Joe put his arm around her waist.

'I got here as fast as I could, I knew I had to get us married before I went back to sea. This little fella has to be born to both of us,' Joe beamed and kissed Mary.

'It might not be a boy, it may be a girl,' Mary scolded, though she was smiling.

'I hope it's not a girl, you were such a bad baby. Your poor mother used to fret herself silly when you cried. I need my quiet time. Perhaps I was a little hasty offering you our home,' Mary's father joked, before picking up his newspaper. He'd had enough talk of weddings and babies and made his way into the kitchen, leaving the three of them making wedding plans. However, the relief of his daughter not being left alone to bring her baby up was overwhelming.

There were dresses to talk about and a bouquet to arrange and although there would be no large wedding breakfast both Mary and Joe agreed that a celebration of some kind would have to take place, if only a cream tea in the centre of York.

The news that Mary was to be married soon went around Rowntree's like wildfire and when it came to the day there were a few surprises for the young couple. The girls from Mary's department had organised a whip-round for their fellow worker and raised enough money to buy a beautiful china tea service that they knew Mary had been admiring for a while, surprising her with their gift. Mary's eyes had filled with tears as her workmates gathered together at lunchtime, making a circle around her and giving her their best wishes. As for the management, it was as usual Seebohm Rowntree that came down from his office and presented Mary with a set of bed linen and a complimentary box of Black Magic with the company's best wishes. It was always the same present, no matter whose wedding. Back home, Mary and Joe put the many gifts they'd been given on display in her father's front room along with the best-wishes cards. Mary and her father had decided that a small tea was to be held at the family home for just a few guests, instead of spending money needlessly on eating in the town. The day was going to be one of celebration but on a budget, and very low-key because of Mary's condition.

Mary looked at herself in the mirror; she was dressed in a loose cream blouse over a plain blue skirt and wore a wide blue and cream headband. Her father had gone around the market that morning and bought her a small bouquet of white chrysanthemums and roses which the florist had tied with a cream ribbon. It was by no means the richest or finest of weddings, but that didn't matter to Mary. She and Joe were getting married and their baby was to have its father's name on its birth certificate and would not be born out of marriage. She turned and looked at Rose.

'Well, I suppose it is nearly time. This will be the last time we will be single together. I must admit I'm a little bit frightened, Rose. We are only going to be married a few weeks and then the baby will be here, what if Joe doesn't return from sea? What if he's marrying me out of pity?' Mary looked at Rose with doubt in her eyes.

'Don't be silly, Mary, Joe loves you and he always has done. Now, come on, your father's waiting, the sun is shining even though it's November, and Joe will be waiting for you. Best foot forward and just enjoy your day.' Rose hugged Mary and kissed her on the cheek. 'I'll always be there for you and the baby, not that you will ever need me. Your father will always be by your side and so will Joe, every time he can,' she whispered as they both made their way to the hastily arranged marriage.

Standing outside the Victorian town hall in the centre of York stood tall, dark and handsome Joe in his naval uniform. Beside him was his brother who was there as a witness, along with Joe's mother and father. In addition, there were Rose's family and numerous employees from Rowntree's, all waiting for Mary, her father and Rose as they walked into the square. They held small bags of confetti ready for throwing at the newlyweds once they were married. Molly stood with a silver paper horse-shoe with a white ribbon on it to give to Mary. As soon as she saw her she ran and placed it in her hand next to her bouquet, and Mary bent down and kissed her as she took it. Everybody cheered as Mary and Joe entered the town hall, and all the best was wished to the couple. Their wedding was going to be a day they would always remember.

'Wasn't she lovely? I know she couldn't get married in white, but she still looked beautiful,' Molly said and sighed.

'She would have done if she could have hidden the bump,' Annie said.

'Aye, I think that baby is due before she says it is, either that or it's going to be a big baby,' Winnie said as they waited for the ceremony to finish. 'Poor lass, I bet she's been worrying about getting married in time.'

'Well, she need not worry any more because here they come, and look how happy they are.' Molly took out her little bag full of confetti from her pocket and ran towards the happy couple.

The air was filled with delicate tissue paper flowers blowing in the light wind and falling upon the happy couple.

The crowd cheered and threw more confetti as they shouted for the couple to kiss on the town hall steps. Which they duly did, smiling at each other, so deeply in love. Rose spotted Ned standing in the crowd and she looked at him; it didn't seem very long since she was thinking of marrying Larry, but now she was looking at Ned with more love than she had ever felt for Larry. Would it be her turn next?

21

Connie looked in the window of the toy shop on Micklegate and smiled. Her little brother Billy would have loved the small brown teddy with a tartan scarf around his neck, she thought, as she opened her purse and wondered if she could afford it for him for Christmas. Even if she could, she didn't dare take it to him, she would have to tell the orphanage why and that would open a whole can of worms.

But the more she looked at it the more she thought how much he would love it and she yearned to see her little brother again, just to make sure that he was all right and still being looked after. It was nearly Christmas, after all, and she was the only relation he had in the world that cared about him. She sighed, opened the toy shop door and went in to make her purchase. He deserved a lot more than a sixpenny teddy, but it was better than nothing, she thought, as she tucked the happy-looking chap into her basket and felt warm with the thoughts of going to see her brother. Whether she had to tell the truth about having left him at the orphanage or not, it was time to put things right for her brother.

*

'I'm going to Selby this morning, Molly. I need to see my brother. I know it's early yet for taking Christmas presents but I keep hearing there's going to be overtime at weekends on the run-up to Christmas so while I have this Saturday off, I'm going to go,' Connie said as both girls got out of bed and started to dress as fast as they could, the warmth of summer long since gone.

'I hope you don't mind but I'll go on my own this time because I think I may tell whoever is in charge about why I left Billy with them. It's only fair that they have his details; who am I to take away his real family? And besides, I miss him even though he is Bill's too, so only my half-brother.' Connie spoke quietly; with Christmas on the horizon her lack of family was really hitting home and for the first time in a long while she was feeling lonely.

'No, that's all right, Connie, looking at the weather, I'd rather not go anyway, it's pouring down out there. You are going to get soaked, borrow my mackintosh because I'm not going anywhere today. I'm hoping that Mam will light the fire in the front room and then I'll just sit in there and finish my knitting.' Molly hesitated. 'If you say who you are they'll not send your brother home with you, will they? It's just my mam won't want another mouth to feed in her house, especially not a baby.'

'No, they can't, I don't think, although to be honest, I do miss him. I thought once I get a bit more settled at work and start earning a bit more I would try and rent myself somewhere to live. It doesn't have to be a palace, just room enough for me and Billy. I was thinking that I could bring him home with me sometime and still work at Rowntree's. They do after all have a nursery for their workers' children, which I didn't know about until I heard Rose and Mary discussing it at the wedding tea. I think that is a wonderful thing for mothers and their children.' Connie sighed and looked at Molly. 'I shouldn't have left him behind, I regret it every day.'

'You were just doing the best you could at the time. If you hadn't left him there, you might never have seen him again, or worse still he could be dead if your stepdad had lost his temper with him,' Molly replied as she sat on the bed next to her best friend and put her arm around her. Since Connie had moved in, the bedroom had become a little cramped and the thought of a baby joining them in their bedroom had worried her and would have felt a step too far.

'I know, but I shouldn't have left him and I'm wondering if I should have told my mam where I had taken him too. Things had just got so bad at home. Anyway, I'll go and catch the train as soon as I have had my breakfast. It will be one less body for your mam to think about today. I might go and see our old next-door neighbours as well and wish them an early happy Christmas, they were always good to me. Otherwise, there's nobody else I will miss in Selby. I don't even know where my mam is at, and she'll not be missing me. She'll probably be losing herself in the bottom of a bottle.'

'Never mind, Connie, we are your family now, and we won't let you down, especially at Christmas.' Molly gave her a quick hug again before they both made their beds and went downstairs to the warmth of the kitchen and the nattering of the family of women that always had something to say.

'You are back with us, are you, Connie? I hope that you've got a ticket this time,' the station master at Selby said to the lass that he had let get away with free travel for as long as he could before deciding enough was enough.

'I have indeed, look, one ticket all paid for and correct,' Connie said and showed her ticket to the man that she had tricked many a time.

'Well, it's good to see you looking well and cared for, the move from Selby has obviously done you good. Are we visiting family on this wonderful day for ducks?' the station master asked as he watched water dripping off the station house roof as the cold, wet rain lashed down.

'Something like that, just need to see a few people to make things right before Christmas,' Connie replied, pulling the collar of Molly's mackintosh up and her woollen hat down over her head before stepping out and making her way quickly up through the town to the orphanage and waving back at the station master that she now knew to be a friend.

Connie was drenched and soaked to the skin as she stood outside the orphanage door and felt sick at the thought of ringing the bell. She peered through the partly stained-glass door into the reception area where she could see children running to and fro across the busy entrance hall.

She breathed in deeply and checked that the teddy bear was still dry, safely stored underneath her coat and cardigan. She swallowed hard, pressed the brass Victorian doorbell and waited.

The door opened and a woman dressed in a nurse's uniform opened the door.

'Yes, can I help you? Have you come to visit one of the children or have you an appointment?' The nurse looked at her but kept her standing on the doorstep despite the pouring rain.

'I've come to see my brother, he was left here in the summer and I just want to see that he is all right,' Connie replied, and wished that she would be allowed in.

'Then you had better come in and see if you can make an appointment and perhaps see him. The lady over there at the desk will be able to help you. I was just the nearest to the door when you rang.' The nurse showed Connie over to the reception and then left, taking a young girl by her hand who had burst into tears complaining that somebody had stolen her doll.

Connie looked at the woman dressed in a tweed suit, her hair tied up in a bun, and plucked up the courage to ask to see her brother Billy.

'I'm sorry to bother you, but I would like to see my brother if I may. He was left here by me in summer out of desperation. I left him outside in his pram with a tag on him saying that his name was Billy.'

The woman looked at her with suspicion and no sense of any emotion on her face. 'And your name is? Did you leave your details with him, else we will have nothing to prove that you are his sister.'

'No, I didn't, I just left him in the hope that you could give him a better home than what he had then. My mother and stepfather were in no position to look after him, nor me.' Connie looked at the woman as she went through pages of a book that obviously told her who had been admitted and when. 'I have a teddy bear for him for Christmas, please let me see him,' Connie pleaded. 'I know he's here, I saw him being walked out in a pram not so long ago.'

'Hmm . . . just wait here a minute and I'll see what I can do. I'll have to speak to the manager.' The woman stood up and knocked on an oak door, entering when she was given permission.

Connie felt uncomfortable and sick as she looked around her. The orphanage, though filled with babies and young children, was quite cold and a little austere, she thought as she looked around at the wooden panelled Victorian walls with pictures of patrons on the wall and a domineering picture of the King looking down upon her.

'Still waiting? She won't be long, I'm sure.' The nurse who had answered the door walked back across the hallway with a doll in her hand. 'She will just be checking something for you, they have to be sure you are who you say you are.'

'Yes, I understand. I just want to see my brother and

make sure that he's happy,' Connie replied with a smile, feeling her stomach churn as the door opened and the receptionist held it open for her to enter the manager's office.

'If you'd like to come this way, the manager would like to speak to you,' the receptionist said coldly.

Connie stepped forward and at that moment she wished she had never stepped foot into the orphanage or left her brother there.

'Please, take a seat.' The manager looked at Connie with an expression of disdain. 'I understand you are enquiring about Billy who was left with us in the summer. You do understand that without proof of relationship, I can't give you any information?' The stern-looking woman behind the desk looked at Connie as she bowed her head. 'Are you his mother by any chance?'

'No, no, he's my half-brother. Our parents just didn't care for us and I couldn't take him with me where I was going.' Connie sighed. 'I just want to know that he's all right and leave him this teddy bear for Christmas and perhaps see him.' Connie pulled the bear out from under her drenched coat and passed it across the desk to the manager.

'I'm afraid I can't give him the bear, you had better take it back. We don't encourage family involvement once a child is in our care. Billy is looking towards a new life now. However, I can assure you that he is healthy and well cared for. Now, I thank you for your concern and if you will excuse me, I have work to do.'

'But . . .' Connie wanted so much to see Billy.

'That's all, thank you, but before you go, perhaps you can give me your name?' The manager stood up in her dark woollen suit and opened the door for Connie in an attempt to make her leave.

'I'm Connie, Connie Whitehead, and I'm his sister,' Connie said, but dared not say any more as she left the office and walked with the teddy bear still in her hand towards the orphanage's main door, the receptionist not even raising her head to say goodbye.

Connie walked out into the pouring rain, her heart heavy and tears in her eyes; she felt so bad, she didn't realise that once Billy was in the hands of the orphanage she might never see him again. She turned quickly in the pouring rain as she reached the bottom of the drive, hearing somebody shouting after her.

'Stop, please stop,' she heard, as she made out the nurse that had been kind running down the drive to her. 'I heard you asking after Billy. Did they tell you anything?' she asked, her uniform getting soaked.

'No, they didn't tell me anything, they couldn't because they wouldn't take my word that I was his sister,' Connie replied as the nurse shook her head.

'I think I saw you a while back, I noticed you looking into the pram when I was walking him out one day. I guessed you were related then as you showed so much care and he seemed to recognise you. However, you'll not be able to see Billy, he is no longer with us,' the nurse said mournfully, touching Connie's arm lightly.

'He's all right, is he . . . he's not ill or anything, is he?' Connie gasped and felt he heart beat quickly.

'No, no, I shouldn't tell you this, but he's been adopted. A well-off couple came around the orphanage not long after you had seen him and decided he was the child for them. He's got a new home and when I say you won't be able to see him it's because they live in America. He's got the perfect life with a couple on a ranch in Montana. I know because I was the one who handed him over.' The nurse looked at Connie and could see tears in her eyes. 'The couple had been looking for a baby boy just like him and they also made a very generous donation to the orphanage, so they are wealthy. The head of the orphanage said it was better he went with them than perhaps return to his family who had shown him no kindness.'

'I know I shouldn't be sad about that, I hope he has a wonderful life, a lot better than he would have done if he'd been left at his home. But I will never see him again, I am his sister, I would have looked after him, once I could afford to.' Connie looked at the teddy bear in her hands. 'Here, take this for one of the children in the home, I have no one to give it to now. Thank you for telling me.' Connie touched the nurse's hand softly and passed her the bear. 'Now go, you are getting soaked, and thank you for what you did for Billy and for telling me.' Connie turned and walked away but was called back by the nurse.

'Give me your address, I'll write to you if I hear anything about him.'

'Thank you, I'd appreciate that.' Connie pulled out a

pen and a piece of scrap paper from her handbag and quickly scribbled her address down, passing it to the nurse with a smile.

'I can't promise, but if I hear anything, I'll let you know.' The nurse folded the address into her pocket and started to run back up the drive.

Connie sighed. Billy was in America, her little brother was thousands of miles away and she would never see him again. What had she done?

'Just look at you, you are absolutely sodden! Go and get changed and I'll make you a drink and something to eat. We didn't expect you back yet, I thought you were going to be out all day,' Winnie said, taking in Connie as she stood dejected and dripping in her hallway.

'I'm sorry, I had to come home, or to the only home that I have,' sobbed Connie. 'I couldn't face talking to anyone else.'

'Whatever is wrong, Connie? What did the orphanage say? Would they not let you see him?' Winnie drew the soaked young girl towards her.

'Worse than that, he's been adopted and he's thousands of miles away in America, I'll never see him again,' Connie wailed.

'Oh, lass, they've been quick in finding him a new home, but hopefully it's a good home. Plus he's young and will know no different as he's growing up. I know your heart is broken, but what a new life you have given him. Plus you can live yours now. Now go and get changed and join Molly in the front room, she was fast asleep on the sofa the last time I put my head around the door, with half her stitches falling off her needles. Go on, go and get changed and I'll make a cuppa for both of you before you catch your death of cold. You have got to look after yourself now and be strong.' Winnie watched as the dejected lass made her way up the stairs; she looked broken-hearted but Winnie couldn't help but think that her brother being adopted was the best thing that could have happened to him. Even if he had gone to America – now that was a long, long way away!

22

'I've never been so busy in all my life. If I see another red ribbon or a red-breasted robin on a holly twig I'm going to scream,' Connie said as she sat down with her tray after the whistle had finally blown for lunch.

'I must admit we are a bit busy, but it is the run-up to Christmas. Think yourself lucky anyway, blinking Big Beatrice has given me the job of gluing that velvet ribbon and fake holly on the posher boxes, it's a blinking nightmare. I'm frightened to death of getting glue all over the boxes and that they'll have to be thrown,' Molly said as she joined the table.

'Don't you two moan, my fingers are packing Black Magic and the fancy chocolates in your fancy boxes in my sleep. Trade must have looked up lately, we have never been this busy before Christmas.' Annie breathed out deeply as she looked at her dinner that she didn't have time to eat. 'Where's our Rose? She is usually here by now.'

'I don't know, she skulks about now talking to Ned Evans, since he's given over sitting with us. It's a devil when your boss can even tell you who to sit with in your dinnertime,' Molly replied and looked up around the dining hall before tucking into her sausage and mash.

'Hey up, she's coming and she doesn't look right happy, things must not be good in her department; either that or she has had a spat with Ned,' Annie said and looked up at her oldest sister. 'What's up with you this lunchtime, Rose? You don't look right happy.'

'Oh, between work and that man of mine, I've had enough. I can't make much sense of either.' Rose sighed and sat down with a bowl of soup.

'Soup, you don't usually just have soup? Are you feeling all right?' Molly enquired, looking at her flustered sister.

'I haven't time to wipe my arse and I apologise but I'm only saying it as it is. There's a promotion with the chocolate crisp bars for Christmas, Ned is leading me a merry dance saying he's no longer happy working here, and then there's a rumour going around that we have a special guest coming to view all departments next week. That everything has to be absolutely perfect before their visit. Just before Christmas as well, surely they could have put whoever it is off for a while.'

'Uh, oh, the man is your real worry, I can tell. You always moan when you are not getting your own way. What is he up to?' Annie asked, and watched as Rose sipped her soup and then pushed the dish half-eaten to one side.

'Oh, don't make me start on it. He says he's had enough of Rowntree's, that he wants to join the Royal Air Force and that he's going to have a ride out to Elvington airfield this weekend. Why on earth does he want to leave a good job like this to go and join an airforce that he knows absolutely nothing about? The man's mad and we have just found one another and his mother needs him to look after her, he can't leave her on her own twenty-four hours a day while he learns to fly an aeroplane.' Rose rattled off all her grievances and then sat back and folded her arms and sighed.

'Oh, other than that, everything's just hunky-dory,' Annie said and grinned.

'I wonder who the important visitor is going to be. I hope that Robert Jones isn't returning to bring them around,' Molly said, looking worried.

'No, he's still in the nick, Molly, and will be for a long time, so don't worry about him,' Connie quickly reassured her.

'It'll be whoever has placed the biggest Christmas order, they did that last year. They brought up the main buyer from down south and treated him like royalty for the day.' Annie looked at Rose. 'Don't worry, Ned will not join the RAF, or he won't if he has any sense, because things are not really settled in the world at the moment. The last thing he wants to do is to learn to fly and then we end up in a war.'

'That's what I have told him, but he is that pig-headed he will not listen. He says that's exactly why he wants to join up. Anyway, I'm invited around to his home on Sunday and to drive out to Elvington with him to view the airfield so he can get a feel of the place. With a bit of luck, we will return and he will have hated every minute there. Why do I always fall for the wrong man?' Rose sighed.

'Well, don't ask me, I'm not exactly the one you should ask,' Annie grinned, knowing full well what everyone thought of her friendship with Josh.

'I'll have to go, I can only have fifteen minutes, we have such a lot of work to do,' Rose said, and left almost as soon as she'd sat down, leaving her sisters and Connie still sat around the table.

'That's why I don't want to ever be management; from what I have seen it's not worth it,' Annie said to Connie and Molly. 'Never be too good at your job else you will end up as worried as her.'

'I don't think it's her work she's bothering about, I think it's Ned talking about joining the RAF,' said Molly wisely.

Rose stood outside the huge aircraft hangars the following Sunday and watched as Ned walked around the airfield with his hands behind his back listening to the advice of his friend who was already a trained pilot in the recently formed RAF. She had been introduced to his best friend Peter, but now they were involved in men talk and she was left on her own. She sighed as she watched the pair of them go into a Nissen hut and disappear from view. In front of her, miles of concrete runway sprawled ahead with hangars and huts dispersed towards the far end, and a tall watchtower with a clear view of the open flat countryside just above her. She watched as a camouflaged plane came in to land at the far side of the field and covered her ears at the sound of its propellers as it taxied and came to a spluttering halt not far from the hut that Ned and his friend were in. She sighed as she watched them go and greet the pilot, who shook Ned's hand and patted him on the back. She could hear them laughing and joking and decided to make her way back to the car and wait for him in the relative warmth of the vehicle. She had no idea that he had so many friends who were pilots; no wonder he was itching to join them instead of working for the pacifist Quaker firm Rowntree's. She wrapped her coat around her and sat back in the seat, hoping that he would not be much longer.

Finally, she saw him saying goodbye to his friends and walking across to her, a smile on his face and a spring in his step.

'Sorry, Rose, I didn't mean to be this long, have you been all right sitting here? I got a bit carried away catching up with my old school friend Peter and then he introduced me to the pilot that just landed that plane. Absolutely fascinating! That is a new Hawker Hurricane, brand new off the production line. Isn't it magnificent?' Ned sighed and started the car.

'If you say so, but I know two things: it's noisy and it smells. Well, what have you decided? Do you think it's for you? Although personally I think you are mad for wanting to leave Rowntree's, you have one of the best jobs in the firm.'

'I don't know, I really want to join but I have my mother

to think of, I couldn't leave her on her own and I wouldn't want to leave you, Rose. We may only have known each other well for a short time, but I do love you and would hate to lose you through my selfish ways.' Ned leaned over and kissed her on the cheek. 'I'd love to learn to fly one of those Hurricanes though, that mate of Peters is a lucky fellow,' Ned said wistfully, then grinned at her. 'Right, let's get back home and I'll stop dreaming and keep my head down.'

'I hope you do because if war ever came to these isles again, it would probably be fought in the air the next time,' Rose said quietly.

'I know, imagine that – defending the country you love high above in the clouds and being part of a team to be proud of instead of making chocolates,' Ned said, equally quietly. Rose looked at him and knew that if he decided to join she would not be able to stop him.

23

'So who's coming tomorrow that is so important?' Annie asked Rose at the supper table. 'Everyone's been told to tidy up their workspace and to make sure we come spotless and clean to work and to mind our manners.'

'I'm not supposed to say, because of security. They are coming to see us, and us alone, on their way up to Scotland. That is all I'm going to say,' Rose said and sighed; she had done nothing but worry about the esteemed visitor to her department since it had been mentioned.

'They! Who are they?' Connie asked and looked at all the questioning faces around the table.

'I can't say, honestly I can't say and I shouldn't say. You'll find out soon enough in the morning. They are arriving at eleven, having lunch with some of the Rowntrees and then carrying on to Scotland. Ned isn't invited though, just the family,' Rose said bitterly.

'Come on, Rose, tell us who it is. We are not going to run out onto the street and tell everyone we know, are we?' Connie said and leaned across the table to look at her.

'No, I can't, you will all be told in the morning when you go to work, so no tittle-tattling until then. I can tell you that it is a big day for Rowntree's, one that none of you will ever forget. That is why I have been so worried – believe me, it is better that you don't know until they are actually in the building. Now, please don't ask me again.' Rose left the table while the others looked at one another.

'She won't even tell me, so it's no good looking at your mother,' Winnie sighed over her brew.

'Well, I'm just glad it won't be Robert Jones showing whoever it is around. I don't mind anybody but him!' Molly said with a smile.

'Forget about him, Mol, he's long gone. And this is someone really important, they have never acted like this, making sure we are all turned out well and the place is spotless,' Annie said and moaned. 'Probably someone that they are wanting to impress and get a big order out of.'

'Well, we will soon find out,' Connie sighed and gazed across to the warmth of the fire. 'Whoever it is, they have picked the busiest time ever to visit and we could all do without them coming.'

The following morning, Rose sneaked down as quietly as she could to find her mother lighting the fire before everyone else came down for their breakfast. 'Mam,' she whispered. 'I know I shouldn't, but I'm going to say who is visiting this morning. If I don't, our Molly at least will be a bundle of nerves and besides, you might want to see her and you'd catch her if you walk up to Rowntree station this morning,' Rose continued quietly. 'But nobody must say anything, especially to any neighbours on this row. It's supposed to be a secret.'

'Lord above, you'd think it was the Queen herself

coming the way you are acting. Nobody is that important,' Winnie said, rising from lighting the coal fire with a smudge of soot on her face. 'I'll not be going to gawp at anybody at the station.'

'Well, Mam, you are quite right, as it happens, but you keep it quiet, promise?' Rose said, pointing out the soot on her mother's face that she quickly wiped off with her dishcloth as her mother looked at her, puzzled. 'It's Queen Mary, Mam, she's coming to look around Rowntree's while she is on her way to Balmoral. That's why we have been sworn to secrecy in fear of assassination.'

'Oh, my Lord, the Queen is coming to Rowntree's, why didn't you tell me, girl? I'll have to make sure that you are all spotless and clean and that Molly and especially Annie mind what they say and are polite. Oh, Lord, and there's me in my old clothes!' Winnie couldn't believe her ears. 'Girls, girls, get up, get up, the Queen is coming, you need to look spotless and tidy. Oh! My Lord, why didn't you tell me earlier?' Winnie said, getting all flustered about her daughters' appearance and wondering whether they would perhaps get to speak to the Queen Consort.

'This is exactly why I didn't tell you, because I knew you'd be in a flap and I knew you couldn't keep it to yourself. Just calm down, the chances of any of us actually talking to her are very slim. She will be advised who to talk to and who not, so stop flapping,' Rose sighed, and watched as her sisters and Connie came tumbling down the stairs.

'What's all the fuss about? Did you say the Queen is coming? Is that who's visiting Rowntree's today?' Annie looked at Rose.

'Yes, Queen Mary, but don't say anything to anybody, do you hear?' Rose wished she had never uttered a mutter as she saw the excitement erupt in the kitchen and then the nerves set in.

'What do we say to her if she speaks to us? Do we curtsy or what do we do?' Connie asked, worried.

'I've been told to greet her with a short curtsy and then say, "Your Majesty". Then, when and if she talks to you, she is addressed as Ma'am. But you won't get to talk to her so I wouldn't worry. I only know that because Ned has been told what to do in case she meets him.' Rose looked at the astounded faces that were gulping their breakfast tea down and for once in their lives wanting to rush to work.

'Well, that's easy, I'll just say "Mam" like I do to our mother. But she'll not look at the side we are on, me and Connie will probably never get a chance to see her.'

'You mind your manners, all of you, I don't want my girls letting our family down in front of the Queen. Now get your breakfast eaten, and be on your way, I have got a lot to do this morning,' Winnie said to her girls. They looked clean and presentable as always, but were they tidy enough to greet the Queen? She definitely wasn't. She was going to have to change and then go and stand near the station and hope for a glimpse of Queen Mary. She knew exactly where she could see her from.

*

'So much for keeping the visit quiet, Rose. The whole place is humming with the news. You should know that something like that can't be kept silent,' Annie said as they clocked into work.

'Well, I did my bit to keep it quiet, at least until this morning. Let's hope that we all get to see her even if we don't get a chance to talk to her.' Rose looked around her. 'There looks to be some of her staff already here, those men standing over there next to the main entrance look like they are watching everybody come and go. They will have to make sure all is safe for her visit. I'll have to go, see you at lunchtime.'

All four looked at the men dressed in dark suits watching everyone as they entered the factory.

'We'd better go, I feel so nervous.' For once Annie confessed to a weakness and smiled as the four of them split up to go to their departments. A visit from the Queen Consort was something none of them would forget.

The Card Box Mill was filled with tension and excitement. No matter how Rowntree's had tried to keep it quiet, the news had spread, so much so that Beatrice had been told to tell her department that Queen Mary would indeed be visiting them mid-morning, but she wasn't expected to stay long in their department. Beatrice herself was a mass of nerves, she had only just been given the news that morning, much to her annoyance and worry.

It was ten thirty when the royal party made its way towards the Card Box Mill. Seebohm Rowntree stood next to Queen Mary, along with her entourage. They walked slowly through the doors and spoke for a brief second or two to Beatrice standing in a group and looking around them at all the workers with their heads down, trying to concentrate on making the chocolate boxes but at the same time wanting to see the beautifully dressed Queen.

Connie and Molly looked up and noticed the group moving towards them, the Queen's maid-in-waiting holding a handkerchief to her face to combat the smell of the glue, but Queen Mary herself walked serenely next to Seebohm Rowntree, listening to what he was telling her. As they got near to Molly and Connie they stopped and Seebohm Rowntree turned to the Queen.

'Would you like to see the full process of how a chocolate box is made, Ma'am? Molly here will be only too happy to show you. Molly only started to work here in summer, but she excels at her skills.' Seebohm looked warmly at Molly.

'That would be very interesting indeed. Please do show me, my dear girl.'

Molly felt her stomach churn as she took in the elegantly dressed woman with her greying hair piled high and her face immaculately made up. Around her neck was a string of pearls and she was wearing one of the most beautiful dresses that Molly had ever seen. Molly remembered what Rose had said earlier that morning and did a small curtsy and replied, 'It will be an honour, Ma'am.' She noticed the smiles on all their faces and knew that she had not let herself down as she picked up a piece of card and started to turn it into the Christmas box that she had been doing for the last many weeks. Only this time she was doing it in front of Queen Mary and her fingers felt as if they had a mind of their own as she stretched the lining paper over the box, glued the sides and finally decorated the box with the chirpy Christmas robin, the red ribbon and the sprig of fir. As she did so, Seebohm talked the Queen through the different stages and explained how many local young girls they employed in that department alone.

'I remember last time I visited, the factory was making gift tins of chocolates as Christmas presents for the troops in the trenches in the dreadful Great War; it seems so long ago. I certainly hope that our country is not heading in that direction again,' Queen Mary said to Seebohm as she watched Molly.

'So do I, Ma'am. War is not at all welcome here at Rowntree's or in any of your subjects' homes,' Seebohm replied.

Queen Mary looked at the box that Molly had just finished. 'That is absolutely marvellous, my dear. May I take the box with me as a reminder of my visit?' Seebohm nodded immediately and Queen Mary took the box from Molly and smiled. 'You are very talented.'

Molly curtsied again and breathed a sigh of relief as the party moved off down the factory floor. She had spoken to the Queen and made her a chocolate box; just wait until she got home and told her mam.

Connie looked across at her friend and whispered, 'Well done! It couldn't have happened to a nicer person. Did you smell her perfume? Wasn't she beautiful?'

'Yes, she was,' Molly said, her legs like jelly.

24

The run-up to Christmas had been hectic and now things at Rowntree's were beginning to calm down as the last boxes of chocolates were dispatched and the factory was wound down for the Christmas holidays.

Winnie was busy in her kitchen, baking and making sure that she had everything that she needed for the big day. She was regretting her hasty decision to ask Ned and his mother to Christmas dinner, especially when they had so much more room at their house. However, she thought that it was only right that she cooked, as Ivy struggled if she stood for too long on her feet, and Rose and Ned seemed to be so much in love. A small Christmas tree had been bought from the market and Connie and Molly had decorated it the previous night, giggling and laughing as they placed the angel that was looking a bit aged on the top and wrapped tinsel around it. Her family was growing and Connie seemed to have been adopted by all the family – and she fitted in well. Winnie looked up from the bread she was baking towards the fireplace and glanced at the two letters that had arrived with a flurry of Christmas cards and wondered what one of them in particular held. It was obvious that one contained a letter from Annie's

299

friend in the Navy, but the other was for Connie and it worried her; Connie never got any correspondence. She only hoped it was not bad news, not at Christmas when everybody should be enjoying themselves.

The four girls linked their arms and sang Christmas carols as they walked down the street. Work was over for a while and the best thing was they were getting paid for having time away from work. There were dances to go to over the Christmas period but most of all they were free to have a much-needed lie-in and time at home where they could just do as they wanted.

'Oh, I am so ready for this Christmas holiday, I am so tired,' Annie said as they reached the corner of their street and a sense of relief hit them all.

'Yes, I won't even mind doing the washing-up after Christmas dinner,' Molly said and put her arm tighter through Connie's. 'Will you be all right with us this year Connie, will you miss home?'

'No, I'll miss Billy and my mam, but we never had a proper Christmas. I loved decorating the tree last night,' Connie replied.

'Come on, you lot, let's sing "We Wish you a Merry Christmas" as we enter the house. Let's make sure Mam knows it's Christmas and that we are all home,' Rose said, and grinned as all four of them broke into song as they walked up the street and opened the door, surrounding their mother with the noise of their singing and laughter.

'Enough, you girls, anybody would think it's Christmas.' Winnie smiled at her girls.

'It is, Mam, and you've got us all at home,' Rose said and then they all shouted 'Happy Christmas!', kissing her in turn.

'I've brought some mistletoe home, it's lost a berry or two because everyone's been teasing everybody else with it at work, but I bet there is only our Rose that will be using it here,' Annie said, taking a sprig of mistletoe out from behind her ear and placing it on the mantelpiece.

'There's a letter on there for you, Annie, looks like it's from your friend in Liverpool, and there's one for you along with it, Connie,' Winnie said, hoping she was worrying unnecessarily about Connie.

'Oh, a letter from Josh, just what I wanted to make my Christmas,' Annie said, and grinned as she picked up the letters and handed Connie hers before sitting down and opening the Christmas card and short letter from Josh. After a few seconds she gasped. 'He's coming to see me between Christmas and New Year!' She beamed as she read the letter again. 'I can't believe that he is coming back to me.'

'There you go, our Annie, Father Christmas has granted you a Christmas wish, you must have been good, even though we know different,' Rose said and laughed.

Then all eyes were on Connie as she opened her letter. Everyone knew it must be something important, Connie never got a letter. Her hands were trembling as she tore it open and read the contents with tears running down her cheeks.

'It's a photograph of my brother, along with a message from the kind nurse at the orphanage. She's stolen the photo for me from his files so I've not to say anything to anyone,' Connie said and showed all her new family as they gathered around her.

'He's being held in his new father's arms on a horse in Montana. Look at the snow-covered hills behind him. He's got a lovely new home, better than he would ever have had if I had left him with my mam.' Connie sniffed and fought back the tears. 'I'm so glad for him, he looks as happy as I am here.'

'Now, that just makes Christmas perfect, girls. All our wishes have been granted. Rose has found her perfect man with Ned, Annie's got a good friend with Josh, Connie has a new family and her brother is safe, and our Molly has met the Queen – what more could we all wish for?' Winnie looked at all her girls with her heart swelling; she loved her family dearly and hoped that the following year would be as happy for them all as this moment was now. That would make her Christmas complete and she could wish for no more. Except perhaps not to find a box of chocolates with her name on it under the Christmas tree.

He just wanted a decent book to read ...

Not too much to ask, is it? It was in 1935 when Allen Lane, Managing Director of Bodley Head Publishers, stood on a platform at Exeter railway station looking for something good to read on his journey back to London. His choice was limited to popular magazines and poor-quality paperbacks – the same choice faced every day by the vast majority of readers, few of whom could afford hardbacks. Lane's disappointment and subsequent anger at the range of books generally available led him to found a company – and change the world.

'We believed in the existence in this country of a vast reading public for intelligent books at a low price, and staked everything on it'
Sir Allen Lane, 1902–1970, founder of Penguin Books

The quality paperback had arrived – and not just in bookshops. Lane was adamant that his Penguins should appear in chain stores and tobacconists, and should cost no more than a packet of cigarettes.

Reading habits (and cigarette prices) have changed since 1935, but Penguin still believes in publishing the best books for everybody to enjoy. We still believe that good design costs no more than bad design, and we still believe that quality books published passionately and responsibly make the world a better place.

So wherever you see the little bird – whether it's on a piece of prize-winning literary fiction or a celebrity autobiography, political tour de force or historical masterpiece, a serial-killer thriller, reference book, world classic or a piece of pure escapism – you can bet that it represents the very best that the genre has to offer.

Whatever you like to read – trust Penguin.